Finding May

Novels and Short Stories by Jennifer Moorman

The Baker's Man

Little Blackbird

Honeysuckle Hollow

Full Moon June

The Legend of James Grey

Average April

Wednesday's Child

Finding May

Starry Sky July

Illustrated Young Adult Novel
by Jennifer Moorman and Julianne St. Clair

The Wickenstaffs' Journey

Finding May

A Novel

Jennifer Moorman

Finding May is a work of fiction. Names, characters, places, and incidents either are the product of the author's imagination or are used fictitiously. Any resemblance to actual persons, living or dead, events, or locals is entirely coincidental.

For May,
who found the grace to rise and shine her light again
and who makes us believe that we can too

1

*F*or her whole life on joyful days, May Wilson absorbed sunlight like a solar panel and channeled warmth and light onto everyone. In contrast, her unhappiness could banish the sun behind gray clouds for hours, and her darker moods brought raging winds and thunderstorms. But these days May felt certain of one thing: this extraordinary ability had deserted her, stealing the light from her spirit when it went, filling her with a melancholy that chilled her marrow.

The embossed words *Grief Counselor* beneath her fingers reminded May of Braille, a language she could not understand any more than a stranger could understand her grief. The counselor's business card felt slick like high-gloss paint, and the cloudy, early afternoon sunlight subdued its pastel color, turning it to dismal gray. Why had she kept the card? She had no intention of calling the counselor, Dr. Helen Douse. Instead, May had worn down one of the corners, smudging away the shiny blue finish, using the card like a worry stone.

Pink and white dogwood petals pirouetted through the air, pushed by a steady spring breeze. May's toes tapped against the cool green grass to the rhythm of a waltz. *Tap, tap, tap. One, two, three. Tap, tap, tap.* Her black flats lay in the shade of the park bench, and her grip on the brown paper lunch sack loosened. She placed her lunch beside her on the wooden slats of the bench, and it slumped forward like a piece of sad, crinkled trash. May told herself for the millionth time that she wasn't lonely; she was alone.

She tugged her jacket around her thin frame and inhaled the potent, nearly cloying scent of blooming Bradford pear trees that lined a section of the city park's sidewalks. A man walking a golden retriever on a red leash paused at the base of an oak tree while his dog barked at a squirrel. The dog's nails scratched at the tree trunk, sending thin flakes of bark floating through the air. A city bus rumbled up the street after picking up passengers at the stop on the corner.

May glanced down at the blue veins just beneath the thin, pale skin of her hands. She could barely remember what the hands of her youth looked like. *Fuller, darker, less veiny, less freckled.* The wrinkles had come slowly, like gentle waves rolling onto the beach, but still pulling away her youth year after year until here she sat. Feeling every bit of her sixty years with skin lined by life, skin as pale as a pearl but less luminescent.

"Oh, knock it off," she mumbled to herself, folding her hands in her lap. "You're only as old as you feel. Only as old as your heart is."

May closed her eyes and sighed. The last six months since John's death had aged her a century. She felt old and forgotten, like something stowed in the back of a museum for safekeeping yet never to see the sunlight again. This venture to the local park down the street from her condo was an almost daily ritual, meant to force her out into a world where she wasn't sure how she fit in anymore, out into a world of sunshine that ignored her now. But the alternative, staying in her condo all day, made her feel as though her life was over, as though she was crumbling apart like brittle, old newspaper. Maybe she was. Time could be a tyrant, demanding payment in the form of vitality and the ease of everyday movement, and every day May paid. At least half of her body ached, her spirit the most.

Why did growing old make one feel like a cast-off? How did some older women come alive and look like they'd swallowed diamonds even as they aged? And yet May felt like a used-up tube of toothpaste—all her good stuff was gone.

"Do you hear yourself?" she asked aloud. "You sound like a Negative Nelly. No wonder no one wants to hang out with you. You're downright depressing."

A woman wearing florescent pink and green skintight pants jogged by and glanced at May. The woman's expression was clear: *Poor crazy old woman.*

"Now people think you've lost it. You need to pull yourself together." *But how?*

May's phone rang in her purse, and she flinched. She rarely received phone calls now. Right after John's passing, her phone had rung so much, she'd flirted with the idea of shoving it down the garbage disposal. The callers were genuine with their sympathy, and she *had* appreciated their compassion. But May hadn't wanted to put on a show for them. She hadn't wanted to repeat, "I'm doing okay," so much that her throat had gone hoarse. She'd wanted to disappear for a while—maybe forever—but there were still arrangements to be made, a book deadline to meet, and a fragile existence to clutch on to.

Most of her friends seemed more worried that her sunshine-y demeanor had also been buried with John. They found her sharp edges and tight lines uncomfortable, and when they were around, they sat on the edges of their chairs, ready to flee at any moment. They shivered in her presence. But May hadn't wanted to feel the warmth; she didn't want the sunshine. And as though the light understood, perhaps even taken a great offense at her ungraciousness, her ability to call the sunlight into her and feel it, let alone share it, had abandoned her, as though saying, *You don't need me? Hmph, let's see how well you survive in the darkness.* In her heartache, May had responded, *I'll do just fine on my own*, but now she knew she'd been wrong. Now the lingering chill had her wearing two scarves and extra socks indoors. Even with an extra quilt on the bed, she still shivered herself to sleep in the gloom.

Her phone repeated its ringtone. Clouds separated, opening up a chasm of blue, and sunlight spilled through the green leaves and spotted her clothes with patches of warmth. The breeze kicked up and blew her shoulder-length auburn hair into her eyes and mouth. She spat it out, dropped the business card into her lap, and dug through her bag.

The number wasn't one stored in her contacts, but it flashed with an area code she recognized from when she was young. *Mystic Water is calling.*

May's heart pounded in her chest like it used to after a sprint across her grandpa's fields. She imagined herself there with the rich, wet scent of tilled earth just before her grandpa planted. She remembered the scratch of corn stalks on her bare arms as she dashed through the rows, playing chase with her older cousins when they were children. She could almost see Grandma Charity sitting on the front porch shelling peas and promising juicy, pink watermelon on a blazing-hot summer afternoon, if they behaved.

"Hello?" she asked, swallowing down a strange sense of panic. She inhaled the scent of green peanuts and sweet corn.

"Is this..."

The young woman's voice paused so long that May thought the caller had hung up.

"Hello?" May asked again.

"Is this Ivylin May MacAdams?" the woman asked, pronouncing each syllable slowly.

May's hand drifted up to her collarbone, and her breath stopped. Chills rushed up and down her arms. No one had used her full name since her parents had been alive.

"Yes," May answered, finally exhaling. The skin on the back of her neck prickled, a sensation she hadn't felt in years.

"Please don't hang up, but I need to get all of this out before I chicken out. You don't know me. My name is Jacqueline, and I found a bunch of letters and poems you wrote to my dad. They were in an old shoebox I found in the back of his closet. I know I shouldn't have opened it, but we were helping him clean...and well, once I started reading, I couldn't stop. I had no idea about you—of course, I didn't.

"But when Dad found me sitting on the floor reading, he confessed, and I couldn't believe he was talking about *you*. I've read all your books. But then I thought, I don't know... I just thought you might come see him. I thought maybe you would like to see an old friend. Because...he's not doing well..."

Jacqueline's quiet voice trembled. May's bewilderment grew. A blackbird swooped down and landed on the grass at her feet. Its black wings, soaking up all the warmth, glistened like an oil slick in the sunshine.

Jacqueline cleared her throat. "He had a massive heart attack a few days ago. They took him to surgery, and now he's in the ICU.

4

He's not stable, and it's been touch-and-go, but when he's conscious, he talks about you, and his face—I just *had* to find you. If you could see his face when he talks about you. I've never seen him look like that. He seems so proud to know you. And not just because you're a well-known writer." She released a thin, shaky breath. "Will you? Will you come home to see him? Just in case...he doesn't make it? I think it would mean so much. He has *no* idea I've been trying to find you for months. You're not easy to track down, even though you're famous. With your author pseudonym and the tightly controlled regulations of your publishing house, I felt like giving up. But after his heart attack, I started searching again because I'm frantic—"

"Honey—Jacqueline, I'm sorry, but I don't know who your father is. I think you have the wrong person. I'm so sorry that your father is in poor health. I wish I could help—"

"Oliver Bisset," she blurted. "Surely, you remember him."

May's hand dropped, and her mouth fell open. The phone plopped onto her lap, bouncing Dr. Helen Douse's business card into the air. The wind swooped in and carried the thin paper high into the sky. May could do nothing but watch it disappear into the clouds. Her chest constricted; snarled emotions awakened in her heart, stretched to make room, and pressed against the cage of her chest. May had always believed that words and names held power. So she shouldn't have been surprised that just *hearing* his name—Oliver—snatched her back to the past faster than she could steady herself or force the memories to stay buried.

Jacqueline's muffled voice sounded from May's lap. May glanced down and listened for a few seconds as Jacqueline called her name. Then she lifted the phone, pressed it to her ear, and closed her eyes. The plastic warmed her cheek.

"You're Ollie's daughter?" *Little Jackie.* An image of the little blue-eyed girl who had looked so much like her daddy appeared in her mind. She'd only seen Jackie once and not in thirty years.

"Yes, ma'am. You remember him?"

May nodded. Remembering Oliver wasn't difficult. Forgetting him had taken years and years and years, and still pieces of him

5

lingered in her heart like ashes floating in the air after a terrible fire.

"Will you come home to Mystic Water?" Jacqueline said the word *home* like it should mean more to May.

Mystic Water was never *my home. If it is anything, it's a place where part of me broke off and stayed...perhaps forever.*

May closed her eyes and leaned forward as an ache built in her heart like indigestion, burning and uncomfortable. Her heart shot electric tingles combined with pain all the way down to her bare toes. It felt like a panic attack building momentum. May forced herself to inhale a full, deep breath and then exhale.

"I'm not sure that's a good idea. Your mama..." May's voice trailed off, and her throat closed. "Is she—"

Jacqueline interrupted. "Mom's gone." She paused then exhaled. "Has been for years now."

May frowned. *She left?*

"Mom's body finally gave out, nearly twenty-five years ago," Jacqueline said in a broken, little-girl voice.

May pressed her back against the hard wood of the bench and stared open-mouthed at the space in front of her. "I am *so* sorry," she said, feeling the truth of her sorrow rattle through her bones.

"Thank you. I'd like to say she fought hard, but she didn't. I think there was too much—too much unhappiness inside her that she held on to more than she held on to life. But that's a whole other story. You know, Dad never got remarried. I wondered if it was because his marriage to Mom was so tough, but maybe there were other reasons."

Oliver had been single for twenty-five years? "I'm sure your daddy had reasons for staying single. Lord knows that being married is hard work sometimes."

Jacqueline asked, "Will you come see him? I think he'd love to see you."

May's hand clenched into a fist in her lap. "Oh, honey, you're giving that short relationship too much credit."

"Your friendship meant a lot to him. Maybe it was a short

6

relationship, but I read your letters," Jacqueline said.

"Those letters were written thirty years ago by a young, foolish girl. I've grown up. I've changed. That feels like another life, and a very *short* time in our lives."

Jacqueline exhaled into the phone. "You wrote the most beautiful letters to him. Your poetry. He's kept them for thirty years. That has to mean *something*."

The truth pushed its way up through the mist in her mind. "Your daddy was special to me." *And I loved him.* She hadn't thought of loving Oliver, of what it *felt* like to be wrapped up in him, not in years. *I loved him desperately. Completely. Like a misguided, naïve girl.* Even now, her pulse quickened with the memories, with the smothering feeling of love that had pressed in upon her.

"I've called his other friends, to let them know. Say you'll come home too. Please."

May closed her eyes and covered her mouth with her hand. She felt like a box had been unearthed in her heart, like a time capsule she'd buried was opening. What would seeing Oliver again be like? Could she travel back down that road? And if she *didn't* go to see him one more time before he died, how would she feel?

A blustery wind pushed through the park, causing every tree to shiver, bending the skinny stalks of the bright orange daylilies. The whole green space looked like it trembled with anticipation, waiting for May to answer.

Should I go back? But I'm so old now. He would be thinking of that girl, and I'm...not her. May lifted her hand and smoothed it down her faded auburn hair. *Should I have colored my hair when my stylist asked me again last week?*

May thought of John, of how the night before he died when they'd sat on the porch, he'd talked about living without regret, about doing the things the heart demanded, about how May would need to get out and enjoy the world after he was gone.

"I'm not saying be reckless and hurtful, but there is a time to live in the moment and to truly live with your heart facing forward," John said. *"I don't want grief to make you feel lost or abandoned. When I*

met you, a fire burned just below the surface. I knew you'd been hurt, but I also knew that with a little time and a lot of care, you'd come alive again. That's what I've always loved about you. I've never felt that burn like you have. Maybe that's the creator in you, but I still respected it. Watching you coming alive...it gave me *life. I know I've dampened your spirit sometimes, and I know I haven't always understood it on a soul-deep level. But I have loved you, May. All these years, I wouldn't have wanted to spend them with anyone else. You saved me from an ordinary life."*

He smiled at her and reached over to pat her knee. May sat quietly, her only response, "I love you too," but thinking how he had saved her too, how he had loved the broken version of her until she found her feet again. John had taken such care of her, had never tried to crush her creative soul, and she had never regretted their life together.

"Mrs. MacAdams, I think it would mean so much to Dad, to *me.* Please."

"I'm Mrs. Wilson now. I haven't been May MacAdams in twenty-five years." May had been devoted to John, and even though their life together had been bumpy at times, weren't all marriages difficult on some days? They'd had more happy days than not. Yet her love for Oliver had felt different—different in the way that young love often feels. *Explosive, desperate, rushing from one high to the next, like jumping from a cliff and laughing all the way down, like living at a deficit every day, never enough, never enough, never enough, forever demanding more to satisfy the insatiable heart of a woman in love.*

Curiosity tempted her with questions. Would she feel anything seeing Oliver again? Would it feel like friendship? Like youth? Like emptiness? John's voice echoed, *There is a time to live in the moment and to truly live with your heart facing forward.*

There is also a time to search and a time to give up, a time to keep and a time to throw away, she thought. *But there is also a time to mend.* May shook her head. Sunlight decorated the grass with orbs of light just out of reach of her feet.

"Jacqueline..." She wanted to say, *I'm sorry.* But was she sincerely sorry she wouldn't be returning to Mystic Water? She cleared her throat and stared up at the sunlight before closing her eyes. "I appreciate you reaching out to me in case I wanted to see Oliver again, but..." But what? *I don't want to. I don't need to. I made a promise.* "But I have a manuscript to deliver to my publisher, and I really can't afford to put it on hold." *Never mind that's it been on hold since John died.* "I live nine hundred miles from Mystic Water now, and it's been a long time. I imagine your daddy would be better served by being surrounded by family and *close* friends."

The phone was so quiet that May worried her cell battery had died. Would she have to repeat herself? She didn't feel confident she could lie again.

The blackbird, with its dark shiny wings, had wandered off, but it returned and stared up at May with black eyes that absorbed the light. It tilted its head as if asking, "What are you doing lying to Ollie's little girl?"

"Jacqueline?"

The younger woman sniffed into the phone. "I understand. Thank you...thank you for your time, Mrs. Mac—er, Mrs. Wilson. You have my number if you change your mind. Just in case..."

Jacqueline said good-bye, and May gripped the phone in her lap. A couple arranged a quilted blanket on the grass nearby, and their laughter drifted toward May. The blackbird cawed and flew off. She sagged against the back of the bench and closed her eyes. Sunlight drifted down through the trees and pooled on the empty spot beside her. Memories rolled forward, wave after wave, and she remembered seeing Oliver for the first time.

2

Grandma, take it slow. Your appointment isn't for another twenty minutes. We have time." Morning sunlight heated their backs and created stumpy shadows on the sidewalk in front of them.

Charity MacAdams, May's grandma, gave May the side-eye and shook off May's helpful hand. "That's the trouble, isn't it? We *all* think we have time, but we don't. It feels like just yesterday that I was falling in love with your grandpa from across the dance hall, and now...now we're out of time."

Her grandma's voice hitched, and she pressed her thin, pink lips together. May saw her jaw clench and release. Her freckled skin looked pale and sallow; the look in her cornflower blue eyes reminded May of the haunted faces she'd seen in history books about the Great Depression. Like they might crumble beneath the weight of their burdens, or they already had and all that remained was the husk of who they'd been, drifting through the days.

Ramsay MacAdams, May's grandpa, had passed away three months ago and devastated Charity, sending her spiraling into a despair so dark and consuming that the whole family worried that Charity would lose the family farm and the house that had been on that land since Mystic Water was founded. Charity, a strong and self-sufficient woman, had refused to get out of bed for the first two weeks. This type of behavior was so out of sync with the Charity her family recognized, no one quite knew how to respond.

Charity's spirit had collapsed inside of her, creating a sinkhole around her heart. The functioning pieces of her that remained were sharp like glass shards, causing her moods to swing back and forth between anger and sorrow. But the farm did not sympathize with her broken heart. It needed to be attended to daily, and due to a complete lack of care and no routine, the troubles had multiplied every day.

Different family members had taken turns staying with Charity to help out at the farm while they hired extra help. They hired farmhands and college kids in need of extra cash. They sought advice from the local farmers who were more than willing to help out one of the oldest families in town. No one wanted to see the MacAdams' farm fail.

The family was also there to sit with Charity, to convince her to keep living, to try and resurrect her zest for life. But Charity had been inconsolable until Little May Sunshine, who was so nicknamed by her grandpa, had arrived a week ago. May's grandpa told her once that she had a sunny disposition, which allowed her to see the positive in most situations. It was common knowledge among the MacAdams family that May seemed able to wrangle the sunshine in her hands and then hand it out to anyone in need. So May became a top contender to pull Charity out of the darkness.

May felt she had not done anything special to ease her grandma's pain, but she'd noticed a change within two days of her arrival. Charity's sight had been failing for years due to macular degeneration, so May read aloud the local newspaper and some of her grandma's favorite short stories. May also crafted original stories to tell her grandma while they shucked corn, shelled peas, and cooked meals in the kitchen. Within three days of her arrival, May heard her grandma laugh for the first time since before the funeral.

Still Charity soured some days, like milk left out in the summer heat, and her attitude made being around her feel like walking barefoot through fire ant beds. Today Charity was extra irritable since she'd tripped the night before and twisted her ankle.

Charity hobbled up the sidewalk toward the doctor's office. The limp was further accentuated due to her left hip that had needed replacing five years ago, but Charity preferred to push through the discomfort. Surgery would have taken her off the farm and made her unable to help for weeks, and before Ramsay's passing, Charity said time off was unacceptable. The only reason she was at the doctor's office now was because May had nagged her until she'd agreed and convinced her that the farmhands would take care of the land.

Charity wore a simple blue gingham dress that accentuated the blue in her pale eyes. "You know I hate being late."

"Good thing we're not going to be," May said as she opened the office door.

May signed in Charity at the front desk, and they sat in the waiting room staring at a muted talk show on the television. Five minutes later, they were moved to a patient room where Charity sat in a rigid, wooden chair rather than on the patient bed covered in a sheet of disposable white paper. Sunlight eased through the slats on the blinds, reaching for May's toes, and warmed the room.

"You should pull your hair back out of your face," Charity said. "That way it wouldn't hang in your eyes like lifeless straw. A little bit more makeup wouldn't hurt either. You're not getting any younger, and another year has gone by. Before you know it, you'll be an old lady with cats."

"I'll keep that in mind," May said, flipping through a magazine meant for young families.

"Being divorced isn't so taboo anymore," Charity continued. "I'm sure a man could overlook that."

May closed the magazine and folded her hands in her lap on top of the slick, shiny paper. A perfectly put-together mom smiled up at May from the cover. "I don't care what people think about me being divorced. Chris was not a good husband—"

"I *know* that. I'm not implying you should have stayed with that Neanderthal. I'm just trying to give you hope that someone will love you again."

The door opened, and a stranger stepped inside. He wore a long, white lab coat with his name stitched over the left breast pocket. He stood more than six feet tall, and his lean frame made his arms and legs appear even longer. His brown hair, lightened by the summer sun, was cut short on the sides and left longer on top. Pieces of hair stuck out in the back, the result of a cowlick. With his thin nose; high, rounded cheekbones; and downturned dark eyes, he reminded May of a little boy with a wide smile that was slow and kind. May guessed he was close to her age based on the faint lines that stretched from the corners of his eyes. Looking at him stirred up a strange, bubbly feeling in May's chest. She sat up straighter, pressing her back against the warm wood of the chair.

The doctor studied the chart in his hands. "Mrs. Charity?" He lifted his gaze, but he looked at May, who sat staring at him as her lips

13

parted. His cheeks lifted, and May involuntarily smiled back.

Charity cleared her throat with a note of impatience. "Where is Dr. Beatty? I only see Dr. Beatty."

The young doctor turned and looked at Charity. "Dr. Beatty was called away unexpectedly to deliver a baby over at the hospital. I hope you don't mind that I'm helping out. I'm Dr. Bisset. You must be Mrs. Charity." He held out his hand.

Charity huffed but never relinquished her manners. She shook his hand with a scowl. "You can call me Mrs. MacAdams."

"Yes, ma'am." Dr. Bisset nodded, and then he glanced over at May and his cheek lifted again in a sideways grin. May returned the expression, as though they were sharing a secret joke.

May stood in front of the full-length mirror in her bedroom. She looped a gray, wool scarf around her neck and poked at the saggy skin beneath her eyes; then she pressed her fingers against her cheeks and lifted the skin, giving herself a temporary facelift. She pulled her fingers through her hair and sighed. "This is what sixty looks like. He's aged, too, ya know. He's not going to look like that handsome thirty-five-year-old."

But she imagined Oliver would have aged wonderfully. He probably looked like a dashing movie star, still in shape, still knocking women dead with his smile and his deep, haunted eyes that downturned in the corners. It didn't seem fair that men were allowed to age while older women could be overlooked for younger, more vibrant models. May had taken care of herself, eaten well her entire life, stayed within five pounds of the same weight from her youth. But...she was still sixty years old, and the signs of a well-lived life showed all over her body.

And he's lying prone in ICU. I could go back. It wouldn't kill me. It's doubtful he'll even know I'm there. I'd be going only to give his daughter peace of mind, not to parade in front of Oliver for approval.

A wild impulse ripped through May, and her back stiffened. She stepped into her closet, creating static charges when her thick wool socks slid past each other. She grabbed her suitcase, opened it on her bed, and stared at it. Was she sincerely thinking about hopping on a plane and flying to see a man she'd promised she would never speak to again?

Another emotion gripped her; it felt a lot like betrayal, all prickly thorns and hollowing disappointment. "A promise is a promise," she said, grabbing fistfuls of scarf in her hands. "I've kept it for thirty years. Why would I break it now, after all this time?" She closed the suitcase and carried it back into her closet. May stared at it for a few more seconds, and then she spun on her heel and hurried out, as though the suitcase might pursue her and beg her to change her mind.

$\mathcal{M}$ ay wandered into her home office with a mug of steaming tea and opened her laptop. Then she leaned back in her desk chair and glanced at the books on her shelves. Novels were tucked all around her condo—some used as bookends for more books, others stacked beneath picture frames, and still more scattered around for decoration. There were books that had been read so many times their spines creaked when opened; their white pages were smudged with chocolate fingerprints, drips of coffee, and salty tears. Those books she displayed in her office.

Shelf space was limited, so these well-worn novels revealed their years of offered and accepted friendship and comfort. Maya Angelou, Roald Dahl, Lewis Carroll, Timothy O'Conner, C. S. Lewis, and Pat Conroy sat waiting for her, always available, always willing to wrap her in ribbons of words that lifted her away into their worlds.

May reached over and touched the spine of Timothy O' Conner's first novel, *Locust Winter*, a mysterious tale of life in a southern marsh town with intrigue, a murder, lost love, and plot twists that coiled more than a water moccasin. O'Conner captivated her from the first sentence on the first page. She'd been standing in a bookstore, circling a display of southern authors, when an image of a Cypress grove on the cover caught her eye. She'd read nearly the entire first chapter while standing at the book table.

O'Conner hadn't written another book for three years, and then he continued to publish a novel every four to five years, with a total of six. He wrote about life in the South, on the beaches, in the backwoods of marsh towns, bringing to life characters who walked through May's dreams like she'd created them herself.

May had wanted to learn more about him, wanted to tell him how he'd inspired her to keep working when she felt certain she'd miss her publisher's deadline. O'Conner didn't seem to work according to anyone's time schedule, but his books rocketed to the bestsellers' lists no matter when they were released or how long between book releases. There were even weeks when his and May's novels vied for top spots.

But no matter how far May investigated, searching for Timothy O'Conner felt like chasing a ghost. O'Conner was a recluse, and the scant information he released to the public offered nothing to reveal the man behind the writing. Still she cherished his artistry with language, and although they had never met, she felt connected to him.

May had similar stories for all of her favorite authors, who were much easier to learn about. Each author inspired her with his or her life and writings. And when she felt stuck on a particular story, she'd pull down their novels and read them while tucked into her favorite chair.

More than half of the shelved books in her office were her own published novels, written under her pseudonym, May James. She'd spent a lifetime writing about heartbreak, true love, serendipity, and connection. Now, after the call with Jacqueline, May's life felt as though she'd tumbled into one of her own novels. This was the kind of story line she'd write about—long lost loves reuniting. But the idea of reuniting with Oliver fluttered her stomach like a rollercoaster ride just before the drop. She pressed her hand to her stomach and thought, *Aren't I too old for this sort of silliness?*

May walked to her office closet, and both knees crackled and popped when she knelt on the floor. The hardwood pressed into her knees, and she readjusted without finding a more comfortable position. May pushed aside boxes of old manuscripts and notebooks containing hundreds of ideas waiting to be given life. In the far back corner, hidden in the shadows, May put her hand on a gray Nike shoebox. She tugged it out and sat on the floor with the box cradled in her lap. She'd taped down the box top years ago, as though that would deter her from ever opening it again. This box had followed her through every move, every major life shift, for the past thirty years, but why *had* she kept it?

May ripped off the brittle tape, tearing away the paper coating on the side of the shoe box. With held breath, she lifted out a letter enclosed in a yellowing envelope. Oliver's handwriting had scrawled *Lovely May* on the outside, and he'd drawn a sun with beams stretching all across the envelope. She turned over the envelope and slipped out the last letter he'd ever written her. An ache trembled all the way down to her toes. The letter quivered in her fingers. May closed her eyes, shook her head, and returned the letter to its envelope without reading it.

She hadn't read it in thirty years, and just *thinking* about reading it now felt like being gripped by vertigo. Oliver's last words echoed in her mind: *I will love you for the rest of my life.* How hopeful she'd been that he had meant those words, that somehow he would find his way back to her. When she'd finally accepted that Oliver would never return, would not love her for the rest of his life, she'd hated those same words.

But were his words being fulfilled now? Had *he loved her for the rest of his life?*

"No," May said, closing the box. "He didn't ask me to come home. His *daughter* did. She's calling *all* his friends from the past. That doesn't make me special. It makes me a name on what is probably a long list." Her mind drifted to when she'd put her hands on the shoebox for the first time.

May sat on a bench in between the aisles of shoes and laced up a shiny aqua tennis shoe. Bright summer sunlight stretched from the long, narrow windows and highlighted the worn spots on the hardwood. The tip of the new shoe glowed in the sunshine. A shadow fell across the aisle, and May glanced up. The detail of the man's face was lost in the halo of light surrounding him, but as he stepped toward her, she recognized him. May sat up straighter on the bench.

"Well, hello, Mrs.—"

"Dr. Bisset," she said in surprise.

He held out his hand.

May stood, lilting toward the right, wearing one flip-flop and one tennis shoe. She shook his hand, feeling his warm skin against hers.

Sunlight traveled around him and pooled around her feet.

"You can call me Oliver. I'm off duty," he said.

"Are doctors *ever* off duty?" May dropped his hand and smoothed her hand down her hair. Something about this man shifted her slightly off center, made her heart fluttery like hummingbird wings.

Oliver laughed. "Occasionally. I was hoping I'd see you again. I didn't get your name when you brought in your grandmother."

She studied him. *He was hoping to see me again?* "Grandma can be pretty demanding of attention when she wants to be. I was just a chauffeur that day. I'm May MacAdams."

He clasped his hands together in front of him. Then he shifted them behind his back, and then into his front pockets. "I bet you're more than her chauffeur. The girls at the office say you're her saving grace, that you've helped bring her back around. They say you've brightened the whole town since you've been here."

May's eyes widened before she calmed herself. "Well, that's certainly not true," May said, but her smile lingered. "It's nice of them to say, though."

He removed his hands out of his pockets and swung them by his side. "It's good to see you again. I've only been here a few months, so I don't know everyone yet," he said, sliding one hand through his hair. "I got the impression that you don't live here."

Is he nervous? Dr. Bisset's energy felt twittery, lacking anxiety but full of pulsing jolts like sunbursts. Light flowed around him, wrapping around his body, but continuing toward May. Her body warmed. "I don't live in Mystic Water. My grandpa died a few months ago, and my family has been taking turns coming to Mystic Water to spend time with Grandma. She's a handful, so we rotate out every few weeks. I've been here a couple of weeks already, so I'll be swapping out once someone else draws the short straw." May covered her mouth and glanced at the floor. She looked up at Oliver. "I shouldn't have said that. Grandma hasn't been the easiest to be with, but who can blame her? She lost her best friend, so that's bound to make anyone lose her bearings and not feel very sociable."

"I'm sorry to hear about your grandfather. Of course that must be hard on her. We all deal with grief differently, and unfortunately, there's no timetable that works the same for everyone," Oliver said, leaning against the nearest shelf. He rubbed the back of his neck. "So...you're leaving soon?"

May's gaze locked on to his, and she leaned back. Sunlight pushed across the floor with a shove of intensity and stretched up her shins and then onto her thighs. May nodded, trying not to stare at the way the sunlight highlighted his tan skin and hair.

"That's unfortunate," he said. "So, what are you up to today? Shoe shopping? Obviously." He glanced at his feet. "Me too. I'm looking for a new pair of running shoes." He looked up at her. "Are you a runner?"

"That depends. Am I being chased by a wild animal?"

Oliver chuckled, and May's smile stretched so wide that she covered it with her hand.

"I'm kidding," May said. "I do a little running. I'm just getting into it, so I wouldn't call myself a runner. I've been running laps around the farm on most days. Being cooped up is hard on my mental health. I need sunshine. I prefer being outside to being trapped indoors."

Oliver nodded. He pointed at the tennis shoe she wore. "Those aren't the best option for running."

"No? They're cute, though, right?"

"What size are you?" he asked. After she answered, Oliver pulled a gray Nike shoebox from the shelf and sat down on the bench. May sat, keeping space between them. Oliver opened the box and handed her a stark white shoe. "These should be perfect."

May thanked him and turned the shoe over in her hand. "Not much of a looker, is it?"

"Don't judge a book by its cover," he joked.

May slipped off the aqua shoe so she could put on Oliver's choice. She laced up the tennis shoe and sat up straight. "Feels good."

"Maybe you judged it too harshly. I'll admit it's not as flashy as that plastic princess shoe you picked up. But put on the other one and walk around. Then walk back over here." Oliver handed her the other shoe, sounding like a man who was used to offering advice and having people follow it.

"Plastic princess shoe?" May laced up the other white shoe.

"I bet these explode with glitter when you run," he said, picking up

21

the shoebox that held the aqua shoes.

May bounced on the balls of her feet. "You're not selling me on these great white whales. They're pretty boring."

He motioned for her to take a walk, and she obeyed. May returned after a jaunt around the store, and Oliver sat watching her. "We should go running," he said, and then he looked surprised by his own statement, as though the words had not come from his mouth. He pressed his palms against his thighs. "If you have time before you go, that is."

"Together?" May blurted, and her heart thumped hard in her chest.

He glanced away from her, shifting his gaze toward the long windows, toward the sun blazing in and reaching all the way to May's waist. He looked at her with a focus that unnerved her. "Would you want to? I'm part of a running group, a few locals who benefit from the motivation and accountability of having to show up. We don't all run at the same pace, but we keep up."

A handsome man wanted to spend more time with her. Why would she say no? Her heart pounded an irregular rhythm. A warning? She tamped down the concern. She couldn't remember the last time she'd agreed to do anything with a man, and certainly not a stranger. "I don't know you at all," May said. "You could be dangerous. What if you're making up this whole running group scenario?" She smiled to lessen the accusation that he was a criminal masquerading as a good-looking doctor.

Oliver's expression shifted from curious to surprised. His dark eyebrows rose on his forehead. "Should I provide you with references?"

May tapped a finger against her lips as though she were thinking. He didn't *seem* dangerous except for how easily his smile drew her in. "Bring them with you on the run."

"Yeah? You want to go with us?" Surprise coated his voice.

Had he expected her to say no? "Grandma won't care."

Oliver looked like he wanted to say more, but he glanced down at her hands instead. "Would tomorrow morning at the main trailhead in the state park work for you? It's already on the schedule. I don't know if that works with your timeline, if you're planning on leaving in the next few days."

"What time tomorrow morning?" She visualized her daily planner in her head. The days fanned out empty except for writing assignments and tasks. She hadn't heard from anyone in the family yet about swapping places with her, so committing to a run in the morning was easy.

"How about early? Five-thirty in the morning?" Oliver asked. "We prefer to get in a solid run before work."

"Fair warning that if these guys are all training for the Boston Marathon, they're going to leave me in the dust."

A genuine smile lifted his cheeks. "They're not trying to qualify right now. You'll be fine. Tomorrow is a yes then?"

May nodded.

"That's easy enough."

May held out her hands, palms up. "I don't have a packed agenda. I'm here to keep Grandma company and to ferry her around, make sure the farm doesn't fall apart, easy stuff mostly."

"Lucky for me," Oliver said, taking his phone out of his pocket. "Send me your number, and I'll text you."

May programmed his number into her cell phone. "It's a date then—I mean, I'll see you tomorrow. Not like a *date*. A run. You know what I mean."

Oliver chuckled. "I know what you mean. It's good that I ran into you. Must have been fate. And someone needed to keep you from buying a lousy pair of running shoes."

"The verdict is still out on these. Guess we'll find out tomorrow." May packed the white shoes back into the gray shoebox. "Thanks for the help. I'll see you and your crew tomorrow."

"Best way to start my day," Oliver said.

The run or with me? May paid for the shoes at the counter, and as she walked out of the store, she glanced over her shoulder. Oliver, sitting in a circle of light, lifted his hand and waved. The sidewalk turned to clouds beneath her feet, and she smiled, thinking, *What am I getting myself into?*

May closed her laptop after thirty full minutes of staring at the blinking cursor. She did have a manuscript to finish and a publishing deadline looming, but her publisher had given her grace and an extension of six months to a year. She'd been with the publisher for more than twenty years now, and they were more like an extended family than a business partner. Losing John had been a shared loss and reason enough for the company to give May time to grieve and then decide how to move forward.

It wasn't as though all of her ideas and creativity had withered like a grape left on a vine. But there were so many additional responsibilities to take care of after someone passed away, especially a spouse. There were forms and signatures and wills and bank accounts and social security benefits and certificates and anything else the government decided was mandatory for officially saying good-bye. Then there were the questions she couldn't answer, like when did she have to clean out his side of the closet? What should she pack up and give to charity? When would she stop pulling down a mug for him when she made her coffee in the mornings? When would she stop hearing his voice in her head? Was it crazy to say never, to admit she *liked* having him still loitering in her mind? Wouldn't losing someone after twenty-five years of living with him make most people feel like a boat shoved out to sea without oars, drifting aimlessly for a while before any wind filled the sails?

But, if she were honest, her manuscript was *not* the reason she didn't want to return to Mystic Water. The truth burrowed much deeper, straight to the pulsing ache in her core, and the idea of seeing Oliver, even as an old man, felt a lot like a boxing match between fear and excitement had ramped up within her, both emotions being pummeled, with no clear victor. May believed promises must be kept no matter what, but was there an expiration date on some of them? After thirty years, would going back on her word not matter anymore? If Oliver were breathing in his last few gulps of air, if his time on earth were ending, could she break a promise she made to herself?

She had not thought about Oliver for longer than a flash in

years, but now her memories tumbled forward like wooden blocks kicked over by a child. She couldn't catch them all and pack them away again, so dozens of scenes replayed in her mind as though she were seeing them through a red View-Master toy. Click, view, click, view. Click, view, click, view.

May parked at the trailhead five minutes before the run start time. A group of seven—five men, including Oliver, and two women—gathered nearby. They stretched and jogged in place. One of the women rotated her arms like windmills, looking like she might take flight. Oliver wore a pair of black running shorts that showcased the muscle definition in his legs, and his royal blue running shirt clung to him like a diving suit. May looked away before someone asked who the gawker was. *Oh, it's just me!* she thought. *I'll be over here hoping I don't make a fool of myself and drooling over the doctor.*

May removed her car key from the key chain and slipped the key down into her sock. The men looked like seasoned runners, with lean muscles and long torsos. Two of them were shirtless, muscled like people who avoided carbs and sugar and anything labeled "treat." Even their running gear was from top athletic brands. This didn't appear to be a hobby; it looked like a lifestyle. The women looked similarly. They were thin with almost waif-like bodies, except the addition of chiseled muscle definition. May pressed her hand to her soft middle. She didn't consider herself overweight, but compared to these runners, she looked like she had double the amount of body fat, like the girl who never passed on dessert. May stretched her neck, rolling it front and back and then left to right.

Oliver met her before she reached the group. He walked toward her, keeping his eyes on her face. She felt the wind push against her back, moving her closer to him. Sunlight danced across her skin.

"Good morning!" Oliver said. "Ready to get in a few miles? I see you're going to test out the new shoes."

May bounced on her toes and then lifted one shoe and pointed her toes toward Oliver. "They feel pretty good. I'll let you know if your advice was any good when we're done. Or if I should have gone the more glittery route." She leaned closer so she could whisper. "These people look like professionals. I'm going to look silly comparatively."

He touched her arm and pressed one hand to his chest. May's skin warmed beneath his fingers.

"I'm only average compared to them," he admitted. "You'll be fine. Plus, they're not competitive on runs like this. They enjoy the company. They're not out here trying to set a PR."

"PR? I don't suppose that means public relations."

Oliver laughed as they walked toward the others. "Personal record. Some people call it PB for Personal Best."

"When you said 'running group,' I imagined a group of moms and dads who were jogging. Not a bunch of marathoners who only eat bark and berries." May gave Oliver the side-eye as they joined the others. "Good morning," she said to them. "Thanks for letting me join you."

They responded with smiles and handshakes. After introductions Oliver stepped up beside her and pressed his arm into hers. She glanced at him, wondering if she should start counting the amount of times he touched her. Maybe he was the touchy-feely sort, making contact with all the women. But when Oliver met her gaze, her insides warmed as though melted by the sun, and she felt like the only woman on the planet who held his attention.

"I'll keep pace with you. It's an easy five-mile trail this morning," he said.

May studied the other runners who were making their final adjustments, starting timers, and preparing their GPS trackers. She felt like the middle schooler who'd somehow been placed on the high school track team. "Easy is relative. Do you have strong legs?" May asked.

"Why?"

"In case you have to piggy back me?"

A couple minutes later the group took off at a steady pace. Oliver was right about them. No one sprinted toward the end of the trail like they were gunning for a trophy or to rip through a ribbon stretched across the finish line. She managed to keep pace with everyone until the last mile when they pulled away, and she slowed. Oliver stayed beside her and chatted. May focused on her breathing and let him do most of the talking. She knew if she tried to carry on a steady conversation, she'd be half talking, half wheezing.

May and Oliver finished a couple of minutes behind everyone else. They were stretching, pushing against trees to lengthen their calves, rolling out their muscles, and laughing while drinking from metal water bottles. May's T-shirt stuck to her back with sweat, and she adjusted her ponytail.

She stood around and talked with the runners for a few minutes until they started leaving to get ready for work or to get the kids off to camp and daycares. Oliver leaned against the trunk of his car, sliding down to half sit on the bumper. His long legs stretched out in front of him, and he resembled a fitness model. May's breath caught in her throat. She wanted to keep staring, appreciating the lines created by his muscles, wondering if his hands were calloused like an outdoorsman or if they were soft like a man who spent his life inside. When he noticed her watching him, his cheek lifted on one side. What was a handsome doctor doing focusing his attention her way?

"You might be a hustler," he said, wiping his hand across his damp forehead. "Or you're humble."

Tiny yellow wildflowers grew in a patch of grass between the cars. Their petals wiggled in the humid wind blowing through the parking lot.

May clasped her hands behind her back and stretched her arms downward. "How so?"

"You say you're not a runner, but I was worried that you were going to outpace me for a while. I thought we might jog along, lag behind, and talk, but you have laser focus. This group runs a nine-minute mile when they're taking it easy, like today. That's still fast, and you weren't dragging behind."

May blew air out through her lips. "You're just trying to flatter me."

"Is it working?"

The way one cheek lifted and created a long line beside his lips when he smirked was adorable. In her mind she imagined her finger tracing that line. "Are you hoping it's working?" Her fingertips tingled. Sunlight, all sparkles and warmth, poured down on them.

Oliver shoved a hand through his damp hair, leaving strands spiking toward the cornflower blue sky. "A little, yeah. Want to run again tomorrow?"

May bent down and retied one shoelace that dragged across the ground. "The group runs every day?"

Oliver shook his head. "I was thinking just me and you. We could run this same trail."

Just the two of us. "Let me check my schedule." May flipped through an imaginary day planner she pretended to hold in her hands. "Oh, look. I'm free." She smiled at him, feeling the tingle spread from her fingers, up her arms, into her chest. "Same time?"

"I'll treat you to coffee afterward."

"Or a gigantic jug of ice water," she said, squeezing her fingers around an empty bottle of water, crinkling the plastic.

"Deal."

May reined in a megawatt smile that wanted to stretch across her face. She had a terrible habit of falling right into relationships without gathering all the information first. When it came to writing, May was the opposite. She went overkill on collecting information and making sure all the facts lined up. But since her last relationship nearly destroyed her life, she'd promised herself she'd be more cautious. *Breathe, May. Slow down.* She leaned down and pulled out her key from her sweaty sock and wrinkled her nose as she pinched it between two fingers. "And in between now and then, I'll come up with a better plan for how to stash my car key. See you tomorrow." She unlocked the car and opened the door. "And thanks. It was nice to get outside and meet new people."

He watched her. "The pleasure is all mine. I assure you."

May gripped the side of the car door. Oliver's expression looked genuine. "I didn't think people actually used that line outside of romance novels."

Oliver's grin widened. "Are you implying this is like a romance novel?"

"Oh, no. With this sweaty hair and blotchy skin? No way. No one wants a disheveled, sweat-soaked heroine."

Oliver tilted his head, pretending to survey her from head to foot.

"From over here, I'd say you're wrong. An athletic woman, just finishing a run? I'd read about her. This heroine is looking strong and happy."

A new wave of heat swept through May's body. She steadied herself with the car door. "You write about her, then. Make her glistening instead of sweaty." She dropped into the driver's seat and waved.

Oliver tapped the back of her car like a cowboy signaling a rider to get her horse moving. He waved. May watched him walk to his own car and get inside. When she backed out of the parking lot, she looked over at his car. He still watched her, and he lifted his hand, causing a flutter in May's stomach, a feeling she hadn't felt in years.

4

$\mathcal{M}$ay walked into her bedroom, opened the closet door, and stood just inside the doorway as if the answers would come to her. Maybe if her suitcase fell from the top shelf in the closet, *then* she would know she should go see Oliver. But no sign appeared. No voice from heaven directed her. Only the *rat-a-tat-tat* of her beating heart answered her from the silence. She would have sworn she was too old to ever feel the nerves connected to love again—those first-date jitters, those long minutes of waiting for the phone to ring, those exhilarating seconds before a first kiss. She shivered in the quiet.

May grabbed her phone and walked out into the sunroom. Late afternoon sunlight streamed through one half of the windows, and May stood in a dreamy, soft glow. She dialed her best friend's number and almost hung up after two rings when her doubts pushed forward. *Should I even talk about this with anyone? Yes, Emily will know what to say. She always does.*

"Hey, May, you caught me right in the middle of dangling little Niki from a hot air balloon ladder." Emily Greene's voice was gentle and slow, like a southern breeze blowing through pines, and richer and thicker than molasses. Just the sound of the twang and the drawn-out syllables caused May's chest to ache for a place she hadn't seen in decades.

"Want to call me back when Niki is safe?"

May heard the sound of a laptop closing and ice being swirled around in a glass. She pictured Emily with her professionally dyed blonde hair styled like Grace Kelly's, sitting at her French country desk, wearing a pink summer dress with matching lipstick. "Niki can wait. The publisher doesn't need this manuscript until Christmas. I'm way ahead of schedule. What's wrong?"

"Why would you—?" May started.

"I've known you for a million years, that's why."

May sagged onto the chaise lounge. She smoothed her hand over the creamy, velvety blue fabric. "Em, I don't even know where

31

to start."

"Start in the middle. The beginning is normally full of boring backstory and unnecessary character introductions. Throw us into the action."

May laughed then sobered. "Oliver had a heart attack, and Jackie wants me to come home to Mystic Water." Dry laughter bubbled up her throat, and she pressed a hand against her scarves when they quivered. "As if *that's* my home."

Silence. Then Emily cleared her throat. "I hate to admit this, but I think I need more details. That was a drop into the deep end. Are you talking about...Oliver? As in, Oliver Bisset?"

May exhaled. The plants in the sunroom shivered. "Yes."

"I think I need something stronger than lemonade." Rustling sounded over the phone. "Andy, where's the Baileys? Would you grab it and an extra cup of coffee?" More muffled voices. "It's May. Yes, thank you. Is it cold in here, or is it just me? A bit more, yes, thank you. Okay, May, I'm...well, to be honest, I'm flabbergasted. No, that's not the right word. I'm...I'm..."

"Stunned? Speechless?"

"Yes. So...what's happened? I mean, *how*? Why do you *know* this? Do you know someone in Mystic Water? What is *he* doing in Mystic Water? Have you even spoken to Oliver since—"

"No. Not in thirty years." May explained Jacqueline's phone call, describing how she'd been searching for May for months and how Oliver's deteriorating health had made the search more frantic.

"And Angelina? Did Jackie mention her?" Emily asked. "Lord, I haven't thought about her in years. We never really hit it off, even when... It doesn't matter. That was a long time ago. I shouldn't speak ill of her."

"She died, Em."

May swallowed loudly in the silence.

"Em? Are you still there?" May asked, tugging her right sock higher.

"Yes. Did Jackie say what happened?"

"Not much. Just that her body gave up. That's so sad for the kids. I had no idea they grew up without a mama. And Jackie wants me to come see him because she's calling his friends. Have *you* heard from her yet? Do you think y'all are on the friends list? Have you even *spoken* to him since you left? I'd assume not or you would have mentioned it—"

"May."

"What?"

"You're babbling."

May huffed. "I *know* I am. Em...should I go? Is that crazy? It's been so long, and after everything. I mean, am I only considering this because John is gone? If John were here, would I tell Oliver he could stick his stethoscope up his—"

"May."

"What?"

"You're not calling me to ask my opinion," Emily said with a sigh. "You just want me to tell you that it's okay that you've already decided to go. Right? If this were one of your romance novels, what would your heroine do? She'd have packed her bag five pages ago. Call me when you get there."

✺

May laughed and sucked in air as she and Oliver raced for shelter beneath the only covered picnic table they'd seen during the last mile of their sprint toward the parking lot. Rain beat down upon the metal roof, lightning streaked across an angry summer sky, and thunder rattled leaves on the swaying oaks. Powerful gusts of wind snatched pine needles from the trees and shot them through the air like arrows.

May dropped onto the bench seat and leaned over, elbows on her knees, sucking in gulps of air and still laughing. Water dripped down her cheeks and plopped onto the darkening, wet concrete slab. She swiped her hand across her eyes as Oliver sat beside her. She glanced over at him through soaked strands of hair that had fallen out of her ponytail. Even though the intense weather created a twisting feeling in her stomach, it didn't dull the happiness she felt. The last time she'd laughed this hard was a memory too faint to form in her mind.

"You were right," Oliver said. "We didn't beat the rain."

"You think?" She rung out the bottom of her T-shirt, creating a pool of water beside her tennis shoe. "I hope you didn't have to be anywhere right after this. You're going to need to wash off."

From the knees down, they both looked like they'd been splatter painted with mud. Oliver's shoes were coated in gray muck, and his white socks might be permanently stained.

"You don't think the patients would appreciate this outdoorsy look?" He laughed. "It reminds me of the time I took the kids to a little canyon trail near our old house, and it stormed the whole drive there. The rain stopped only a few minutes after we parked, but they still wanted to go on the hike. We were *covered* in mud and red clay. I had to have the car detailed afterward."

May's head jerked toward him, and her eyes darted down to his left hand. She blurted, "You have kids?"

Oliver leaned back against the picnic table, stretching his long legs out in front of him. "Two. A girl and a boy. Jackie and Michael."

Rain hammered against the roof as the wind swept in angled sheets of water. May looked away from his gaze. She'd been imagining this handsome doctor was single and childless. Like her. Not that him having children mattered, but she shifted on the bench, wondering about the rest of his story and why he didn't wear a wedding band. Was he divorced? Widowed? Was this the warning she'd felt at the shoe store? May wrung her hands together, feeling the absence of the diamond she'd worn for five years. Five years of hollowing out like a dying oak.

"Does that bother you?" he asked over the howl of the wind.

Rivers of mud gathered speed on their downhill course. She blinked away the old memories of raised voices and the sound of boots stomping up the stairs. "Which part?"

"That I have children."

May swiped her hand across her wet forehead and pulled her hair into a tighter ponytail. She slipped into information-gathering mode, like she would when researching an article, and shook her head. She could approach Oliver like a local she would interview instead of like a potential date. *Do you even* want *to date?* she wondered. "How old are they?"

"Jackie is ten, and Michael is eight."

"Are they here with you? In town?"

Oliver met her gaze and held it for a few seconds before looking away, staring out into the saturated forest. "They're with their mother for the summer."

"Oh..." She paused. "Is it hard for you to be away from them for so long?"

He nodded. "I miss them a lot. It's quiet without them around, and the house is too big with just me in it. It's hard, but some days go by faster than others."

"Is this a new adjustment? Have you been divorced long?" *Did he move to Mystic Water to be farther from or nearer to his ex-wife? He'd mentioned he'd only been in town a few months.*

Oliver pressed his palms against his thighs and sat up straighter. He cleared his throat, and thunder boomed, rattling May's teeth. She crossed her arms over her chest and shivered as the temperature dropped. The storm held strong right over them.

"I'm not," Oliver said, barely louder than the wind. "I'm not divorced."

Rain slashed beneath the metal roof, wetting the tips of their shoes. She pulled her feet toward her, tucking them under the bench seat. May sat still, replaying their conversation from the shoe store, from the run the day before, when she had felt as though he'd been *flirting* with her. She recalled his smile when she'd agreed to meet him today. But... *He's married?*

"You're not wearing a wedding band."

Oliver rubbed the back of his neck and looked at her from beneath his dark lashes. "It's complicated and uncomfortable to talk about."

Oliver lifted his left hand and flipped it over, studying it, perhaps remembering how the band used to circle around his finger, remembering the feel of the metal against his tan skin. He rubbed the empty space with his thumb. Then he sighed and turned to face her on the bench.

"Short version. Angelina and I have had a contentious relationship for years, but we've managed to do our own thing and stay together for the kids. She had an affair with another doctor in my practice this past winter. We decided to move. We—*I* needed a change. Mystic

Water is as good a place as any, but she hated it here right away. Too small, too suffocating, too saccharine—her words, not mine. I think she hates everything." Oliver shrugged. "The fighting got worse. After the first six months here, she decided that divorce was the only way she'd be happy, but I'm doubtful she'll ever be happy.

"Anyway we're separated right now. I'd be lying if I didn't say her leaving wasn't a relief. But she took the divorce paperwork to her parents' place at the beach to make sure it's what she wants, which translates into making sure she *gets* what she wants. I barely care anymore. What we *do* agree on is that we both want to do what's best for Jackie and Michael. Right now the kids think they're on vacation with their grandparents. They know I'm working, so there aren't a lot of questions. Angelina and I have agreed that I can come down every other weekend to spend time with them."

Because she had no idea what to say, she opted for a cliché. "I'm sorry." May's brain worked double-time trying to refile Oliver from "available" to "friends only," but the idea burned in her stomach like too much lemonade, and disappointment caused it to churn even more. *That's odd,* she thought, surprised by the intensity and persistence of her reaction.

Then she added, "Although I would love for it to be, marriage isn't always sunshine and daisies. My daddy used to tell me that who you marry is one of the most important decisions you ever make. At the time I was young and thought choosing a college was pretty rough. I believed finding Prince Charming would be much easier. But once you marry a toad, you know my daddy was right. People feel differently about divorce once it enters into their sphere. How are *you* feeling about it?"

"You want to know the truth?" he asked. "I feel like I'm coming up for air. I miss the kids, but I talk to them every day." He placed one hand on his chest. "But I feel like *me* again. Not just a dad. Not just somebody's doctor. Not an irritating husband. And then you showed up the other day, and you brought this light with you, and I knew I had to get to know you. You are a jolt of positive energy."

May's chest warmed. "That sounds uncomfortable."

Oliver shook his head. Water dripped down his temples. "Quite the opposite. I've been feeling disillusioned about a lot of things. About love and relationships and those notions I had about what my life would be like by the time I was in my thirties with kids. No starry eyes for me. Since Angelina left with the kids, the empty's gotten bigger, like my purpose...if I'm not Dad, and I'm definitely not a husband, then what am I? What am I *doing*? Maybe it doesn't matter. Maybe this is all there is. Get up. Go to work. Repeat. There's nothing new under the sun, right? From a certain angle, it's all meaningless. Those hopes and dreams we have...do they really matter? Do we *really* make that much of a difference?"

"That's a crappy outlook on life," May said. "Life is hard, sure. The world is broken. The people in the world are broken. We do stupid things. We hurt one another. But the sun rises again every morning. And there's a lot of good to be thankful for in life. We also love one another. We dream together. We help, we grow, we change. And every day *isn't* the same. I bet if you wrote down five things you noticed or said or things that happened every day, by the time a week passed, you'd see that your days are all different. There is something interesting and beautiful and worth seeing in every day."

Oliver's expression softened and he exhaled. "See that's what I mean. You showed up, and just sitting here, I feel comfortable and peaceful for the first time since we moved...since before we moved actually. The girls at the office say that the *weather* is better when you're around. They say your grandpa had stories about Little May Sunshine and how she spread joy like she was tossing wildflower seeds."

May squirmed on the bench. He'd asked about her at the office? "And you believe them?"

Oliver looked toward the sheets of rain rushing through the forest. "It sounds farfetched, but I can't remember the last time I felt peaceful and *warm*. I could get used to it, and having someone to talk to is nice."

May smiled down at her lap, but there was an uneasy ache forming in her stomach. When she looked back up at him, she imagined yellow police tape crisscrossing his chest, telling her, DO NOT CROSS. *Back away, May. He's off limits.*

✦

May stood on tiptoes and pulled down her luggage with a grunt. How could an empty bag still feel heavy? She carried the suitcase to the bed, opened it for the second time, and stared at the gaping insides. She rubbed her cold hands together, creating friction between her palms. When she had left Oliver, she had felt as empty as this worn suitcase, felt gutted of every ounce of her being. Now, after thirty years...could she return and look at his face again? Would a damaged part of her heart resurrect, all wobbly and tattered and full of ugly? Why, now, after all these years had he decided to tell his daughter about her? *Only because his daughter found our letters. He would have taken me to the grave.* Her hands trembled so she fisted them at her sides.

She thought about John, about what he would say and think. He had been her biggest supporter, telling her to take an adventure and follow wherever it led. Would he offer the same advice now? Would he say, "Sure. Go see a guy who tried to destroy your light."

May huffed. "Oh, I know very well John would *never* say something so dramatic." May almost smiled. "And Oliver didn't try to destroy my light. If anything, he amped up my light so high, no human could possibly live at that level of brightness for very long. A total burnout would have been inevitable. I just accelerated the shutdown. So, in reality, I turned off the light."

Had there been any other option? No. Every other choice was more heartbreaking than the path I chose.

She opened her laptop, typed an airline's web address into the search bar, and looked for flights into the biggest cities close to Mystic Water. After comparing flights and pricing, May booked a ticket for the evening, which gave her a couple of hours to pack and catch a taxi to the airport. Then she booked a rental car at her destination. From the closest airport, she'd have to drive the remainder of the way to Mystic Water.

May called Jacqueline, and the young woman answered on the second ring. May updated her on her travel arrangements. "I booked

38

a flight and rental car. I live nine hundred miles from Mystic Water now. I won't be in town until some time tomorrow afternoon."

"You're coming? Oh, thank you so much." Jacqueline's voice sounded watery with emotion. "I know it's been a long time, but to know that my dad has a chance to see an old friend... Thank you. Get here as soon as you can, and call me when you're in town. Do you think you'll want to stop by and see us tomorrow? Can I tell *him* you're coming home?"

"I'll call you when I get settled in Mystic Water. As for telling Oliver...I don't know him anymore. I don't know how he'll react. I'll leave that decision to you."

Jacqueline thanked May again and hung up.

May stared at her reflection in the full-length mirror. A bright beam of sunlight pushed through the bedroom window and swathed her shoulders. Strands of her auburn hair shined in the light. She turned to look at the sunshine, wrinkling her brow as though a stranger had walked into the room. "Are you seriously going back? After all this time? After what happened?" Her reflection shrugged.

"How can I *not* return?" she asked, and her beating heart punctuated every word. "I thought the story was over, but there is another chapter."

5

*S*trong easterly winds pushed against the taxi as it raced toward the airport, smearing the passing landscape into green and gray streaks. The impressive winds rushed beneath the vehicle and vibrated the whole car. May clutched her small, leather purse.

The driver gripped the steering wheel, his bony knuckles sharp and white, and in the rearview mirror, May saw a line of concentration form between his bushy eyebrows and stay for the entire ride. Halfway to the airport, May pulled out her phone and checked the weather. An unexpected storm zigzagged across the state, with no clear direction, like it enjoyed surprising towns with torrential rains and high winds. Based on its current path, the storm looked like it might hit the city. It has been months since May felt confident of any connection with the weather. *A sign I shouldn't be going to Mystic Water? Or a sign telling me to get out of town as soon as possible?*

The taxi dropped May off outside the terminal. A mighty blast of supercharged air shoved her right into the airport, whipping her hair around her head. Everyone inside looked just like her, windblown and worried.

After passing through security, May found the gate and checked the departure time on the overhead screen. The flight, even though an ominous storm brewed outside the windows, would still leave on time. Flying toward Mystic Water appeared as though she would be flying away from the coming tempest, so perhaps she would be safe.

A half hour later, the flight boarded, and May tucked her bulky carry-on beneath her seat rather than in the overhead. She didn't want it too far out of reach. What if someone crushed it? What if someone walked off with it, thinking it was his? What if she opened the overhead, only to find her carry-on had turned to dust like something from the past? *Could you be any more ridiculous?* Earlier on an impulse, May had grabbed the gray Nike shoebox full of Oliver's letters—the same box she'd been dragging around for

41

thirty years—and shoved it into a carry-on bag. If she were going back to Mystic Water, so were these letters. She didn't even want to analyze what that meant, so she'd turned off the annoying voice in her head wanting to pick apart her actions and slung the bag over her shoulder like the Ancient Mariner's albatross.

May had also packed Timothy O'Conner's first novel, *Locust Winter*, into her carry-on. The worn spine creaked when she opened the book. She propped the book in her lap while she snuggled into her jacket. The man in the middle seat eyed May—in her scarves and winter pea coat—and opened the tiny air vent above his seat, rotating it on to full blast. The pilot flew them out of the city and out of the path of the storm. By the time May reached chapter 7, the setting sun pulled her attention. She watched the sun set high above patches of darker clouds, swathing the sky a brilliant golden orange, but unease grew in her stomach. After another half an hour, soon after a stewardess served drinks, the pilot's voice came over the loud speaker.

"I apologize for the inconvenience, but it appears as though the storm has split in two. This newer storm has taken a sharp turn and is now making our original landing zone impossible. I apologize to inform you that we will not be landing—"

The plane lurched to the left, and May's paper cup slid across her tray table like an air hockey puck, headed straight for the floor. She caught it, sloshing lukewarm coffee all over her hand. A collective gasp arose from the passengers. A flight attendant stumbled into a row of seats, and May leaned toward the window. Darkness shrouded everything. Then a lightning bolt rocketed out of the clouds nearby, and she flinched.

When the pilot's voice returned, he explained they would be making a quick landing at the nearest airport in a small town still a few hours from their original destination. Raindrops popped against the small, oval window like BBs; May pressed her fingertips against the cool glass and remembered sitting with Oliver as a rainstorm trapped them beneath the park shelter, remembered that stormy day that clenched her stomach as much as this one.

A part of her had known then that she should toss out the hope she'd had when she'd first met Oliver. He wasn't a single man looking for a date. He was in the middle of a complicated, potentially messy situation, and she had *no business* inserting herself into his life. Even when most people tried to keep a divorce "nice and easy," it could turn faster than a weathervane during a storm. Bitterness surfaced when emotions heightened. Words sharpened, hands clenched tighter, and patience stretched too thin.

May believed a man and a woman could be friends without the worry that it needed to be complicated. Not every man and woman were desperately attracted to one another. They could be friends and care for one another without it ever developing into anything more serious or risky or hurtful. So logically, May understood that she and Oliver *could* be friends. In theory.

But even if May had been naïve enough not to notice the way he smiled at her, she couldn't ignore the tingling in her body or the way her skin shivered up the back of her neck when he focused his brown eyes on hers. May had felt the delicate threads connecting the two of them together; she had felt the spark of attraction flaring inside of her. May *should have* ignored it. But she hadn't.

The lines for airport rental cars curved more than Lombard Street in San Francisco. Airport workers tried to cram everyone into a space that wasn't equipped for such a crowd. May understood without being told that there wouldn't be enough cars to satisfy the demand. The zigzagging storm forced too many people into a town not big enough to hold them.

May shifted her carry-on bag to the other shoulder. Frustrated passengers and exhausted children filled the room with their grumbling voices. College students, wearing their university's colors, laughed and jiggled fast-food cups of ice and soda and slurped through straws, which sounded like off-beat music. The man in line behind May hummed "Dancing on the Ceiling," and May caught him staring up at the fluorescent lights.

May checked the time. Even if she were one of the lucky ones who received a rental, she'd need to find a hotel and sleep. She'd never make it safely to Mystic Water driving through the middle of the night. She stifled a yawn with the back of her hand. Her cell phone dinged, alerting her of a text message.

Let me know when you land, Jacqueline wrote.

Grounded three hours from Mystic Water. There's a huge storm forcing planes in the area to land. I'm waiting for a rental car. I'll keep you updated, May replied.

A minute later Jacqueline wrote, *Be safe! I told Dad you were coming.*

May stared at the words and felt her pulse throb in her neck. *He knows.* The past felt like two powerful hands gripping her waist and yanking her backward. She struggled to remain in the present, to not return to the young woman she had been. May unbuttoned her jacket.

A couple of minutes later Jacqueline sent another message.

Same response from him. Silence. He pressed his hand to his heart, closed his eyes, and he's been sound asleep ever since. Keep in touch.

The hotel bed was ultra firm, and May sat on the edge and bounced a few times, feeling little-to-no give. She rubbed her hand across the tufted comforter. "This should be a restful night."

May lay back, fully clothed, and spread her arms at her sides, palms toward the ceiling, as though in Shavasana. She exhaled. After a few minutes, she looked at her carry-on sitting beside her on the bed. May pushed herself up and unzipped the bag to find her shoebox. The brittle tape would never stick to the cardboard again. May dug down through the pile to pull out the letter at the bottom.

The plain white envelope had never been sealed, but instead the flap was tucked inside. May pulled out the letter and inhaled. She put on her bifocals, lay back, and read the first note Oliver had ever left beneath her windshield wiper.

Dear Marvelous May,

When I asked you to write me a poem, I admit I was expecting something rhyming like my kids gave me in elementary school. Instead you put words together that surprised me and left me feeling slightly inadequate (even though I hate to admit it). I thought, "Who is this girl? Who writes like this?" Not many, and no one I know personally. Thank you for the poem. I am beyond impressed. Never stop writing, May. And if I can be so bold, never stop writing me.

Sincerely,

Overbold Oliver

Ghost words, drifting and bumping into one another in a back corner of her memory, tried to form the first poem May had ever written Oliver. She'd only written one copy and had given it to him. Perhaps that poem was in the box Jacqueline found. May spent a minute thinking about how she had felt that summer day, coming outside one morning and finding the envelope pressed against her windshield like a treasure. She unwound a scarf from her neck. Then she put away the letter, changed into pajamas and took off her socks, and lay on top of the sheets, hoping her heart would settle.

The next morning May felt like she'd slept on hard-packed ground all night. She rubbed her fist into her lower back and stretched. The thermostat had never cooled off the room, and everything in May's suitcase felt damp. The humid air reminded her of her grandparents' barn in Mystic Water. As a young girl, she'd spent hours in the barn during the summer, playing pretend, climbing the ladder to the hayloft and using it as a fort or a castle. Even though the barn's interior was always shaded and provided shelter from the intense southern heat, it *never* felt cool inside. Sweat still soaked through May's clothes, even while sitting in the shadows of the barn.

She rolled her suitcase down the hotel hallway and onto the elevator. Continental breakfast goods spread down a long table covered in a white cloth. Misshapen circles of grape juice and blobs of strawberry jelly stained the cloth. Fruit loops had escaped a box and littered the floor near the milk dispenser. People sat at every table, sipping coffee, complaining about canceled flights, reading the daily newspaper, or shoving powdered eggs around on melamine plates.

The electronic doors whooshed open, and May pulled her suitcase out into the parking lot. She'd noticed a Waffle House next to the hotel last night. She tossed her luggage into the trunk of the economy rental car and walked to the bright yellow sign.

May chose a booth in a corner nearest the parking lot and slid in so she could see out the window. Pollen collected in the bottom corners of the outside window ledge and scattered through the puny holly bushes like yellow confetti. A young waitress stepped up to May's booth. A tattoo of a vine peeked out of the blue collared shirt she wore.

"Morning," the young woman said. "Coffee?"

"Regular, please."

"Know what you want to eat?"

May shook her head. "I need a minute to look over the menu."

The waitress smiled and walked away. May dug through her purse for her eye glasses. She'd chosen a bright blue pair, with legs the deep blue color of the Caribbean Sea. When she'd first been told she'd need to wear glasses because she was "getting older," May had walked out of the ophthalmology office in such a daze that she'd tried to unlock a car in the parking lot that wasn't hers. In frustration, glaring at the key fob, she'd grumbled at the curse of technology, only to realize seconds later that her car was on the other side of the lot, blinking its tail lights at her.

Bifocals?! What's next? she'd thought. *Forget my own name? Wrinkle like a prune? Pluck gray hairs from my chin?*

May had called Emily and babbled about needing glasses and growing old. Emily's voice arose in May's mind, *Beauty is wasted on the young! We're expected to give up our youth and beauty in exchange for wisdom. God forbid we keep them both. Well, except for us, of course. We'll be beautiful* and *wise and the envy of all our friends until we're well into our nineties.* Emily's husky laugh had rippled through the phone line and caused May to laugh with her. Then Emily had told

May to march back into the office and buy a pair of glasses that would make her smile every time she saw them. All those years ago, May had bought a candy-apple red pair because it reminded her to be bold. Now she loved her blue pair because the color brought to mind trips to the Caribbean with John, and it was also the exact color of the summer skies in Mystic Water.

May slipped the bifocals onto her nose and reached for the laminated Waffle House menu. Sticky drops of syrup dotted the breakfast offerings. She glanced out the window and breathed in the scent of warm maple syrup. Images of cinnamon star bread and a maple-glazed scone bobbed to the surface of her pool of memories, reminding her of a breakfast she hadn't thought about in years.

6

May parked around the corner from Bea's Bakery in downtown Mystic Water. The summer heat shoved itself into the car as soon as she opened the door. May inhaled the muggy morning air. She reached back into her car for the bag that held her notebook, travel article notes, and pens. The sidewalks were empty except for a few early-morning shop owners sprucing up their front walks or adjusting their window displays. May glanced up at the sun and squinted. Temperatures climbed toward ninety degrees.

She heard the muffled voices from the bakery as someone pushed open the door and stepped outside. The rattle of dishes, spoons knocking around in coffee mugs, and morning chatter greeted her on the sidewalk before she entered. The scent of hot, sticky-sweet sugar and warm vanilla wrapped around her and pulled her straight into the bake shop. Downtown might be empty of pedestrians, but patrons jam-packed Bea's Bakery.

A young girl wearing a blue gingham apron with large blue eyes and unruly black hair tugged into a high ponytail greeted May. "Eating in or taking out?"

May glanced around the sugar-filled room; the small interior seating area hummed with voices, and nearly every seat was occupied. May had smelled the bakery's goods outside the shop, but inside the smell was even more divine, more intense. She inhaled and then felt a warm tingle trickle down her back. She saw Oliver the same time he saw her. He sat in a far corner near the front windows. He lifted his gaze from a book held in his hand, the paperback cover folded over backward. His other hand lifted his coffee, which he had stopped midway to his mouth. A spoon clanged against a coffee cup. A handful of napkins blew straight off the nearest table, flapping through the air like birds before landing at May's feet.

"Order to go, pl—" She said, but Oliver smiled, lowered his blue mug, lifted his hand, and pointed at the empty chair across from him.

The bakery worker's expression softened, and she followed May's gaze. "Oh, you joining Dr. Bisset? Go on and have a seat. Our dailies are on the board, but if you have any *special needs,*" she winked, "you

49

let me know. Do you want coffee?"

The whole town knew about Bea's Bakery and how it offered cure-alls in the form of pastries, sweets, drinks, and baked goods. Even Grandma Charity swore that treats from the bakery could soothe the town's heartaches, set flight to their hopes, rekindle friendship and love, and spark their passions. When May had laughed at her grandma's confession, Grandma Charity had pointed to the lemony-yellow ray of sunshine that spotlighted May in the kitchen. "This coming from the girl who attracts and collects sunshine," her grandma had said.

May wanted to stick with her to-go order because she could walk to the library and find a secluded table void of a handsome, unavailable man. But Oliver pointed again at the chair and looked like he had been waiting on her to show up all morning.

"Hmmm?" May asked the young girl.

"Would you like coffee?"

May glanced at a chalkboard sign displaying the bakery's daily specials. "Yes, please. Do you make Americanos?"

She tapped her pencil against her notepad and nodded. "Anna makes the best around. Go ahead and have a seat."

May weaved through the scattering of tables and people, and Oliver's gaze never left her. Sunshine streamed through the windows and created a sunny path on the tile floor. "Follow the Yellow Brick Road" played in her mind, and she tamped down the impulse to skip. She glanced at her wrinkled khaki shorts and wished she'd worn something more attractive than her white college T-shirt. The closer she got to Oliver, the warmer her body became, making her feel as though she were approaching the sun.

Oliver dog-eared a book page, closed the paperback, and pressed on the cover, but it splayed open like a paper fan. She slid out the chair and sat across from him, tilting her head and reading the upside-down title, *The Great Gatsby.*

"Good morning," May said, wondering why she sounded so breathless. She pointed to the paperback. "You know they make bookmarks, right? You don't have to ruin a perfectly bound book." She leaned forward and whispered, "Don't let a devoted reader see the book in this state. She'll call you a monster."

Oliver's eyebrows raised, and he pressed his palm against the book cover again. Then he took a paper napkin and shoved it into the book to mark his page. "For the sake of my safety around book lovers. Thanks for looking out for me, and good morning to you too. This is a nice surprise. Do you come here often?"

He and May both laughed. "Worst and best pickup line ever. But no, this is my first time. Grandma likes to make breakfast, and I usually eat oatmeal, but she started talking about Bea's Bakery and their cinnamon star bread and how Grandpa loved all of their baked goods, and how everything here is *so magical—*"

"So I keep hearing. Frances Dotson, a regular according to her, told me the cinnamon star bread will protect me against unhappiness and ill will. I can also expect my reverence and awe to increase at least twofold, maybe more."

Sunshine draped across their table. "And you believe her? After Grandma went on and on about the bread, I decided I had to have it, magic or not." She hung her bag on the back of the chair.

Oliver folded his arms together and leaned forward over the table. "You're not going to believe this, but it's your lucky day."

His smile felt like an enchantment cast over her. She leaned in and whispered, "Why is that?"

"Today's special is an extra-large cinnamon star bread. The people swear this fancier, larger version is powerful enough, not only for all of the stuff I mentioned, but to also make you fall in love."

May's eyes widened, and she glanced around to see if anyone had ordered the special. A highly designed cinnamon roll the size of a dessert plate, sprinkled with sparkly sugar and dripping glaze, sat on most of the tables. Even from a distance the pastry looked flaky and buttery and shining with icing sugar. May looked at Oliver. "Did you eat one already?" She leaned away as if falling in love might be airborne and contagious.

He shook his head. "I was waiting on you."

May raised her eyebrows. "You're not buying into the whole 'falling in love' line are you?"

"Only one way to find out," Oliver said. "Let's share it and see what happens."

The warm tingle spread to her lips. "You're going to get me into trouble. That much is obvious."

The young girl placed May's Americano and water glass on the table. She pulled out her notepad. "Ready to order?"

Oliver said, "We're going to need an extra plate for that special. And let's add in a maple-glazed scone."

"Great choices," the waitress said. "You won't be sorry. The real maple we use will give you a spring in your step with a touch of sweetness. I like to say it adds a bit of sparkle to your day."

Oliver leaned back in his chair as he watched an elderly couple holding hands pass by on the sidewalk. May cupped her mug in both hands. Sunshine reflected off Oliver's dark hair, making it shine, and his lips parted into a slow smile. *More sparkle isn't necessary,* May thought.

May scooped the last of her Waffle House scrambled eggs onto the fork using a slice of toasted wheat bread. She placed her hand over the top of her mug as her waitress breezed by with a coffee carafe. Her zippy nerves didn't need another boost of caffeine or else she'd have the jitters all the way to Mystic Water.

She paid her tab and walked through the hotel parking lot to find her rental car. The scent of warm vanilla carried on the breeze. May dropped into the driver's seat and inhaled. She plugged in the coordinates to Mystic Water on her cell phone and checked for the shortest route. In four hours, she would be crossing the state line and entering a town she hadn't wanted to see in more than twenty-five years.

The cinnamon star bread was everything it promised to be: hot, flaky, still soft and absolute perfection inside with melted, sticky cinnamon and sugar. She wanted to say it was bogus that eating this bread would make someone fall in love, but her insides felt as gooey as melting dark chocolate. May pulled off a small piece of the bread, while listening to Oliver talk about how he'd ended up being a doctor instead of pursuing other interests. Thin bits of pastry and cinnamon sugar stuck to her fingers.

"A writer?" May said as a piece of bread tried to lodge itself in her throat. She thought of the notebook she had crammed into her bag, of the words that crowded the lined pages. Could they really have another interest in common? One more connection drawing them together.

"A doctor or a writer? Can you imagine what my parents would have said if I'd rejected medical school?" He chuckled, but it sounded forced. Oliver lifted his hand when the waitress neared them. He pointed to May's coffee mug when she stood by their table. "Could we get a refill? I'd love another cup too." He looked at May. "Americano, right?"

May nodded and leaned over to glance into her cup. She hadn't even noticed it was empty.

"Anything else?" The bakery worker asked. Oliver shook his head and thanked her.

"Thank you," May said to Oliver once the worker walked away. "You chose to be a doctor because of your parents' expectations?"

Oliver tapped his fingers against the side of his coffee cup. "Not entirely. Health and wellness have always interested me. My mom was a health nut, feeding me whole wheat sandwiches and quinoa well before it was any kind of national obsession. I understood the importance of keeping the body in good working order, so a medical profession wasn't a bad option or a far leap from what I enjoyed."

"Did you lose interest in writing?" May couldn't even count the number of people she'd met who'd *talked* about wanting to be writers but who hadn't even started a story or who had started a dozen stories they'd never finished. Most people lacked the discipline needed to be a successful writer. Even though there was a magical, dreaminess attached to being a writer, any great writer understood the amount of nonglamorous work involved in completing a project. Writing on less inspiring days is what killed off half of the wannabe writers she knew. The rest didn't want to make actual time to write because they'd rather complain about *not* having time.

"Good question," Oliver said. "Not exactly. Medical school happened.

I crammed in reading a book or two around my school studies. The kids were born. Between school, my residency, and the family, I didn't leave a lot of room for writing. I wrote two short stories over the years, probably terrible ones at that, but it was something. If I'm honest, I didn't give writing much thought. Now, with all the quiet, I've been thinking about it a lot more. I have this story about the beach and an absentminded beach bum who gets wrapped up in a drug deal gone wrong and drags his two best friends into the mix. It's not autobiographical, but I've created some of the characters loosely based on people I knew growing up."

May quirked an eyebrow. "Were you involved in a drug deal gone awry?"

Oliver laughed, and May loved to watch how it relaxed his features and lifted his cheeks, creating crinkles around his eyes. "No, but I've known a few beach bum friends who've done some stupid things to help pay the rent a time or two, including getting mixed up with some colorful characters."

"Like the beach mafia?"

Oliver pointed at her and then leaned forward on his elbows. "You laugh, but the mafia is still kicking."

May laughed more. "I'm not doubting you. But your story sounds fun with lots of opportunity for tension and humor. Tell me again, why aren't you writing it?"

Oliver shrugged. "I know better than to try and give you an excuse."

"So don't give an excuse. Get to work," May said, leaning back in her chair. "If you want to write, you have to start. If you want to find the time, you will, and if it's important to you, you will find the time."

"This sounds like a talk you've had to give before. But I could use a good swift kick in the pants because I think it would make me feel good to write this story. To actually *finish* it. And I'm hogging the conversation." He popped a piece of scone into his mouth. "What about you? We've talked about aliens and Yellowstone and traveling and farming in this intense heat, and you've inspired me to get serious about writing something, but I'm doing all the talking."

May sipped her water. It was easier to let him talk, creating less opportunities for her to babble or sound silly or say something that would turn down the light in his eyes. "Asking the right questions is important, and listening is a skill."

"And you have mastered both," he said. "Michael is the same way. He has the most intense focus, and when it's turned on you, you feel like he can see right into your soul."

May wiped a napkin across her lips. Imagining Oliver didn't have kids and that he wasn't going through a divorce was easy when the two of them sat talking and laughing over breakfast pastries. But as soon as he mentioned his kids, May felt like someone shoved off a diving board. She *was* interested in learning all she could about Oliver, though. The last intelligent, well-traveled, humorous man she'd had a conversation with was her British Literature teacher in college. But Oliver was a complicated add-on to the easier, freer life she'd worked hard to create. Did she *really* need to toss him into her story?

Oliver leaned back in his chair. "It bothers you that I have kids."

It wasn't a question. May folded her napkin and slid it under the lip of the plate. She traced the blue inner circle on the ceramic plate before looking up at him. "No, of course not."

"Your face changes."

May sighed. Her gaze drifted out the window. A cardinal landed on an outside bench. She couldn't hear its chirp, but she imagined it each time the bird's beak opened. She looked back at Oliver.

"It's a strange juxtaposition. Sitting here with you, having a wonderful conversation, sharing a pastry, like two old friends. It's fun and exciting and interesting. And I get lost in it and forget that you're married with kids. And then that idea, even saying it out loud, feels strange. Because we're *not* old friends, and yet we've gone running together twice, and now we're having breakfast, and I don't want to be unintentionally inappropriate or disrespectful of your family." *And maybe I shouldn't want to spend time with you.*

The truth startled Oliver, but he nodded. "I respect that. And I respect you. I *am* married. I don't want to make you uncomfortable, so I apologize if I have. I'm happy to have a new friend, that's all."

The skin on the back of her neck prickled like someone standing too close to a fire. She rubbed it and then folded her hands together in her lap. "Friends. Of course. I don't mean to imply that I think you're trying to be anything more than a friend." Her cheeks burned. *She* was the one letting her emotions traipse off through a field of daisies holding hands with Oliver. *He*, on the other hand, was not. "Did it sound like that? It did, didn't it? That's embarrassing." She groaned. "Here you are being a friendly guy and we're having a nice chat, and off I go telling you not to hit on me because you're married with kids. Makes much more sense now that I let you do all the talking, right?"

Oliver laughed. "May, I know what you meant. It's easy to see why someone *would* hit on you, but I will keep it clean. You keep your hands on your side of the table, and I'll keep mine over here." He drew an imaginary line across the center of the table. "Like I tell my kids, don't cross that."

She leaned back in her chair, mimicking his pose, and blew air out through her lips. "Thanks for trying to make that less awkward."

"I understand. When I'm sitting here with you, it's easy to push aside, or even forget, all the mess right now. This feels like me getting to know a really interesting person. It makes me wonder how our lives would be different if I had met you twelve years ago in my college class instead of meeting Angelina."

May pressed her lips together as she studied his face. His downturned eyes revealed genuine curiosity. She shook her head. "First of all, I was just graduating high school, so I wouldn't have been in your class. Secondly, I was twelve years more naïve and more ridiculous than I am right now. You'd have overlooked me. Imagine my awkward responses times one thousand."

Oliver spun his coffee mug around and around in a slow-moving twist. "I don't see how anyone could overlook you. But you haven't told me what you do for a living. How is it that you're here and not working? Wait, let me guess. Circus performer? Independently wealthy? Hobo?"

May snorted. "Nobody uses the word *hobo* anymore. I'm a travel writer."

Oliver's smile wavered. "Seriously? You're a writer?"

May nodded. "I write more than travel articles, but right now, that's the bulk of my job. I can work from anywhere."

Oliver shook his head. "May MacAdams, you grow more interesting by the minute. Would you write me something?"

May drew her hands into her lap. "Like what?" She hadn't written anything personal for anyone. Ever. Chris believed writing was a waste of time, and the one night he had found and read a few of her poems, he'd made jokes for weeks about how girly and emotional and ridiculous they were. She'd stopped writing *anything* for nearly a year.

"Anything," he said. "Do you write poetry? I'd love to read something you've written, even if it's not new."

"I don't normally write for others, not outside of work, but I'll see what I can dig up," May said, doubting instantly that she'd ever offer up her writing to anyone again. Allowing someone to read her personal writings felt like that old dream people always talked about, the one where they're standing naked in front of colleagues or at school or any place where they're dying of embarrassment but are frozen and forced to endure.

"Fair enough. You have to meet my friend and neighbor Emily. She's a children's book author, and she and her husband live on my block. I bet you two could talk about writing and the writer's life. Since we've established that you and I *are* friends, does eating grilled meat and drinking moonshine tonight count as something you do with a friend?"

May scrunched up her face. "Moonshine? Are you serious? Tell me you don't actually brew moonshine in your backyard."

"I don't but I've been invited to a barbecue tonight at my neighbor's house. And although I swore to secrecy, I do believe there will be moonshine as part of the beverage selection. The rest of the evening will have music and dancing and food and what I hope will be a decent party. Emily will be there, and I bet you two will have a lot in common. Why don't you join us? How could you turn down moonshine?"

"Easy." She laughed. "If I wanted to drink gasoline, I would stop by the 7-Eleven and fill up."

Oliver leaned forward on his elbows and whispered, "Have you ever tried moonshine?"

She mimicked his posture and voice. "No."

"I'm not saying it doesn't taste like gasoline, but I wouldn't turn down an opportunity to try it at least once. But it's the lesser of all that's offered. There will be dancing, music, food, friends. Unless you have plans."

May looked toward the ceiling and sighed. She knew she should say no, but her curiosity multiplied. What would hanging out at a party with Oliver be like? "Have I mentioned that you're going to get me into trouble?"

"That has yet to be proven," Oliver said.

May's cheeks felt hot. In slow motion, she pressed her fingers against her skin as her lips parted. May hadn't felt *hot* in months. She unwound the scarf and dropped it into the passenger seat. Then she cranked the engine on the rental car and blasted the air conditioning. She rotated all the vents to face her so the cold air could chill her cheeks and lower her body temperature. She wiped her sweaty palms on her jeans. The carry-on bag with the box of letters sat in the passenger seat. May felt tempted to read another one. Instead, she reached over to turn on the radio. Ella Fitzgerald sang "Dream a Little Dream of Me." May sank back against the seat, closed her eyes, and exhaled.

"It's as though the universe is conspiring to make me remember you, Ollie. I'd almost forgotten this song...that dance," she whispered. Dancers whirled around in her mind. The scent of pine tree sap and tart lemonade. The fiery sensation of moonshine burning its way down her throat. The lights strung through the gazebo. The fireflies blinking in the forest.

After a breakfast of shared tasty pastries and more than an hour of conversation, May spent the rest of the day debating whether or not to go to the backyard party with Oliver. Grandma Charity encouraged her to "get out and live a little or she'd turn into an old maid." As if there were only two options that the rest of her life hinged on: go to the party and have a life or skip the party and become a lonely cat lady.

Later that evening, May parked her car on the curb outside of the address Oliver had written on one of the bakery's paper napkins. She leaned forward over the steering wheel and peered out through the windshield. Oliver lived in one of the historic homes, a two-story brick and stone Tudor, on Dogwood Lane. When he'd mentioned his house felt too big for just him, May had imagined a three-bedroom ranch-style home with outdated wallpaper, not a three-thousand-square-foot manor.

May's nerves caused her stomach to feel like she'd eaten too many Pop Rocks chased down by Coca-Cola. But she grabbed the grocery bag and strolled up the stone pathway that led to the front door. She pushed back her shoulders and lifted her gaze. She practiced deep breathing and felt the nerves lessen. The scent of charcoal filled the air, and laughter carried on the breeze. Two kids, bent over their handlebars, rode their bikes past her car and challenged each other to pedal faster.

The manicured boxwoods created a square border around the front of Oliver's house. Bright pink flowers bloomed in the flowerbeds. May admired the crosshatch windows lining the front of the house and the stone archway that welcomed people onto the front stoop.

Something moved out of the corner of her eye on the side of the freshly cut lawn. Oliver stepped into view. "Right on time. How are you?"

May paused on the path. Oliver wore khaki shorts and a gray T-shirt with an image of an antique camera on the front. The casual clothes made him appear like a guy May could have met at a book festival. She could almost forget the reality of who they both were.

"Grandma sent blueberry hand pies," May said, holding up the bag. "She informed me that it would be rude to attend a party without bringing a gift for the hosts."

Oliver held up a bottle of wine and pointed at the label. "Jack, the owner of the store, informed me that this was a favorite among townsfolk for a summertime shindig."

"Did he actually use the word *shindig*?"

Oliver closed the distance between them. "I added that for drama. Want to walk on over? Sounds like they've already started."

59

May studied his profile in the early evening light. What was Angelina like? Had they gone running through parks together, had they laughed over birthdays, traveled to foreign countries and strolled down cobblestones? Had he brought her wildflowers for no reason, or had they shouted for their university's team from the football stadium bleachers? What would have caused his wife to seek love and affection somewhere else? Was he a workaholic? A closet drinker? Had she always found it difficult to feel satisfied? What were their children like?

She stepped around her questions, and they drifted behind her like shadows. Oliver glanced over at her as they walked down the sidewalk. He walked close enough so that every few steps, their arms touched. May's skin burned beneath the contact.

Oliver asked, "The most important question of the night will be, do you prefer hotdogs or hamburgers?"

"Hotdogs or hamburgers?" May repeated. "Do I have to choose? Can't I have one of each?"

Shock rippled over Oliver's face before he chuckled. "*That* is the perfect answer. No dainty eaters over here."

May lifted the bag that held the hand pies. "Do I look like someone who is a dainty eater? I'd eat this whole bag if I didn't know it would be bad manners because I'd be eating someone's gift."

"I could help you," he added. "If we eat the whole bag before we get there, they'll never know you ate their gift."

May smiled. "I think you mean *we* ate their gift. It seems like you want to join in with the deception, but you don't want to get caught. So you'll leave me hanging out to dry by myself. Have I got that right?"

Oliver pressed his elbow into her side, and May pulled away with a playful laugh. "I can see my first impressions are lacking. I'll prove to you that I'm the good guy."

"We'll just have to see about that. For now, I'll mind my manners and show up with the gift. Because if Grandma finds out I ate all the pies, she'll have my hide and have me pulling weeds for days." May grinned at Oliver, bewitched by the wide smile on his face.

People stood in small groups on a manicured back garden behind another Tudor, one even larger than Oliver's. Partygoers drifted from one pod of people to another, holding sweating bottles of beer, plastic wine glasses full of rosé and white zinfandel, or red SOLO cups with hidden contents. Two men stood over the grill, flipping burgers and talking about a baseball summer league. A long card table sat beneath a gazebo strung with white, fat-bulb lights. Bowls and food containers crammed every available space on the tabletop. There were fresh berries, vegetables and hummus, an assortment of condiments, various potato and pasta salads, baked beans, coleslaw, bags of potato chips, and chocolate chip brownies.

Most of the people at the party knew May's grandparents, and they expressed both sympathy over the loss of her grandpa while seeming happy to meet another MacAdams family member. Oliver caught a football and tossed it back to a wiry teenager across the bright-green lawn. A tall, curvy blonde leaned back her head and laughed, sending the deep, husky sound into the star-speckled night sky. She caught May's gaze and lifted her hand.

"Oh, yes, coming right over," the woman said in a slow, Southern drawl, and then she spoke to the women standing around her, looking as though she were excusing herself.

May glanced over her shoulder. Was the woman talking to someone else, someone behind May? The blonde sashayed with purpose, making a straight line for May.

"I've been trying to get to you all night," she said, holding out her hand. Three gold bracelets jingled on her thin, feminine wrist. The red-and white-polka dot dress she wore pulled tight across her buxom chest, but drew in at the narrow waist before flaring out again at the hips. Gold loops decorated her shiny, white sandals. "I'm Emily Greene. Oliver told me that we *had* to meet, but I've been trapped with the president of the Garden Club, who insists on talking endlessly about enforcing that all knockout roses on the block be red, rather than white. Hello, Queen of Hearts, crazy much?

"Anyway, Oliver said you and I were kindred spirits like Anne Shirley and Diana Barry. He didn't actually use that exact comparison, but I gathered as much."

Emily's firm and short handshake surprised May because she had expected dainty and soft instead. May introduced herself and added,

"Oliver hardly knows me."

Emily looped her arm through May's and led her to the drink table. "Pick your poison."

May grabbed a red SOLO cup of ice and filled it with water.

"Total party girl, I see." Emily's chuckle reminded May of a blues singer's raspy, throaty tone. She poured moonshine and lemonade into a cup and then pulled May toward the back of the garden. "Let's take a walk."

It wasn't a question.

May followed in silence until they stood at the edge of the yard where pines soared high into the star-studded darkness. The night air smelled thick with tree sap and heady, blooming wild honeysuckle. Thousands of fireflies flickered in the forest, looking like flashbulbs.

"Are you imagining you're a Hollywood starlet and these are your adoring fans and the paparazzi snapping your photograph? Cause I am," Emily said.

May heard the smile in Emily's voice. "Has anyone ever told you that you look like a real-life Barbie doll?"

Emily's deep laugh sent out a ripple through the branches and startled the nearest fireflies. They dimmed and flew away. Within moments, they returned, blinking and darting around. "Only my husband." Emily leaned toward May and whispered. "He looks like a dark-haired Ken doll. No lie. And the truth is, I always wanted to look like Hawaiian Barbie. Dark skin and hair. I suppose we always want what we don't have." She sipped her mixed drink and winced. "It sure does burn going down."

"Do you know how many women would love to look like Barbie?"

"Too many. It's not that glamorous. You can't find regular clothes that fit. Everything I own has to be altered, unless I decide I want to wear muumuus exclusively. Want a drink?" Emily held out the lemonade-moonshine mix.

May shook her head and watched a firefly zip through the trees like a woodland fairy.

"Enough about me. The more interesting conversation is, how did you meet Oliver? I just about fell out of my chair when he showed up with you. Course I wasn't sitting, but did you know him already?

They just moved here a few months ago, and I didn't think they knew anyone else. But Angelina has been gone for a few weeks now, so we haven't seen him as often to catch up."

May rocked on her heels. "I don't know him. Not really." The plastic cup dented and released in her grip.

Emily turned to face May. Her dark eyelashes fluttered. "That's all I get? Oliver said you're a writer, and you're leaving out important details. Are you keeping me in the dark on purpose so you can reveal your plot in a surprising way later? Or are you being vague in the hopes that I'll drop it?"

May laughed and shuffled her sandals on the prickly grass.

"Can I be honest? Tell you a secret?" Emily asked. "I haven't seen that man smile—and I mean a real smile—since they moved here. And a face like that, it's a shame it doesn't smile more often. Am I right? I couldn't figure out why he never smiled until I met Angelina. She's..." Emily sipped her drink. "She's a real piece of work, as they say. Unhappiness drips off her like acid, scorching everything around her. She acts like she can't stand him, which is such a strange thing to see once you've met Oliver because he's so damn nice and mannerly. Their kids are well mannered too, and then you meet Angelina, and it's like she's being eaten up from the inside by a terrible darkness. I shouldn't talk about someone I don't really know, but just seeing him acting so happy is like seeing a completely different Oliver. He looks genuinely joyful." Emily lifted her cup in May's direction. "I'm not a betting woman, but if I were, I'd bet that's all you."

May's eyes widened. A breath hung in her throat when she inhaled. "No. No, we hardly know each other. Honestly, we've only had, like, four conversations." May's heartrate increased as her stomach knotted. A combination of excitement and terror wrestled deep in her gut.

"Only four? That's exact." Emily shrugged. "Did you know there is a stat that says it takes men 8.2 seconds to fall in love?" She held her mixed drink toward May again.

May grabbed Emily's cup and took a drink. The acidic juice and the potent moonshine burned a trail from her tongue all the way down her throat. May coughed and Emily laughed while she slapped May on the back.

Fireflies circled around them and surrounded them like a protective shield. "Don't say that," May whispered. "He's married, and you shouldn't talk about falling in love like it isn't dangerous."

Emily sighed. "Love is the most powerful emotion, and that's why it will always be the most dangerous." The lightning bugs separated and dashed toward the trees.

"Who wants to dance?" Oliver asked.

May wiped the back of her hand across her lips. Oliver stood with a man who May guessed was Emily's husband because he *did* look like a Ken doll. May's gaze drifted toward the gazebo. "Dream a Little Dream of Me" played from large speakers.

"Oh, honey, they're playing our song," Emily said, sliding her arm around her husband's waist. "To be fond of dancing was a certain step toward falling in love." Emily looked at May.

"Jane Austen," May responded.

Emily smiled. "Oliver was right. You and I *are* kindred spirits." She and her husband walked toward the couples dancing and swaying on the grass.

Oliver held out his arm and hooked it, offering it to May.

"I don't dance," she said.

"Is that the moonshine talking? Come on. One dance?"

"Is this going to be like potato chips?" May asked.

Oliver tilted his head. "How so?"

"You can't have just one?"

Lightning bugs flew close the ground at their feet, creating a blinking path toward the dancers. Oliver reached out, grabbed May's hand, and hurried toward the music, singing along with Ella Fitzgerald about bright shining stars and night breezes. Oliver wasn't making it easy to isolate him in the friend zone in her brain. She counted off 8.2 seconds, measuring time in heartbeats.

7

*F*our and a half hours later, the Mystic Water city limits welcome sign appeared. The sign's vibrant lettering looked freshly painted. The wording and design hadn't changed since the last time she'd seen it. For a moment, as she crossed the line and entered the city, May imagined she was traveling back through time.

Sunlight enveloped her car like a hug from a longtime friend, wrapping her with warmth and light. She rolled down the window and whispered, "I missed you," before she realized what she was saying. The smell of smoky heat rising off the black-tar asphalt pushed into the car. The scent of sap from the mature pine trees that lined both sides of the road mingled with the sweet honeysuckle breeze. Time slowed around her car even as her foot slipped off the gas pedal and she coasted into town.

May entered downtown Mystic Water and scanned the new shops shuffled in with ones she remembered from her youth. Townsfolk walked the sidewalks eating ice cream from Scooper's. Children skipped toward the sunny park. Her brow wrinkled when she noticed Bea's Bakery was gone, and in its place looked like a newer structure. Scrambled, possibly a diner, was full of people eating inside the cool interiors. The sticky scent of cinnamon rolls drifted into the car as she drove past. People dined in Mackie's Café and grabbed sandwiches and pickles wrapped in brown parchment at Cavelli's Deli. A sparkling, glass front window on a corner building displayed a red sign with the words For Sale printed on it.

May turned the car away from town and drove toward Dogwood Lane. During her earlier search for lodging, she found that Mystic Water didn't offer many rentals. There was one bed and breakfast, but May wasn't in the mood to share living spaces with anyone. However, one other option popped up as available—of course it was located near where Oliver had lived thirty years ago. The rental was too large for what she needed, but in a pinch, staying in a restored Victorian manor offered more pros than cons. May turned onto the street and slowed her speed even more. She crept past Oliver's former home, leaning forward over the steering wheel, and peered up at the Tudor. Nostalgia swept in through her window and loosened her hands on the wheel. If she concentrated, she could almost hear Oliver's laughter, almost see the two of them standing on the front lawn. It felt as though she'd left a younger version of herself—a ghost of who she was then—with Oliver in Mystic Water.

On the next block, May pulled into the driveway belonging to Honeysuckle Hollow. May had read all about the manor on its website—how it had belonged to a local family, the Hamiltons; how it had then fallen into disrepair, but how it had also been rehabbed by another local, Tessa Andrews Borelli. Honeysuckle Hollow hosted weddings, family gatherings, parties, and the occasional traveler. May could almost believe fate had caused everyone to avoid these particular dates so that she could return to Mystic Water and stay in a house that was down the street from where she'd spent her summer with Oliver.

The Summer of Oliver is how Emily referred to that time in May's life. May, in contrast, had often called it *The Summer I Died* because nothing else described what happened to her at the end of that season.

May grabbed her suitcase and found the keys to the house tucked beneath a turtle on the back patio. She stood in the garden, turning full circle, admiring the flowering roses and the honeysuckle vines cascading all across the fence. A river weaved through the garden, and white, orange, and golden koi swam and opened and closed their mouths at the surface of the water. Herbs grew among flowers, and May imagined tossing up a tent and staying in the middle of it. Wouldn't John get a laugh out of her camping outside on the ground? She heard his voice warning her of how such a terrible idea would end only with back pain. May smiled. She and John hadn't camped since their thirties; they'd learned to appreciate cabins and beds instead. But returning to Mystic Water slipped May back in time to when she was younger, when camping in a backyard felt fun and silly, when eating a melty, gooey grilled cheese was the best dinner.

May unlocked the heavy back door, and it swung open into a spacious, light-filled kitchen.

"Wow," May breathed out. She pushed closed the door with her foot. May shrugged out of her pea coat and draped it across a kitchen chair. Leaving her suitcase in the kitchen, she grabbed her phone and called Emily.

Emily answered on the second ring. "Are you there?" Her breathy voice sounded as though she'd run to the phone.

"I'm staying in Honeysuckle Hollow." May peered out the dining room window at the front yard. "Your old house is across the street."

Emily laughed. "Any reason why you chose a mansion for your accommodations? I'm not judging you, of course. Every princess deserves a stay in a castle."

May lowered her shoulders from her ears and rolled her head on her neck. "I had two options. A mansion or a bed and breakfast."

Emily hummed in her throat. "You know what my first question is. How many bathrooms in the B&B?"

"A couple of the rooms have toilets. One has a toilet and shower, but it's booked. Then there's a communal bathtub and toilet upstairs."

Emily groaned. "Shared bathrooms, forced conversation, pretending you like the dry biscuits at breakfast served by a hovering host? Good choice on going with the mansion. Now be honest. How does our old house look?"

A blackbird landed on the lawn and turned its soul-searching eyes toward May.

"Still in great shape, but their knockout roses don't look as wonderful as yours did." May let the curtains fall back into place. "The house doesn't shine as much without you in it."

"You're just trying to flatter me. It's working. You know I was a terrible gardener, but I love you for saying so." Emily exhaled. "What's next?"

May shrugged, even though Emily couldn't see her. She peered up the grand staircase. The chandelier sparkled like diamonds in sunlight. Dozens of rainbows spotted the hardwood in the foyer. May scattered them with the toe of her shoe. "Let Jackie know I'm here."

"How are you feeling?"

"The truth?" May rubbed her stomach. "Queasy."

"You can always back out. You don't *have* to do this," Emily said, slowing down her words even more, placing extra emphasis on *have*.

May shook her head. "I've come this far. He might not even know I'm there."

"May, he'll know. I talked to Andy, and he agrees."

"Agrees with what?" May asked, pacing through the living room.

"Oliver has *never* gotten over you."

May rolled her eyes and stood at the long windows. "Oh, don't be such a romantic," she argued. "That's absurd."

"You're standing in Mystic Water about to go see a man whose daughter has been *tracking you down* for weeks just so her dad could see you one last time."

One last time. "I feel sick."

"Of course you do. How long are you planning on staying?"

"A day or two, maybe less."

Emily's exhale traveled through the phone, falling heavy on May's shoulders before drifting away. "Call me as soon as you can? Let me know what happens. I'll be on pins and needles until you do."

"How do you know I'm not going to bail?" A cardinal swooped down from the oak tree in the backyard and landed on the patio. It tilted its head and looked at May through the kitchen windows. Then it chirped twice before flying away.

"Because you've never left a story unfinished, and this one has another chapter or two to go."

After the party with dancing, moonshine, and a yard filled with as many fireflies as stars in the sky, May stood on the sidewalk in front of Oliver's house. A streetlight's beam cast them in a small, pale-orange circle of light. She covered her mouth and laughed. "You'll get us kicked out of the neighborhood if you don't stop making me laugh."

Oliver leaned toward her and whispered, "I don't think they can kick you out of a neighborhood."

"Were you even *listening* to the president of the Garden Club? She sounded serious about enforcing both flower choices and neighborhood quiet time after 10:00 p.m."

Oliver folded his hands together behind his neck and looked up at the stars. "I tuned out around the time Emily started snickering. Somewhere around the part about chicken dung in the flowerbeds."

"We shouldn't fault her for having a healthy obsession about keeping Mystic Water lovely and clean and...what did she call it? Free of what?"

"Noise pollution," Oliver said. "According to her, anything that happens after ten is definitely pollution, mostly to the mind and soul. And can you really have a healthy obsession? Doesn't the word *obsession* mean something akin to mania?"

"Mania sounds threatening. I better be getting on home. Right now you're polluting my brain and evidently my soul, which is serious business."

Oliver wiggled his eyebrows. "Serious indeed. Well, Ms. MacAdams, this has been a real treat. I hope we can do this again sometime." As soon as the words left his mouth, his smile drooped. "Is it wrong to say that? Because it's true. I'd like to see you again, and I have enjoyed getting to know you more. There's never enough time to talk about all I want to."

May held her breath for a few seconds. Then she exhaled, deciding on admitting the truth. "I had a nice time tonight too."

"I still want you to write something for me. I know you have talent. I can tell."

May glanced away. "I could be a horrible writer." She caught his eye. "Or someone who only writes depressing and miserable poetry."

"Not the May I know."

Her lips quirked. "You don't know me."

"I know enough," he countered.

69

"Enough for what?"

"Enough to know I want to see you again. Soon."

May wanted to hug him, to grab his hands and thank him for an evening of laughing so hard that her stomach ached. She wanted to feel him up close again, like she had when they were dancing, when she could close her eyes and imagine they were alone on a dance floor, surrounded by twinkling lights, fireflies, and summertime magic. Instead, she held out her hand, and Oliver tilted his head and looked at it.

He gripped her hand in his and shook it. "The safest option for saying good-bye after 10:00 p.m."

"My thoughts exactly. Have a good night, Oliver. Thanks for moonshine and dancing." She grinned. "Bet you've never been thanked for those two things together before." She unlocked her car and opened the door.

"Can I see you again?" he asked just as she moved to get inside the car.

She paused too long. He fidgeted on the sidewalk.

"I only know Emily and Andy," he added, "and now you. It's nice... having a friend. I'd forgotten what that was like."

May felt an urge to say no. Even when she tried to shove Oliver into the friend space, he didn't fit well; trying to compartmentalize her feelings for him felt a lot like trying to shove a dozen inflated balloons into a clown car. One or *all* of the balloons were bound to escape. And her heart reacted to him in a way it didn't respond to her other guy friends. She made the mistake of looking into his hopeful eyes, and that one glance dismantled the shoddy wall she was trying to construct between them. May kicked her toe against the pavement.

Just because she *could* spend time with Oliver didn't mean she *should* continue doing so. Her mind zoomed into the future, piecing together a few dozen scenarios for how her relationship with Oliver could turn out. Fifty percent ended with her feeling devastated because she had become too attached to someone she should not be attached to, and the relationship severed, leaving her with empty hands and a broken heart. The other fifty percent played out images of them sitting together, holding hands, loving each other until they were wrinkled and white-haired. "Grandma Charity can only tolerate me for so many hours a day. She'll probably be glad for me to give her some quiet time."

Oliver shoved a hand through his hair. "I'll call you. Now you better get out of here before you're polluted any more. I wouldn't want to damage that soul of yours."

May shook her head and waved as she drove away, wondering if she were already leaving a part of her heart with Oliver as he stood on the sidewalk watching her disappear into the night.

May left her suitcase in the closet of Honeysuckle Hollow's master bedroom. She dragged her fingers across the sky blue and white quilted comforter on the king-size bed. May pulled O'Conner's novel and the shoebox out of the carry-on, dropping them both onto the quilt. She flipped off the shoebox lid. The more she opened the box, the less fear coiled in her stomach. The emotions she'd had trapped and chained inside of her had already been loosed. Now standing in Mystic Water, there seemed to be no reason to hold her memories at bay. The unleashed memories trampled over every boundary she'd created. *Wild horses,* she thought. *Running free.*

May pulled out the next letter, which had been tucked inside a card adorned with a three-dimensional sun and beams carved out of wood and glued to the front of bright yellow cardstock. The interior card read, *You are the sunshine in all my days.* Oliver had signed his name, but he'd also included a note.

Dear Magical May,

Before a few days ago, the perfect evening would have been some distant time in high school or college with me sitting with friends in the football stadium. Too much soda or beer and enough nacho cheese to make us sick. What is that stuff anyway? Plastic? I don't want to know. There would have been lots of yelling at the ref and singing along with the band.

Now I'd admit that spending hours putting up a backyard tent and sitting in the grass eating a grilled cheese with you is what I'd put on repeat. I haven't looked for constellations since I was a kid. How do you do that? Make everyone feel young and happy and special? I've never had a more magical friend.

Sincerely,

Awed Oliver

May dropped the letter and card on the bed. Then she removed her shoes and wool socks, wiggling her toes, waiting for a shiver of cold that didn't appear. She wandered back downstairs, with wispy sunlight trailing indoors behind her like fairy dust. She grabbed her phone off the kitchen countertop and dialed Jacqueline's number as she stood on the warm kitchen tiles.

"Hey," Jacqueline said, whispering a word so full of hope that May's heart stuttered. "I'm so glad you finally called. How are you? Are you in Mystic Water?" A door clicked closed. Muffled voices filled in the empty spaces.

"I'm in town, yes, staying at a rental on Dogwood Lane—"

"Dogwood Lane? That's where Dad's house is. We lived on Dogwood Lane for a couple of years, but I guess you know that. We moved from Mystic Water to be closer to my mom's family at the beach and sold the house, but Dad moved back once we were grown. Same house. He said he'd been waiting on it to go up for sale ever since we moved. He finally got his wish just before he was ready to retire. He's been back in Mystic Water for a few years now, working at the clinic again."

May's eyebrows lifted on her forehead. "He bought your old house? The Tudor-style one?" She walked through the dining room and looked out the front windows that faced the street. The thick drapery rustled beside her when the air conditioner kicked on. She couldn't see Oliver's old home, but she knew it was only a few houses down from Honeysuckle Hollow.

Jacqueline made a humming noise in her throat. "He loved that house. I thought he was a little crazy for wanting to move back to a town where he had no family or friends, but it makes more sense to

72

me now. He has fond memories of Mystic Water, of the friendships he made here. He said it felt like coming home.

"We're still at the hospital. He's having a restless day today, so they gave him some medicine to help him sleep. Would you like to come visit? He's still sleeping now, but he'll probably wake up in the next hour."

Do I want to go see him? May's stomach clenched. She rolled her neck on her shoulders, working out the tension. *What's the big deal? He's just a man, and what you had with him is fathoms-deep water under a bridge you burned to the ground years ago.* May had forgiven Oliver—not that what happened was exactly his fault, but she *had* blamed him for months after she left. Blamed him for letting her fall so hard in love with him, for letting her break herself into pieces over an ill-fated romance. The brokenness had healed, and the more years that passed, the less she felt he deserved *all* the blame. But it had all been *too easy* with Oliver. Too easy to spend time with him, too easy to laugh, too easy to love him madly.

May knew that if she had the chance to do it all again, to make the decision to leave him again, she would still leave. There had been much larger, much more precious hearts involved than her own. If she could go back and avoid the heartbreak by never allowing herself to fall for Oliver, would she? She imagined herself taking those steps toward him, letting him slip his hand into hers, giving him control of her heart.

"Mrs. May...are you still there?"

"Yes," May said. "Yes, I'll come there. What room are you in?"

May carried her cell phone upstairs and dropped it on the bed beside the opened shoebox. *Should I change my clothes?* She fanned her shirt away from her body, feeling the dampness of perspiration on her back. She dug her toothbrush out of her suitcase and stood in the bathroom. Holding the toothpaste in one hand, she reached out and pressed her fingertips against the silver glass of the mirror. She felt as though she were looking beyond her reflection and straight through the layers of the past, seeing a young woman with a scattering of freckles emphasized by the hot summer sun and with a smile that lasted for weeks. Her auburn hair hung around her shoulders, and the sensation of kisses whispered over her neck.

May exhaled and dropped the toothpaste tube on the bathroom counter. She glided through the bedroom, opened the French doors, and then stepped out onto the second-floor balcony. Breathing in the air of Mystic Water triggered a storm of memories, each one rolling forward, expanding, with thunder rattling her bones, bolts of lightning flashing past. Sunlight stretched through the leaves of the great oak in the backyard and highlighted May in a spotlight of warmth.

She stared out into the garden, but she didn't see the present. She watched scenes from her past, as though her life rewound itself back to the summer thirty years ago when she'd fallen in love with Oliver Bisset.

The long-absent sunlight drew her out, highlighting the memories in her mind, and May walked barefoot through the downstairs of Honeysuckle Hollow and stepped out into the vibrant backyard. The summer air was weighted heavy with moisture, coating everything with a fine layer of damp. She lingered in the shade of the oak tree. May glanced around, not seeing Honeysuckle Hollow's backyard, but Oliver's.

She knelt and touched the prickly, green grass, running her hands over the blades, remembering how the tiny pin pricks of Bermuda grass had poked into the backs of her bare legs when she and Oliver had lain, elbows touching, staring up at the stars. Crickets had chorused from the darkest shadows while lightning bugs blinked against the fence line and in the tree branches.

May rubbed her elbow, feeling the ghost of Oliver's skin pressing into hers. Who had spotted the Big Dipper first?

8

*M*ay fell into a hole that yawned wide in her mind, tumbling back thirty years ago when she'd spent one long summer in Mystic Water.

Grandma Charity's voice came from the kitchen, sounding as though she were having a conversation with someone. May hadn't heard anyone drive up. When she peered out of her bedroom window, the driveway was empty of anyone else's car. Had someone called? May hadn't heard the house phone ring. She'd been writing a poem. For Oliver. *What has gotten into me? Now I'm writing poetry for men?* May closed her notebook and dropped her pen into a coffee mug on the desk.

May walked up the hallway, with floorboards creaking beneath her bare feet. Grandma Charity laughed, and May's eyebrows rose.

"I'd like to see *you* try to catch one," Grandma Charity said. She stood in front of the kitchen sink, her head leaned toward one shoulder holding a cell phone tight, and washed her hands. The makings of a pie crust covered the countertop with a dusting of flour, pats of butter, a bowl of blackberries, and cling wrap. Grandma Charity dried her hands and then glanced over her shoulder. She laughed again. "Oh, here she is. You have a good day, young man." She held out the phone for May.

May stared at it without moving.

Grandma Charity lifted her hand higher. "Go on, take it. Quit standing there and blinking like a toad on a log. It's a call for you."

May grabbed the phone. She pressed it to her ear. "Hello?"

"Good morning," Oliver said.

She heard the smile in his voice. She lowered the cell and wrinkled her brow. "You answered my phone?" she asked her grandma.

Grandma Charity shrugged and turned back to her pie dough. "That's what people do with phones."

May hurried from the kitchen and pushed open the front screen door to the wraparound porch. "Hey," she breathed into the phone. "Sorry, I didn't hear the phone ringing. I was working on a writing project."

"That's okay. I had a nice chat with Mrs. MacAdams, and I was careful to properly address her this time. How are you? I've wanted to call for days, but the office has been busy, and I needed to get a few things before I was ready to call."

May exhaled. "That's a strange thing to say. What things did you need to get before you could call?" She sat on the top porch step. Squirrels raced through the yard and up a pecan tree. A riding mower rolled into view on the side acre lot, and the warm summer breeze brought the scent of freshly mowed grass. Morning sunlight shined through the trees and dappled the front yard with pockets of light. May wiggled her toes in a ray of sunshine.

"It's good to hear your voice," Oliver said. "Before I answer, tell me...how are you?"

"Oh, we've been good around here. I sent off an article to *Travel and Leisure*. And I've been working on a piece for *Southern Living* about Southern cities that are real gems. One of those types you read about the best-kept secrets."

"Did Mystic Water make the list?"

May smiled. "I'm tossing it in for luck. It really is a special town. I'm hitting only the high points, like the world's most delicious cinnamon star bread and how it protects you from unhappiness and kindles love. If I read my article, I'd want to visit Mystic Water."

"Make sure you include the dashing and brilliant local doctor." Oliver and May both laughed. "What else have you been up to? Not all work with no play, I hope."

"Grandma and I went blackberry picking early this morning. I'm not saying I ate my bowl of berries before we got back to the house, and I'm not saying that Grandma gave me a stern talking to about it, but that could have happened. Now she's baking a pie from the looks of the kitchen, and I'm outside talking to you. How are you?"

"Doing well. The office has been overflowing this week, and the kids and I are planning a camping trip toward the end of the summer, which is why I called. Have you ever been camping or pitched a tent before?"

76

May's lips parted. Her heartbeat paused. *Is he asking me to go camping...with his kids?* "If camping in Grandpa's fields count, then I've been camping. We used my cousins' boy scout tents, and I helped pitch them."

"I had a feeling you'd know. I already asked Mrs. MacAdams if she minded you being out this evening, and she gave you permission, but I'll ask you too," he said and chuckled. "Are you free tonight?"

"It seems I am." She wanted to ask, "Does Grandma know that you're separated, not really single? Because I don't know how she'd respond to me being out with you. She's old fashioned in that respect." But instead, May asked, "What's on your agenda?"

"I ordered a giant, family-size tent for the kids and me to use, but I want to practice putting it up before we go. It's a two-man job. Or an Oliver and May job. If I buy dinner, would you want to come over and help me figure it out?"

Two blackbirds swooped down and hopped around an oak tree, pecking at the ground. A blue jay dove down toward them like a fighter jet, and the blackbirds flew off, cawing and flapping, leaving behind black feathers.

May asked, "Backyard camping?"

"That's the general idea."

"What's for dinner?" May wandered into the front yard and stopped to admire the blooming daylilies lining the front porch. Sunlight followed her like a beloved pet, and May smiled up at the sky.

"Good question. I'm not a great cook, but I can handle simple things. Or I could order takeout from somewhere in town."

"What simple things can you cook?"

"May, you're putting me under pressure!" he said and laughed again. "I want to impress you and say I can cook fish tacos on the grill or chicken kebabs, but really my specialty is grilled cheese. I can make it fancy with bacon or tomatoes."

May watched a sunflower-yellow finch land on the nearest bird feeder. It chirped at her. "Don't undersell the grilled cheese. That's a winning dish if done properly."

"How about you come over at six and you can judge my grilled cheese skills? I'll even throw in a couple of specialty treats from Bea's Bakery."

"Now you've properly bribed me. I'll see you then."

"Can't wait."

May said good-bye and disconnected. She pressed the cell phone to her chest and grinned, feeling like she was sixteen again. She spun around in a circle, even though she knew better than to unleash the happiness she felt expanding inside her. A voice in her mind said, *Rein it in! Get ahold of yourself!* But another voice said, *Don't miss this.* She glanced toward the kitchen window where Grandma Charity stood watching. From a distance, it was difficult to see her grandma's face, but it looked as though she was smiling too.

Later in the day May parked in front of Oliver's house, grabbed her purse and the blackberry pie Grandma insisted she take, and walked up the path leading to Oliver's front door. She'd reread the poem she'd written for him a dozen times, and she'd argued with herself about whether to bring it with her. The poem, now folded like a secret love letter, heated her purse like a lava rock and warmed her hip as she walked, and the bag swung back and forth against her.

May hesitated before knocking. Would it feel strange to be alone with him in his house? Was it inappropriate? *If you're friends,* she thought, *then there is absolutely nothing wrong with hanging out.*

9

*O*liver chewed on the side of his thumbnail. He'd spent a solid hour cleaning the whole house—sweeping, vacuuming, polishing, and dusting. How *did* that much dust collect on the top of his framed college diplomas? The frame glass sparkled, highlighting the certifications of his Bachelor of Science and Doctor of Medicine degrees. He cracked his knuckles and scanned the living room again. Then he blew out a candle he'd lit on the coffee table. Too much, too touchy-feely. The candle had been a house gift from his neighbor Emily, and now the whole room smelled like bourbon pecan pie. A car door slammed outside. Oliver flipped on the ceiling fan and waved his hands through the air, hoping to get rid of the Betty Crocker smell. He felt squirmy—like high school squirmy before his first date, which had been an epic failure. But this wasn't a damn date. He cracked his knuckles again and walked into the foyer.

Oliver flung open the door. "Right on time."

May stood on the front stoop in a beam of sunlight. She balanced a wrapped pie on one hand and clutched her purse strap in the other. Her green eyes looked jittery like a rabbit that's been spotted in the brush, but she smiled. Heat rolled toward him like flames and circled him.

"I was taught that being late isn't an option," she said. "Terrible things happen to late people."

Oliver raised his eyebrow. "What kinds of terrible things?" He opened the door wider and waved her inside the cool interiors.

She stood in the foyer and shivered. "I've never been late, so I don't know." She craned her neck back to see the two-story entry with its wrought iron chandelier. She touched the dark, carved wood railing of the staircase. "This woodwork is so intricate, I bet it's original to the house." She looked at the two rooms that branched off from the foyer, one to the right and one to the left. Then she peered around him, straight ahead, at the living room that led to an outdoor terrace. "Wow, Oliver, this is something else."

"Something...good? I like historical homes. The character and the workmanship. They don't build modern homes like this anymore."

May slipped off her flip-flops. She stepped onto the Persian rug centered in the foyer and wiggled her toes. "Give me a tour, please?"

Oliver took the purse from her hands, dropped it on a side table in the foyer, and carried the pie into the kitchen while she waited. When he returned, he motioned for her to follow him.

He led her first to his favorite room, a library off the front of the house with built-in bookcases that stretched all the way to the ceiling. May dragged her fingers across the spines and smiled, leaning back her head and scanning hundreds of titles.

He leaned his hip against the edge of his oversize writing desk, watching her, wondering if she knew how stunning she looked. Her smile was contagious. "I knew you'd love this room."

Her expression softened as her pupils dilated. "You're right. I'm done with the tour. We don't have to see the rest. If you need help with the tent, I'll be in here." Sunlight glinted off his diplomas, and May stepped closer to read them. "What was your undergraduate major?"

"Biology."

She stepped closer to his medical degree. Oliver saw her reflection in the glass. "Why didn't you major in English?"

"And let everyone know I'm a science *and* an English nerd? No thank you." Oliver laughed and pushed off the desk.

"You're right," May agreed. "It would have been too much for the ladies to handle. Great at both science and English *and* being handsome. Mind explosion."

May's back stiffened. Her eyes widened in the glass, and Oliver's pulse quickened. She thought he was handsome? Silence stretched.

Oliver almost laughed at how uncomfortable she looked. She hadn't meant to call him handsome; that much was obvious. So he said, "Come on. There's more to see."

He showed her the master bedroom with its Roman bath and Turkish blue tiles, the formal dining room with its too-big table for twelve, and the living room centered around a stone fireplace. The modern kitchen with its dark woods and rich granite countertops opened into a breakfast area with floor-to-ceiling windows that welcomed in the sunlight. An additional room connected to the breakfast area.

"This is called a keeping room. I'm not sure what it's keeping, but it's basically another sitting room."

May nodded as she stepped into the small, square space. "It's a name dating back to Colonial America. Most of the cooking was done around the family's only fireplace, which was also the warmest area of the house. You can imagine that made the kitchen a crowded space, so to avoid annoying the cook, these rooms were created off the kitchen. That way everyone could gather nearby, in the keeping room. Think of it as a cozy nook where you can talk to the cook, stay out of the way, and still enjoy the warmth and company."

He crossed his arms over his chest and leaned against the room opening. "Are you also an expert in colonial times?"

May shrugged. "I've done a bit of research. Travel writer," she said and pointed at herself.

Oliver showed May the three bedrooms upstairs, each with its own ensuite, and the media room that had been intended for the kids but sat quiet and empty. Untouched and dusty like rooms no one ever uses. May stepped into Jackie's doorway, not quite entering, but studying the pink-striped wallpaper, the poofy duvet that looked like a cumulus cloud had landed on her twin bed, and the bright-white bookshelves full of colorful stories. The scent of strawberries and plastic lingered. A small purple pony sat on the windowsill looking out into the front yard.

A picture of Jackie sat on her desk, and May's eyes drifted there and stayed. "She's got a lot of spirit," he said. "She wants to be either an architect or a nun."

May smiled. "That's quite the spread. Are you Catholic?"

Oliver leaned against the doorjamb and crossed his arms over his chest. "No, but she read a biography on Mother Teresa and decided being a nun should be added to her list of possible life paths."

"She could do both," May said as she walked toward the staircase. "Design and build nunneries or convents." She glanced at Oliver over her shoulder. "She's beautiful."

"Thank you." Oliver's chest filled with both warmth and longing. He imagined Jackie's laughter and the way she said *Dad*, dragging it out when she was thought he was being frustrating on purpose. "My biggest worry is that some boy will break her heart, and I won't be able to do anything about it. I can't keep her innocent forever." His fists clenched and released.

"That's guaranteed," May said descending the staircase, sliding her palm along the smooth railing.

He hustled to catch up and walk closer to her. "Which part? The broken heart or the innocence?"

"Both," May said. "I hate to sound like my daddy, but heartbreaks and failures are some of the ways we build character. Love is always a risk, isn't it?"

"Do you think it's worse to never take the risk?" Oliver asked, stopping in the foyer and watching her.

"Do you?"

She had him there. *Did* he think love was worth the risk? Was it worth ending up where he was now? He looked at his feet and then up at her. May's pale eyes and gentle expression relaxed him, making him feel as though he'd stepped outside into the morning light. "A few weeks ago I would have said no. I would have told you that taking that risk was too great. I didn't believe the kind of love—attraction, whatever you call it—worth risking heartache for even existed. We're all just confused people muddling through and making a disaster of relationships." He tilted his head toward the living room. "Walk with me to the terrace?"

He didn't wait for her to respond, so she followed him through the living room; he felt the push of heat behind him. He opened the French doors and stepped out onto the stone terrace. A winding stone path accentuated the landscaped grass and led off to the left. Oliver stopped at the edge of the terrace and stared into the yard. He'd already opened the oversize tent box, and he'd taken out all the pieces and parts and arranged them on the grass.

May stopped beside him. Sunlight reached for her. A breeze meandered through the yard and swept away the heat. "What changed? You said *a few weeks ago*, so what's different now?"

Oliver stepped off the terrace and loped across the yard toward the tent supplies. Excitement sparked in his chest, fueling a feeling of boldness. He turned around, walking backward a few paces, and pointed at her. "I met you. I've never had such an interesting friend." His face burned, but he smiled. Then he laughed and motioned for her to follow.

May hesitated, pressing her hand against her stomach, and then she stepped right off the terrace, right toward Oliver, looking just as brave as he felt.

Two hours later May snapped the last piece into place while Oliver held the pole steady. She stood and stretched her back and wiped the back of her hand across her forehead. "This thing is a monster of greatness." She glanced at the backyard fence; the sun was slipping away in the distance, leaving behind a sherbet orange sky. "We almost didn't beat the sunset."

Oliver bent over and stepped through the tent's front opening. He turned full circle in the first room, checking to make sure all the poles were tight and that all the zippers worked. The kids were going to love this. He could hear their excited voices as they darted through the rooms. He stepped into the second room meant for sleeping. "Thanks for your help, May. I'm 100 percent sure I wouldn't have been able to do this alone."

May pointed to the empty box. "It says so in large letters. Two man or woman job."

"Does it say 'two woman'"? Oliver stepped out of the tent and squinted at the box.

"It has two little silhouette men. I'm adding extra details they forgot to include. If you have a Sharpie, I can put a couple of dresses on those guys."

The sunset reflected off May's auburn hair. His fingers itched to run his hands through it. He cleared his throat. "You're staying for dinner, right? I'm not ready for you to go. Unless you need to."

May nodded. "I vaguely remember you inviting me to have dinner and that you were going to impress me with grilled cheese and baked goods."

"The pressure is on." He gathered up the remnants of the tent box and torn-open plastic baggies while May filled her arms too. She followed him inside and when Oliver thought, *I could get used to this, playing house with May,* he tripped over the lip of the French door frame.

May laughed but made sure he was okay. As they gathered the dropped trash, Oliver shoved the thought way-far to the back of his mind.

Half an hour later May sat cross-legged in the darkened backyard. Tiny blades of freshly mown grass poked into the backs of Oliver's bare legs. Gooey provolone and pepper jack stretching from her lips as she pulled away from the sandwich distracted him, and he stared at her mouth. Her fingertips glistened from the melted butter on the bread.

"What's the verdict?" Oliver asked and then shoved the last bite of sandwich into his mouth.

"Cheesy perfection. You could start a food truck," May said. "Travel across the states."

He wiped his hands on a napkin. "Are you going to be my sidekick? Writing about our travels?"

May's smile wavered. Warmth radiated toward Oliver, stretching over his body, stirring up a feeling of need within him. Her expression turned unreadable.

"Why do I have to be the sidekick?" she asked, reaching for a napkin.

"You're right. You're the hero in this story. I can already attest to that."

May leaned her head back and stared up into the branches of the trees in the backyard. "Oh," she said and inhaled. "Lightning bugs."

It was as though May had called them into existence. A few flashing fireflies multiplied. They appeared everywhere in the yard.

Dozens of blinking, dashing lights. They twirled and dived around her and Oliver as they pulsed their mesmerizing signals.

May leaned back on her elbows. "It's hypnotizing, isn't it? I could watch this all night." She sighed.

Oliver shifted over closer to her and stretched his long legs out alongside hers. He propped on his elbows and leaned back his head. "So let's do that."

Two hours later, after they shared an oversize slice of blackberry pie and two chocolate chip cookies from Bea's Bakery, they were stretched out on an unzipped sleeping bag, staring up at the stars. Thanks to the noise and light pollution policies working to be enforced in the neighborhood, the house lights were dark, making the constellations visible. Oliver had told her about growing up on the beach, about the summers spent with his three best friends bicycling and learning to surf, about his parents splitting up when he was six, and about how he'd been shuffled back and forth between their homes and their dysfunctional dating relationships. He had wanted something different, more stable, for his own children, but he and Angelina had not agreed on much of anything in years.

May told Oliver about summers spent in Mystic Water on her grandparents' farm and about her own unusual family dynamics. May's dad was a quiet, serious man who earned his PhD in agriculture and biosystems engineering so he could make the MacAdams farm more efficient. Then the university in a nearby city offered him an air-conditioned job with benefits he couldn't turn down. May's mama taught art to middle school kids and offered private lessons to anyone in their city. They'd even built a modern art studio on a side acre of their land. May was the youngest of three, with an older brother and sister. Both siblings were now married with three kids each, following a traditional path, while May had always been the child hacking her way down an unbeaten trail. Single, thirty, and childless, working a job that let her be what her sister called "a hippie wanderer."

"A travel writer," Oliver said. "Have you always wanted to travel or drift from place to place? Do you love that free-bird lifestyle?"

He might not need to worry about his earlier thought about playing house with May. She didn't sound like someone who desired that.

May blew air out through her nose. "You make me sound like a boat without an anchor."

"Are you?" Why did the thought of her leaving give him a stomachache?

May stretched her legs by pointing her toes and exhaled loudly. "I don't consider myself a restless spirit, if that's what you mean. I don't have to always be *on the move*." May's head shooshed against the slick fabric as she shook her head. "I appreciate security and the idea of having a home. I don't travel to every location I write about, and having a home base gives me stability, which I like. But, yes, I love seeing the world, even this country. I can find anywhere interesting, so boredom or being travel weary don't affect me much, if ever."

"But you do write other things, right? Not just articles?"

May closed her eyes. "I would like to publish a novel or two one day," she admitted. "I have a few ideas, a few outlines started. But they're all in pieces. Nothing completed or fully fleshed out."

"I could ask you what you asked me," Oliver said. "What are you waiting on? Why aren't you working on them now?"

"That's a good question. Time is a factor. Motivation maybe is too."

"Someone once told me that if it's important to you, you'll find the time."

May looked over at him. "Whoever said that is brilliant. Keep her around."

May's smile mesmerized him. "Where do you consider to be your home?"

"That's the strange part. I don't feel like I have a solid home base right now. My parents' home feels a little like home. Being in Mystic Water, because we came here every summer as kids, feels a little like home. I used to own a cozy house outside of the city where my parents live, but I had to sell it." May closed her eyes. "I guess I'm still looking for a place that feels like home, that place where you walk into the door at the end of the day and sigh."

Oliver folded his arms behind his head. "You've not mentioned it. But have you ever been married?"

"Yes."

"And now you're not?"

"That's correct. I am most definitely not."

A minute passed before Oliver spoke again. A rush of questions tied up in his mind. When she didn't elaborate, he finally asked, "That's it? No details? You know that only piques my curiosity. What type of man would May MacAdams marry?"

Her laugh sounded clipped and dry. "Dr. Jekyll and Mr. Hyde. It was a combo deal."

Oliver snorted. "You're teasing. I can tell."

"Nope. He was a real charmer and a real monster. Chris swept me off my feet because that was one of his skills. His charisma and intelligence could draw anyone in. But underneath all that was a mentally imbalanced man who was just as dominating and controlling as he was charming. It didn't work out, as you can imagine."

Oliver pushed himself up on one elbow and looked down at her. "You're serious? Was he abusive?" His hand fisted.

Lightning bugs drifted around May's silhouette. She closed her eyes and inhaled slowly. She blew the air out and vibrated her lips. "Yeah. But it's done now. We learn and we move forward."

Oliver lay back down and frowned up at the sky. "I don't like that. How could anyone abuse you? You're so...easy."

May laughed. "Careful now. That could be misconstrued."

Oliver elbowed her in the ribs, and she wiggled away. "You know what I mean."

May rolled her head to the side to look at him. "The real question is, am I easy like Sunday morning?"

Oliver laughed. He shifted beside her. "Can you make out any of the constellations? I haven't seen this many stars jumbled together since I was a kid." Oliver lifted his arm and pointed a finger straight above them. "Is that—"

"The Big Dipper," May said.

Oliver lowered his arm and rolled his head to the side, his cheek sliding against the slick fabric of the sleeping bag. May looked over at him and smiled in the dark. When their eyes met, a fire started low in his stomach, and all he could think about was kissing her. Heat rushed through him like gas tossed on a fire. But May turned her face away.

"I should be heading home." She pushed herself into a sitting position.

Oliver lay still without moving as the heat seeped into the ground beneath him. Lightning bugs blinked in the yard. Some had found their way inside the tent, flashing and darting around, making it look like a dance party behind the dark fabric.

Oliver stood and reached out his hand to her. May let him help her to her feet. "Thanks, May." Her small hand felt so warm in his.

"For what? Helping with the tent? It was a learning experience for me."

They walked toward the house. A single lamp on a living room end table illuminated the otherwise darkened house. They paused in the foyer so May could grab her bag and slip on her flip-flips.

"For all of it," Oliver said. "I'm not sure I've had a more enjoyable evening."

"Pffft," she said with a short laugh. "I highly doubt that. Putting up a tent and eating grilled cheese and pie and cookies sounds easy to top on a list of memorable moments."

"It's not so much what we did as it is who I spent my time with."

His brown eyes met hers, and she shivered. She placed a hand over her stomach and smiled when Oliver did. "I had a nice time." She glanced down and fiddled with the strap on her bag. "Thanks for dinner and stargazing." May walked to the front door, unlocked it, and swung it open. She stepped onto the front stoop and glanced at him over her shoulder. She shoved her hand into the bag, retrieving a piece of folded paper. "Here."

Oliver's brows rose as he reached out his hand. His lips quirked in one corner. "Did you write me a letter?"

May's eyes looked twitchy, and she lifted her hand before dropping it to her side. "A poem."

But as soon as Oliver smiled at her, her expression softened. He stared down at the folded paper. "I *wanted* to read something of yours, but I didn't think you'd actually let me. Thank you, May. This is the best thing I've gotten in a long time."

She shuffled her feet on the stones. "You haven't even read it yet. It could be dreadful."

"Not a chance."

She waved. "Night."

Oliver leaned on the half-open door and watched her walk away. *Where has this girl been all my life?* "Good night, Marvelous May."

10

$\mathcal{B}$ack at the farm, May eased her car door shut and then bumped her hip against it to click it closed. Grandma Charity's room faced the front yard, and May didn't want the noise to wake her in the silence of the night. Fireflies moved around the nearest tree, and May stood for a few moments, watching them and smiling. She walked toward the front porch but stopped. She leaned back her head and stared up at the brilliant stars burning against the midnight black sky. She hugged her arms around her chest, feeling the warmth of Oliver lingering on her skin. His words blew through her mind, caught on the summer breeze.

"Only two reasons a girl stands outside staring up at the stars in the middle of the night."

May jumped at the voice. Grandma Charity stood on the front porch in her white, cotton nightgown like a ghost. An interior light illuminated her from behind, accentuating her wide hips and the tilt of her stance as she favored her right leg.

May hurried up to the front porch. "What are you doing out here? It's late. We should get to bed."

Grandma Charity made a tsking noise in her throat. "What am I doing? Watching you watching the sky. So which reason is it?" She made no move to go back into the house.

A porch board groaned beneath May's shifting feet. "What are my options?" She pressed a hand against her stomach.

"You're in love or you're heartbroken."

May shook her head and walked for the door. "That's easy. Neither."

Grandma Charity turned to look at May. "You think because I'm old, I don't know anything?"

May opened the screen door. The hinges screeched, and the crickets quieted. "Of course I don't think that. But I'm *not* in love or heartbroken."

Grandma Charity pursed her lips. "You've spent the entire

evening, well into midnight, with a young man who is interested in you."

May held open the screen door for Grandma Charity, who did not move to enter the house. May eased the door shut. "It's not like that. He's...we're friends."

Grandma Charity laughed, sending a succession of short bursts of noise into the night. "Are you fibbing to me or to yourself?" Her smile was genuine, but her expression revealed she did not believe May's words.

May huffed. "We *are* friends. It's just that... He's married, Grandma. He has two kids, and his wife left him. They're separated, I guess, and they're working through divorce papers. It's a mess really."

"And you've decided you want to be part of a mess?" she asked with raised eyebrows. Even in the dim light, May could still see traces of the red tint to her grandma's hair, leftover from her youth.

"I haven't decided anything." May reached for the rusted metal handle on the screen door again.

"But you like him," Grandma Charity said.

May lowered her arm. "I'm trying *not* to."

Grandma Charity reached for May's hand, a surprising show of affection. "Oh, Little May, has that ever worked for any woman before? This situation sounds like a pigsty, muddy and full of slop. I'm not scolding you. Lord knows if your grandpa hadn't wrestled me to marry him when he did, I would have been all over the place with my heart. Plenty of men would have wrung that sucker flat, but not your grandpa. He knew how to handle it and care for it. He knew how to tame me enough so I wouldn't bolt like a wild filly. I don't seem like it now, I know, but I was soft and sensitive once, restless too, a lot like you." She cast her darkened gaze toward the fields. "Farming makes you tough, so I formed callouses because I had to survive and we had to be strong to make it through the lean seasons. But you're not calloused, not Little May. Not yet." Grandma Charity looked at May. "I hope not ever."

May blinked in the silence, struggling to find the words to

respond to her grandma's honesty. She tried to imagine her grandma as a restless young woman but failed. She'd only known the tough, steely woman who could raise a family and keep a farm running, who could feed a family on rations and keep them unaware when food was scarce. But Grandma Charity *had* been young once; she had fallen in love and stumbled her way through a marriage. "What do I do?"

"What are your options? Love him or don't?" May nodded, and Grandma Charity reached for the screen door. "Be his friend. It sounds like he could use a good one."

"Be his friend. That's all?" May asked.

"That's the best place to start, Little May," her grandma said. "I think he'll have more trouble keeping control of his feelings than you will."

"Why do you say that?"

Grandma Charity's gaze drifted out into the yard. "Your grandpa used to tell me that the sunlight followed you wherever you went. He was right. I think you know that too. Being near you is like being in the sunshine. And nearly every living thing needs sunlight to survive. We crave it, we bask in it, we stand and smile in it. So when someone who has been standing in the shadows steps into the sunlight, he feels alive and happy, and it won't take long for him to *need* that feeling every day. Like Oliver will."

May shook her head. "Grandma, that sounds bogus."

Grandma Charity shrugged. "We never see ourselves clearly."

"What if...what if I struggle to stay just friends?" May stomach rolled as she followed her grandma into the house. She locked the front door behind her.

"What if, what if, what if. We don't know a lick about what we will wake up tomorrow and find. Be his friend, right now, right this minute. That's all you have to think about. Now go to bed and don't let me find you pacing the floors overthinking. You're not getting any younger, and you need your sleep or else you'll be pretty sorry looking in the morning."

"Grandma!"

Grandma Charity grinned and switched off the lamp in the hallway. "Good night, Little May."

11

*T*he next day May woke up to a good-morning text from Oliver. He was up early, going out for a predawn run, and he wanted her to know he was thinking about her. She'd been unable to wipe the smile off her face, even while drinking coffee. After a light breakfast, she laced up her running shoes, whipped her hair into a pony tail, found an up-tempo playlist, and ran laps around and through the fields before sunrise. She returned to the farmhouse with her sweaty clothes sticking to her skin and removed her shoes and wet socks while sitting on the front porch stairs. She watched the sunrise turn the skies over Mystic Water fuchsia and blazing orange. When she felt confident her legs were steady, she went inside to shower.

An hour later, May finished her article for *Southern Living* and sent it off to her contact editor at the magazine's main office. As she closed her laptop and gazed out the window at the quiet farm, verdant corn bent in a hot summer wind. Tornadoes of dust kicked up on the edges of the dirt driveway and twirled away into the fields. Wispy white clouds speckled the bright blue sky. She flipped through her notebook, looking at the pages she'd written for plots and novel ideas. *Could I actually write a book? Would it be any good?* She wondered if she should ask Emily how she got started writing books and creating a habit of it.

May's phone rang, and she stared at the unknown number. It rang another three times before Grandma Charity yelled from the front of the house.

"Are you going to answer that or not?"

"I don't know the caller!" May shouted back.

"Take a chance, Chicken Little!"

May groaned. She could imagine her grandma rolling her eyes and tsking in the kitchen. May answered the phone. "Hello?"

"There you are," a husky female voice said. "I was disappointed to think I might miss you. It's Emily. Emily Greene from the party. Oliver gave me your number. I hope that's okay. I promised him it was only for friendly purposes. What he doesn't know won't kill him, right?" Emily laughed, and it traveled through the phone, finding May's smile and causing her shoulders to relax.

"I was just thinking about you. It's good to hear from you." Sunlight splayed across May's writing desk and reflected off the silver casing on her laptop. She rubbed her hand over the smooth, warm metal, letting the sunlight flicker across her fingers. Then she closed her notebook.

"How about lunch?" Emily asked. "I need to get out of the house. I've been writing all morning, and I have a crick in my neck. Andy says I'll go blind if I stare at a computer screen all day every day. Could you use a break too?"

"I'd love one. Where are you thinking for lunch?" May walked to the bedroom closet and looked for a change of clothes. She remembered Emily's fashionable dress at the party, and her own yoga pants and white tank top weren't going to measure up. Sitting around the house working was one thing, but being seen around town in athletic gear was not acceptable. *What if I run into Oliver?* May groaned.

"How about Cavelli's Deli? They have a shady outdoor eating spot. It'll get us outdoors without setting us on fire in the sunshine. Meet me at noon?"

May pulled a sky-blue sleeveless blouse from the rack and inspected it. She nodded and tossed it out of the closet and onto the bed. "Perfect. That'll give me time to do something with my hair."

"Oh, are we getting fancy? Should I wear my red lipstick?"

May laughed. "Whatever you wear will only enhance what you already have."

"Oh, May, you charmer."

May pulled a white skirt from a hanger and tossed it on the bed. "Thanks for inviting me."

"Thank *you* for giving me an excuse to get out of the house and get out of making lunch for Andy. That wonderful man insists on coming home every day and having lunch with me."

"A man who wants to spend time with you? Sounds awful," May teased.

Emily laughed again and said good-bye.

When May walked out to her car, a rectangle of white lay beneath her windshield wiper, with one end of it flapping in the breeze. May's name had been scrawled across the front of an envelope. She tugged it free of the wiper and glanced around the yard. May pulled a piece of folded notebook paper out of the envelope, and as soon as the letter unfolded, she glanced at the bottom to see the sender's name. *Oliver.*

He'd read her poem. And he *loved* it. May was surprised Oliver thought a poem about stars and whispers and fragile hearts was interesting. His response was so different and so kind compared to her ex-husband, Chris', words years ago. May's throat tightened, and she pressed the letter to her chest. She'd never let anyone read her poetry, but now Oliver offered her praise and wrote he was *beyond impressed*. May drove to the deli with a grin stuck on her face.

If not for the breeze, which felt a lot drier and smelled like a dusty field today, May and Emily would have roasted on the patio attached to the side of Cavelli's Deli. The ice in their mason jars had melted a half hour ago. Scooper's ice cream thawed as soon as it left the frozen plastic tubs, so people carried paper bowls with upside-down waffle cones propped on top of their double scoops. They drank cookies and cream and triple chocolate fudge ice creams through red paper straws while walking down the sidewalks. Shops blasted the air conditioner on high and fogged up storefront windows.

Emily stirred her straw around through her watered-down lemonade. Condensation rolled down their glasses and pooled on the cardboard coasters advertising local brews from the Corner Pub.

Sitting in the shade of the outdoor awning, Emily talked about growing up in Mystic Water and how she and Andy dreamed of moving to the mountains where there were four distinct seasons and the changing of the leaves didn't happen in a heartbeat, the way it did in Mystic Water.

"You blink and it goes from summer to winter. Not that the winters are much to complain about. I don't think it's snowed here but twice in fifty years, but still..." Emily said, pausing to sip her warming lemonade. "It would be nice to see the leaves changing over the course of a few weeks. Rather than falling off dead in a couple of days. You wake up one morning, the leaves are red and gold, blazing like the trees are on fire. Everyone gets excited and starts talking about pumpkin pie and Halloween and the Fall Festival and then *bam*! The next morning, they're lying all over the ground, shriveled and brittle, like they couldn't die fast enough. Then we spend the next few months shivering and waiting for spring." Emily stretched out her long legs. "Listen, to me, going on and on, sounding like a bitter old lady. I'm being dramatic of course. The fall sticks around for more than a few days. I do love Mystic Water. But I was meant for the mountains, a cabin somewhere in the Smokies."

May finished her turkey BLT and crumpled up the brown parchment paper that had been tucked around it like a blanket. "Why haven't you moved yet? What's keeping you here?"

"Our parents," Emily said. "Andy has oldest-child guilt. He feels responsible to make sure someone takes care of his folks, not that they need it. Those two have more energy than a couple of teenagers. And I just have guilt. Anytime I mention moving, my mama gives me the sad eyes." She sighed and then smiled, flashing her straight, white teeth accentuated by the scarlet lipstick. "One day maybe." She poked the last two potato chips into her mouth.

May watched people come in and out of the shops across the street. The smell of melting chocolate and warm vanilla drifted from the bakery and lingered around their table, coating the hot air with a pink, sugary sparkle. "I can't stay here much longer, or I'll walk right over there and order a few dozen—"

The hardware store's door swung open, the aluminum handle on the door shining in the sunlight, sending a bolt of light straight across the street into May's eyes. She blinked a few times and sat up straighter in the metal patio chair. Oliver walked out of the store talking on the phone, frowning. His words were unintelligible from across the street, but his raised voice indicated his unhappiness, his anger—so different from his easy laughter and peacefulness the night before.

Emily followed May's gaze, turning in her seat to find the source of May's fascination. "Uh oh," she said, watching Oliver too. "Looks serious."

Oliver paced up and down the sidewalk. Then he stopped by his car, which was parked a few spaces down from Bea's Bakery. He fumbled with his car keys, before dropping them on the pavement. He bent down and snatched them up again. His voice lowered, but his anger did not abate. A few leaves wilted on a nearby dogwood tree.

The burning sun offered the townsfolk a break and coasted behind a few wispy clouds, filtering softer light down onto the street. Oliver's expression sagged as he unlocked his car; his head pitched forward as his shoulders drooped.

May pushed back from the table, gripping the black metal edge with her fingertips as though ready to sprint away.

Emily nodded in her direction. "My thoughts exactly."

May's attention focused on Emily. "What?"

"You're going to run over there and see what you can do, right? Get going before he drives away. You can't leave him alone when he's having the worst day ever."

"No. No, I can't. That's a total invasion of his privacy," May argued, bouncing her legs up and down beneath the table.

Emily narrowed her gaze, but her expression was compassionate. "Really, May? You mean you *aren't* thinking that you should rush over there? You *don't* want to console him? See if you can help?"

May swallowed and glanced away from Emily's knowing stare. "We're just friends—"

"If that were me, would you let me get in the car and sob alone? We're *just* friends, aren't we, May?"

"Of course I'd check on you," May said. She *wanted* to dash across the street to Oliver. To ask him if he was okay, if there was any way she could ease his frustration, but...but part of her wanted to be his friend from a distance. Because being too close to Oliver felt dangerous, like she might cross the friends to more-than-friends line faster than she could inhale. When she and Oliver were close, it was as though his internal core burned hotter like the center of the sun and his gravitational pull intensified, pulling May straight to him. She glanced at her purse where she'd stashed the note he'd left on her car. She'd read it a half dozen times, memorized his words.

Emily started clearing their trash from the table, stacking their sandwich baskets and combining their trash. "What are you still doing sitting here?"

May clenched her jaw, exhaled the breath she'd been holding, grabbed her purse, and said, "Wish me luck!" Then she hurried across the street, stopping only to make sure it was clear of traffic.

Oliver opened his car door and dropped into the driver's seat, leaving his door slightly ajar. One leg still dangled out of the open car door, the toe of his dress shoe touching the sizzling pavement.

"You *should* have talked to me first," Oliver argued. The steering wheel creaked beneath his grip. Anger burned him from the inside, pulsing at his temples.

"So now I have to run *everything* by you before I speak to *my* children?"

Angelina's voice scalded his ear.

He inhaled slowly, taking his time before answering or else he'd completely lose his temper again. When he spoke, his voice was even, controlled, and quiet. "*Our* children. We had an agreement—"

"Shut up, Oliver. Don't you ever get tired of the sound of your own voice? I know *I* get sick of it. They're *my* children. I gave birth to them. I raised them. I've wiped their snotty noses and taken them to doctor's appointments and fed them and dressed them for school every day, and what have *you* done?"

"Paid for all of those doctor's appointments and school and the food and the *home* you live in—"

"I can't *believe* you would throw *that* in my face! It's *always* about money with you!"

"No, it's not—"

Angelina hung up. Oliver tossed the phone into the passenger seat. He exhaled and waves of heat rippled over the car. Someone knocked against the car's side panel.

"Oliver?"

He didn't flinch at the sound of her voice; he looked up at her like someone trying to peer through dirty glass, like his vision couldn't focus on what was on the other side. Oliver blinked, staring at May, who seemed to appear like magic. She dropped her hand from the car door.

"Are you okay?"

"May?" he asked. "What are you doing here?" He sat up straight in the seat, tried to smile. He unclenched his hand.

May jabbed her thumb over her shoulder. "Emily and I were having lunch across the street, and I saw you and wanted to say hey and thank you for the letter you left for me. But it looks like I caught you at a bad time. You don't have to tell me, but is everything okay?"

Oliver looked away from her and put both of his hands on the steering wheel. He squeezed the leather, causing it to creak beneath his grip, but then he dropped his hands into his lap. He was *not* going to talk about this with her, not when she was standing there looking at him like she wanted to hug him. Oliver shook his head and said, "Just frustrating divorce details that would be..." He paused, rubbed the back of his neck, and then looked up at her. "It'll be okay."

"Would be what? You want to talk about it? I know we don't know each other well, but I've seen that look before, and you look like you could use a friend."

Oliver tried to chuckle, but it sounded dry and uncomfortable. He rubbed his hand across his chest. "I don't want to bother you with this. There are lots of other interesting conversations we could have."

May pointed to the passenger seat. "Mind if I join you? You could blast the air so we don't have a heatstroke, and we could talk."

On an impulse Oliver reached out and wrapped his fingers around hers. She felt warm to the touch. "May, that's really thoughtful, but I'm not going to talk to you about my divorce problems."

She glanced down at his hand before looking him in the eyes. "Why not? Because I'm a stranger?"

He sagged against the driver's seat and let go of her hand, dropping his arm against his side with his hand dangling out of the car. May didn't seem like a stranger to him. In fact, he felt *too* comfortable around her. "No, because...because it's weird."

May didn't wait for Oliver to say more. She walked around the car, opened the passenger door, picked up his phone, and sat. She closed the car door and reached over to turn the keys in the ignition. Then she dropped his cell phone into the cup holder. May cranked up the air to high and turned the nearest vents toward her face.

"Why is it weird?" she asked. "We're friends, aren't we? You said so yourself." May bent one leg beneath her and turned in the seat to face him.

Oliver closed his car door, but he didn't look at her. Friends, sure. He rested his hands on the bottom of the steering wheel and stared out through the windshield. She made it so easy to be around her, to think about her long after she *wasn't* around. If he said he didn't like her as more than a friend, then he was a liar.

May poked him in the arm. "Why is it weird?" she repeated, interrupting his thoughts.

"Because, May...I like you."

"I like you too, which means I'm a great person to confide in." May smiled at him, but she stopped as soon as he turned his face in her direction.

The words rolled out like they had no idea they shouldn't. "No...I *like* you. As in I'm attracted to you."

May pressed back against the seat and inhaled as her eyes

widened.

Oliver groaned. "Good Lord, I can't believe I just said that. But it's true, and now it's out there." His laugh sounded sad and embarrassed. He massaged his fingers against his forehead and then his temples. "It's been a helluva day already, and if possible, I made it worse." He looked at her. "My apologies, May. My brain-to-mouth filter is malfunctioning."

May pressed her top teeth into her bottom lip. Then she said, "Don't apologize."

The wispy clouds blew away in a rush of wind, and sunlight beamed into the car, stretching across the two of them like a blanket of buttercup yellow. Oliver released the steering wheel and stared at his palms covered in sunshine.

"I don't want to make you uncomfortable," he admitted, his low, quiet voice barely audible over the blasting air conditioning.

"I'm not."

"Or scare you off."

"You haven't," May said.

Oliver closed his eyes and shook his head. "May, why are you so great?"

May's laugh burst out of her. "Uh, I'm not." She reached over and covered his hand with hers. "You've had a bad day, right? We can toss out everything you've said and blame it on stress."

"Doesn't make it untrue," he said, flipping over his hand and squeezing her fingers. He could get used to the way he felt when she touched him.

May squeezed in response before pulling her hand back into her lap. "One thing at a time. Since we've confirmed we're friends, tell me why you've had a helluva day. It doesn't matter if it's about the divorce, and it doesn't matter if it's icky. If we're friends, then we're honest with each other, even about the not-so-pretty parts of our lives. And you said you could use a friend in town," May pointed to herself, "and here I am."

Oliver half-smiled at her before turning back toward the steering wheel. He leaned his head against the headrest and sighed. "It would help to talk to someone about it. I *know* that. But I don't want to talk about it with you. Not because it's *you*, but because I don't want to...now don't laugh at me, but I don't want to dim your light with my darkness. I know how it spreads. I feel toxic right now."

May laughed anyway. "Ollie, I had no idea you were so dramatic! Come on, you aren't going to *dim* anything around here, and you're hardly toxic. One bad day doesn't make you a hazard to be avoided at all costs." She poked him in the arm.

He rolled his head to the side and looked at her. His heart raced.

May squirmed beneath his stare. "What?"

"You called me Ollie."

"Oh," May said. "Slipped right out."

"I like it. My childhood friends used to call me Ollie. Takes me back."

May blushed, and she looked out the window. "Talk, *Ollie*," she said, "and quit stalling." She rubbed her hand across her collarbone.

"You sure you want to do this?" he asked. "Once we cross this line, we can't go back."

May caught his gaze. "Which line is that? Cause I think there are a few that we're trying *not* to cross."

Oliver studied the darker green line circling her pale irises. "How about we agree not to cross any other line right now except the one that allows me talk to you about my *whole* life, not just the shiny parts."

"I can handle that," May said.

But could he handle letting her in more? And if yes, how long could he keep a handle on his feelings?

12

Oliver pulled his seat belt across his chest and clicked it locked. "Buckle up, buttercup," he said, putting the car into reverse. "As much as I love the small-town-everybody-knows-your-name vibe of Mystic Water, I don't want to have this conversation sitting outside the bakery for any tempted gawkers to watch."

May buckled her seat belt. "Head over to Jordan Pond. You know where that is?"

Oliver nodded and slipped on his sunglasses. Her reflection watched her in his silver-coated lenses. May lowered the sun visor and settled into the seat, trying not to wring her hands together in her lap. Thoughts about what could have happened today on the phone call bounced around in her head like a ball shot through a pinball machine. Every second her mind created a new, more extravagant scenario.

"There are a few benches scattered around the shore. At least one or two will be in the shadow of a willow."

Oliver drove to the pond and parked the car, and they walked down to the edge of the water where a bench was situated beneath a great weeping willow. Sapphire and violet dragonflies buzzed along the lakeshore and darted in and out of the whispering branches that swayed in a steady breeze.

Once they were seated, May bent her knee beneath her, switched her brain to friend mode, and turned toward Oliver on the bench. "Let's hear it."

"No small talk, huh?" He shoved one hand through his hair and made sure his cell phone ringer was turned off. "Jackie, she's my daughter—"

"I remember."

Oliver nodded. "She called me this morning, and I could tell she was upset. She's normally upfront with her feelings, not much of a filter. Like me today. But she was having trouble articulating what was bothering her when I asked. Finally, she blurted, 'Why are you

105

leaving us, Dad?'"

"*Leaving* them? Oh..." May's lips parted. "They know about the divorce? I didn't realize the kids knew."

Oliver's jaw clenched. "They don't—they didn't. Angelina and I agreed *not* to tell the kids. They thought they were at Grandma and Grandpa's for a while this summer so their mom could spend time with her family, and they could go to the beach."

May covered her mouth with her hand. "She told them without your permission?"

Oliver cut his eyes over at May. His hands clenched into fists in his lap. "She told them *something*, but it's not the truth. I'll preface this by saying that two days ago Angelina called me to discuss the divorce agreement, and she didn't feel as though her alimony was going to be sufficient to keep her in the type of lifestyle she's accustomed to, which is ridiculous. She's spoiled, and she doesn't want to work, and Lord only knows why she thinks she needs to live in a mansion. What's she going to do all day when the kids are in school? She's going to lie around a pool and drink Mai Tais." Oliver exhaled and rolled his head on his neck.

"I'm digressing quickly, but it pisses me off," he said, clearing his throat. "It's a complete joke to think she needs to live the high life while I work my ass off and support her *and* the kids." He blew out a huge puff of air. The grass along the bank bent at a sharp angle. "Let me get back on track. I said no to her childish demands, and she's been stewing over it since then. She told the kids I don't want to help them have a nice house or nice clothes. That I'd rather spend my money on who knows what—booze and loose women. She told them that I've decided to leave them because I've found other things that interest me more."

May gasped. "She did *not* really say that. What would interest you more?"

Oliver shrugged. "Jackie said my job, my friends, some girl—"

"What girl?" May blurted.

Oliver reached over and touched May's knee. The heat from his hand felt scorching, even through the cotton fabric of her skirt.

"It's no one. Just something Angelina made up so that she could seem like a victim."

May frowned. "Didn't Angelina have an affair with your work associate?"

Oliver grunted a reply. "The kids don't know that. We agreed there was no reason to tell them since it would only color their opinion of their mom."

"But it's okay to sully you?"

"The point is that she and I agreed that when the time came to talk to the kids about separating, we'd talk to them together. We'd explain that it wasn't about them and that Angelina and I were going to be better parents if we weren't married. We were going to be better *people*. But we weren't leaving *them*. We weren't deserting them in any way. We would still see them and love them and be there for them in every way that we could be."

"What did you say to Jackie?"

Oliver stared at a mallard swimming across the pond, creating ripples that drifted all the way to the shore and splashed tiny waves onto the bank. "I told Jackie that none of that was true, and I asked her if I could speak to her mom. Angelina got on the phone, which was like talking to a screeching owl. Angelina has done this before. Fallen off the wagon with alcohol, and I'm fairly certain today that she was tipsy, if not on her way to intoxicated. There was no reasoning with her." Oliver's shoulders slumped forward; he pressed his knuckles into the back of his neck. "Somehow the entire reason she told the kids is *my* fault. For trying to hurt her and make her suffer after the divorce. None of which is true. It makes me wish that when I met her, I could have seen how this whole story would play out. I could have seen it wouldn't be worth it."

Frustration surged off Oliver like heat waves. Dragonflies that flew close to him darted away as soon as they neared. The branches of the willow lifted in the wind, pulling their leaves out of his sphere.

May scooted a few inches away, seeking relief from the rising temperature. She folded her hands together in her lap. "If you'd never met Angelina, then you wouldn't have Jackie and Michael.

And you're not sorry you have them, are you?"

"No," he said, straightening. "I'm never sorry about having them. They're the only bright spots in this situation."

"Then wishing you'd never met Angelina is pointless. Not meeting her means not having your kids. Moving forward to what's happening now, are you worried about the kids being with her if she's drinking?"

"I'd be more worried if they were alone with her, but her parents are there, and they're more than capable to help. Jackie told me her cousins were there, so that means Angelina's sister is with them too." He shook his head. "The kids will be fine physically. But mentally...I mean, what do you *say*? I can't lie to Jackie and tell her that part of it isn't true. But how do you explain that you're not staying married but you're also *not* leaving them? In a way I will be leaving them. There's no way I'd get full custody, and I wouldn't do that to Angelina. She loves the kids. And she's a great mother. When she's not drinking, of course. But I know *why* she's drinking. She's not handling this well."

"Will she *start* to handle it better? Will she stop drinking?" May asked. A dragonfly zipped through the air in front of them; its florescent blue wings sparkled in the sunlight.

Oliver nodded. "Her parents won't put up with that nonsense for long. She's incensed with me. Nothing new, but I can't let her rob me blind, now can I? I don't want to roll over like a neutered dog. I work hard to provide for my family."

"I'm assuming she's a stay-at-home mom," May said.

"With a PhD. So she's not helpless or lacking sufficient intelligence. The university has offered her an adjunct position multiple times through the years, even after the kids were in school, but she didn't want to work. She'd rather wear yoga pants and drink Starbucks for two hours." Oliver pitched forward, pressed his elbows onto his thighs, and dropped his face into his hands.

"Who wouldn't?" She hesitated before reaching over and rubbing his back. She felt Oliver's muscles relax beneath her hand. He felt hot to the touch, like the lingering heat of a stove eye.

Sunlight trickled down to them through the willow leaves, and May glanced up at it. Oliver sat up and gazed over at her.

"This was already a wreck," Oliver said, "now it's worse."

"The mess seems unavoidable no matter how hard you try," May said. "I don't know much about kids, but my suggestion would be to stay honest with them. Now that they know, don't try to keep anything from them. I think they'd respect you more and have more comfort knowing the truth, even if the truth is uncomfortable. It sounds counterintuitive, but if they trust you to be honest, then they'll feel like you're more of a team going through the tough stuff together."

Oliver stretched out his long legs as the sunlight sprinkled down on him. He inhaled and exhaled a few times before reaching over and patting her hand. "That wasn't as bad as I thought, telling you."

May chuckled. "Thanks, I guess."

He wrapped his fingers around her hand. "You know what I mean. You're easy to talk to. And I feel better, too, so thank you. Just *sitting here* with you makes me feel better." Sunlight spread around them. "Thank you for being that friend I needed." He rubbed his thumb across the top of her hand, leaving her skin tingling. "I don't want to go, but I have to be back at the office in half an hour."

May jerked her hand away and sat up straighter. "Work! I completely forgot you have a normal job."

"We aren't all traveling hobos."

They both laughed, and May rushed Oliver back to his car because he didn't want to get off the bench. On the drive back to town, they listened to songs on the radio but spoke little. Oliver pulled into a parking spot by the deli, and May clicked her seat belt free. She grabbed for the door handle, and Oliver held on to her arm.

"Thank you, May."

"Enough already," she said, opening the door. "That's what friends do. Don't let this helluva morning ruin the rest of your day, okay? You can still have a good afternoon. I'll see you later."

Oliver leaned over into the passenger seat and pointed up at her as she looked down at him. "Not if I see you first."

May closed the door to the sound of his laughter, and she waved as he backed out of the parking spot and drove away. Her phone dinged, alerting her of a text message. Emily's message read: *Were you his knight in shining armor? You know it's been longer than 8.2 seconds, right?*

Later that evening an explosion rattled the windowpanes, echoing through the quiet farmhouse with its concussions. May bolted upright in bed, gasping for air. Flashes of light illuminated the bedroom, and she squinted, lifting her hand to block the brightness. The scent of sulfur hung in the air. Stillness and darkness returned. Then angry rain slammed sideways against the side of the house. May exhaled. *A thunderstorm.*

With her heart thumping hard against the thin fabric of her T-shirt, May swung her legs over the side of the bed and walked to the window. When lightning flashed, sheets of rain came into view, sweeping across the fields in great swaths of water. After ten minutes of pounding rain and thunder rattling the house, the night quieted, the crickets chorused from their hiding spaces, and May lay back down. But her restless heart filled with questions about Oliver and friendship and the feel of his hand in hers. She flipped to her side, pressing her cheek against the warm fabric of the cotton pillowcase, and felt a twinge of guilt spreading discomfort into her heart. She dreamed of a crumbling, buckling paved road with a hand-painted sign staked in the ground on the roadside that read, *Turn Around While You Still Can.*

The next morning when May awoke, the house appeared too dark for morning. The bedside clock read 6:00 a.m. The sun should have been shining a half hour earlier. Gray, low-hanging clouds drifted over Mystic Water, looking like someone had draped a wool blanket over town. May pulled on a pair of lounging shorts and shuffled up the hallway. The air in the house felt heavy and damp, like the wooden walls could not keep the outside humidity at bay.

Grandma Charity stood at the kitchen sink holding a mug of coffee in both hands. "Coffee is still hot in the pot."

An empty mug sat beside the coffee pot. The ceramic lid sat at a tilt on the sugar bowl, with a spoon shoved into the sweet grains.

"Anything you want to talk about?"

May stopped halfway to the carafe. "Anything *you* want to talk about?"

Grandma Charity nodded her head toward the window where the overcast morning barely lit the interior of the kitchen. "You brought that gloom home with you yesterday. I could feel the storm brewing when you entered the house." She tapped her chest. "In here first," she opened her arms wide, "and then it spread."

May laughed, but the sound pinched at the edges. She poured coffee from the carafe and reached for the sugar spoon even though she didn't want to add any to the black liquid. The niggling of guilt returned, and she rubbed a hand across her stomach. "That's interesting. I didn't know I had the power to bring storms."

"Don't sass me, Little May." Her grandma turned from the sink and faced her. "You think darkness doesn't follow you home the way light does?"

May sighed. "Grandma, it's too early for this cryptic talk. I'm *fine*. A little tired because of the loud storm. But otherwise, I have a lot of writing to do today. If you don't mind, I'm going to get started." She lifted the coffee mug into the air. "Thank you for the coffee."

An hour later May finished her article for *Travel + Leisure* and her coffee mug sat full on the desk. After a few sips, the acidity had burned her stomach like a bad decision. And the feeling in the pit of her stomach had turned into a ball of thorns that rolled around, making her feel squirmy and agitated. She grabbed her cell phone.

It's early, but are you free? she texted Emily.

A few minutes later Emily responded, *I had a feeling you were going to text or call. Is this storm your doing?*

May frowned, staring down at Emily's words that matched her grandma's. She gazed toward the window. She stopped short of typing, *There's nothing wrong,* but she knew that was a lie. Her cell phone beeped.

Want to come over? We can have breakfast on the patio.

May replied that she'd be over in half an hour. She jumped in the shower and wound her hair up into a loose bun. She took out a knee-length blue skirt and a white button-up blouse from her closet and dressed, finishing off her outfit with the only pair of strappy sandals she owned. On her way down the hallway, she called to her grandma and told her she'd be home in a couple of hours.

As May walked out the door, Grandma Charity said, "Take an umbrella. I don't think the storm has passed yet."

13

"Cookie Crisp or Lucky Charms?" Emily picked up a cereal box and shook it. Her red nails stood out against the blue box. "Don't laugh. Were you expecting Eggs Benedict or a breakfast casserole?"

May reached for the Cookie Crisp box. "Actually? Yes. You're so 'put together.' I even imagined we'd be dining on some hard-to-find Wedgwood place setting only found in the South."

Emily dumped Lucky Charms into a melamine bowl covered in poppies and laughed. The husky sound fluttered the pink hydrangeas' leaves. "You're sweet, you know that? Not that fake Southern sweet that some people ooze, but genuine. I appreciate the compliment, and although I make a delicious breakfast casserole, this morning seemed like keeping it simple would be best." The top three buttons on her navy blue blouse were left open to allow room for her voluptuous chest to be less restricted. Her blue jeans looked like she'd ironed them. Emily had twirled her blonde hair into a messy bun, which still looked carefully arranged. She made casual look classy and beautiful. And *easy.*

Even though May's clothes were nice and clean, she felt frayed and awkward in comparison, mostly because of the stormy emotions brewing inside her. The thick, damp air clung to her skin. She filled her bowl with tiny, crispy cereal bits that resembled chocolate chip cookies. "Why did you say I'd brought this?" She pointed to the ominous sky that hinted of more rain soon.

Emily unscrewed the top on a bottle of Baileys Irish Cream and poured more than a shot's worth into her steaming coffee. "Want some?"

May shook her head, worried the addition of alcohol might catapult her emotions into a deeper, darker place. Buoying her feelings already felt like a desperate struggle against a rising tide.

Emily twisted off the cap from the jug and poured milk over her cereal. She passed it to May. "I woke up thinking about the storm, and you were also on my mind." She leaned back in the wicker chair and wrinkled her brow. "It sounds silly when I say it out loud, but the two *felt* connected to me." She shrugged, but she cut her eyes over to May. "Why? *Did* you? Do you have superpowers? Because that would be exciting."

May rubbed her earlobe. "Pretty sure I'm just a regular person."

Emily made a scoffing noise in her throat. "You'll never be *just a regular person*. But I understand. You're saying you aren't able to rain dance storms into Mystic Water. You *do* know the town thinks you're a sunshine dealer, don't you?"

"A what?"

Emily slid the diamond on her necklace back and forth on the chain before dropping it against her chest. "You can be honest with me when you're ready, but I know you're different than most folks, and I like that about you. If I'm in need of a shot of happiness and sunshine, I have a direct line. Something's bothering you, though. It's hanging all over you like an ugly sweater." Emily blew across her coffee mug and sipped. Then she grimaced. "A bit heavy handed on the Baileys this morning."

May pressed the chocolate chip cookies into the milk and watched them bob back up to the surface. Maybe one day she could tell Emily about how she felt connected to the light, and also how there were days when she wanted to disappear into the darkness and hide from the sun. Her marriage to Chris had eventually been more full of shadows than light, but it had been a few years since she'd felt like a sky filled with storm clouds was her own doing. "How would you feel if another woman were falling in love with Andy and he wanted to spend time with her?"

Emily's spoon thudded against the side of her bowl. She swallowed her mouthful of cereal but coughed. Then she swiped a paper napkin across her mouth. "Good heavens, May. That's a shocking change of conversation."

"How would you feel?" May asked again.

"I'd be furious," Emily said.

May's gaze moved toward the charcoal-gray clouds rolling over the tree line. "And if she said they were just friends, would that be okay?"

Emily put down her spoon and turned her body toward May, leaning forward on the wicker chair's armrest. "*Are* they?"

"Just friends?" May said and shook her head. "No. They both are attracted to each other. They're *saying* they're friends, but it's just what they're saying so it sounds and feels less...wrong."

Emily pressed her pink lips together, turned back toward her cereal bowl, and picked up her spoon again. "Forgive me, I'm a little slow this morning. I see where you're going with this." She spooned Lucky Charms into her mouth and chewed. "Eat your cereal before it turns to cookie mush." She washed down her cereal with a swig of spiked coffee. "Andy and I aren't like Angelina and Oliver. That's a completely different kind of animal."

"Is it?" May asked, staring at her warped reflection in the spoon.

Emily motioned for her to keep eating, but May's appetite deserted her. Thunder boomed in the distance, sending shivers up her arms.

"You haven't seen or met Angelina," Emily said. "You have no frame of reference. Has he talked about her at all?"

May explained what had happened the day before with Oliver and the kids and how Angelina had broken her word and told the children about the divorce. Emily listened and ate her cereal while May talked.

When May finished, Emily said, "I hate that for him. He loves those kids, and it's a rotten way for them to find out. Without bad mouthing Angelina, oh, why the hell do I care? I might as well be honest with *you* and quit trying to be all prim and proper. I'll tell you that their relationship is not a healthy one. In fact, it feels poisonous when you're around it. Like one of those toxic waste dumps that you're dang sure you're going to catch something from it if you stand too close. Their relationship is not one that should continue if they can't change their ways and habits, and it's better for everyone if they do separate. I'm not pro breaking up a family, but those two...they're a sick pair together, if I've ever seen one."

May frowned. "I can't even imagine Oliver being part of a *sick pair*. He's so easy to be around."

"For *you*," Emily said. "You bring out the good in him." She pointed a red fingernail at May. "That's *your* thing. One of *your* qualities. I'm going to go out on a limb and say that you not only *see* the best in people, but you drag it out of them, even if they don't want you to or don't realize that's what you're doing. So, of course, Oliver is Prince Charming with you. Why wouldn't he be? You're like a breath of fresh air in a house that's been sealed up and quarantined for years while the disease lives and multiplies on the inside."

"I don't see *how* she could be that bad. He says she's a great mother to the kids," May argued.

Emily shrugged and reached for her coffee. "I'm not saying she's a monster and he's innocent. I've seen them together, seen them interact, and they bring out the worst in each other. I don't know what happened to them or when it happened, but when I've been around her, she gives off bitter vibes, and Oliver...I hate to admit this because he's a good guy, too, but when they're together, it's like he's seething with contempt and disgust. Seriously, it seems like they detest each other but they're faking nice in public."

"I'm not trying to condone his behavior, but one thing that might make him seem angry is that she had an affair with his coworker."

"*Did* she?" Emily asked. Both eyebrows rose on her forehead. "Isn't that a twist in the narrative? Then why on God's green earth does she act like she despises *him*? Either way, they don't need to be together because they're not going to just wake up one morning and decide to work it out. If they were, it would have already happened."

Lightning zigzagged across the sky. "And because they are miserable together...that makes what he and I are doing okay?"

"If he's happy and you're happy..." Emily sipped her coffee. "You've not *done* anything, have you?"

"No." May shifted in the chair. Then she leaned her elbow on the table and pressed her forehead against her hand. "It's still wrong. He's married. And I *know* it. We're not pretending he's not married, and I keep telling myself that I can be his friend and that's all, but... but that's a lie." Thunder boomed and they both jumped. May lifted her head and watched the rain fast approaching them from across town. "When we're together, I kinda forget about her, but then yesterday after we talked, it's *all* I could think about. If someone were doing this with Andy, I'd be indignant on your behalf." May looked over at Emily when Emily touched her arm. "But I've never been good at letting go when I should. I *always* stay way past when I know it's only going to hurt me more. Even after the damage has occurred."

Emily's expression offered sincere care. "Past mistakes don't guarantee you'll continue to make the same ones now. Do you think you're falling in love with him?"

May shrugged, but then she nodded. The truth wiggled in her stomach like a slippery eel, and lightning flashed again.

"Let me repeat this and please listen to me. I am *not* condoning adulterous behavior, but Andy and I are nothing like Angelina and Oliver. We are not falling apart nor have we been *staying together* for the kids. I have to imagine that Oliver is not sitting idly by why you give him lovesick puppy dog stares. You're not tempting a man beyond his ability to control what is happening. You light that man up. He *wants* to spend time with you—"

May interrupted her. "It doesn't make what we're doing any less wrong. Angelina could be Cruella de Vil, but it's still not okay. I want to be better than that. Stronger than that."

"Better and stronger than what?" Emily asked.

"Than what I always do. It's like I abuse my heart on purpose sometimes. Even when it's telling me to go, I don't always listen. But in this situation, I'm not *sure* I should let go. Logically, though, it makes sense for me to leave, right? He's not...free. But I feel connected to him, so I'm being indecisive."

"You didn't target Oliver and go after him with complete disregard for his family life. You aren't out to destroy his family. He and Angelina have done a fantastic job of that on their own. You just showed up to find a lonely man who needs a friend."

May exhaled. "We both know that we would be more than friends if we could. So what do I do?"

"It sounds like you know what you should do. If you can't be just friends with Oliver, then you need to tell him and you should stop seeing him. At least until the divorce is final."

May looked at Emily. "You think he's going to want to be with me after his divorce?"

"Uh...yes, May." Emily took a bite of her soggy cereal. "He would be with you right now if he thought he could without tarnishing your reputation. Do you want to be with him? If he were single and you ran into him on the streets of Mystic Water, would you date him?"

May sagged against the chair and leaned her head back. She stared at the blanket of dark, churning clouds. Thunder boomed and shook the trees in the backyard. May pressed her hands to her stomach. "Yes."

Emily offered her an understanding yet sympathetic smile. "Give yourself some grace here. The soul reacts differently when it finds another soul that ignites it with passion. It's difficult to contain that, especially when all we want to do is wrap our arms around it and run off, screaming and laughing like we've been overcome with madness."

Emily held out her hand, and without giving it much thought, May grabbed it, squeezed, and said, "That's a great description. You should be a writer."

"I think we're going to be best friends forever." Rain burst into the yard, zipping straight toward them. Emily reached for half the items on the table. "Let's get inside before we're soaked!"

They cleared the table and shrieked as the rain beat down on them before they were safely indoors. Lightning sparked sideways like glowing spiderwebs and lit up the sky like white fireworks.

Emily set her armload down on the kitchen counter top. "Can I request that you calm your heart down so that this storm settles, since you're rain dancing storms into town?"

An hour later Grandma Charity called and asked May to run a few errands for her in town. May dodged rain puddles, jumping around the sunken-in places in the grocery store parking lot, and she lost her umbrella to a fierce gust of wind that swooped down and snatched it from her hands. She watched the umbrella disappear like a struggling blackbird pulled into a tornado. In town May leaped underneath awnings downtown while making her way toward the hardware store. Still the rain poured from the sky, ranging in intensity from a severe summer storm to a pitiful drizzle.

By the time she'd finished her errands, the rain had moved on, but dense gray clouds blocked the sunlight. Everything in town looked drained of color, blurry and smudged like an out-of-focus photograph. On her way home May reached a crossroad and felt lured to take the long way, which would lead her by Jordan Pond. As she neared the pond, the desire to stop and sit on the bench beneath the willow intensified. Her insides quivered, and she tightened her hands on the wheel.

Used to the urgings of her subconscious mind, May assumed her brain was telling her she needed to write, to get down on paper the cluster of feelings she'd been collecting over the past few weeks. Perhaps a new story idea was being born in her mind. She parked the car and grabbed her notebook and pen. But as she walked toward the bench, she realized why she'd been led to Jordan Pond. It wasn't her creative brain calling out to her; her heart had been sending up smoke signals. Someone needed help.

14

Oliver sat on a bench beside Jordan Pond with a cardboard six pack next to his shoe. The thin, dangling limbs of the willow trembled in the muggy breeze, whispering caution, but Oliver batted one of its tendrils off his shoulder.

Three empty beer bottles lay strewn on the sodden grass. He heard footsteps squishing around patches of mud and water. He *felt* her before he saw her.

"You know it's kinda illegal to have an open container of alcohol outside of a drinking establishment or your home, right? We're not a dry county, but you can't willy-nilly drink anywhere you want."

"It's *kinda* illegal or it *is* illegal?" Oliver looked up at her and tapped his temple. "I had a feeling you'd show up."

"You did?" May asked, eyeing the waterlogged slats of the bench. She puffed out her cheeks and sat. She hooked her ballpoint pen onto her notebook and rested it in her lap.

He strangled the half-empty beer bottle between his knees. "I was thinking about you." He lifted the bottle and drank.

May pressed her teeth into her lower lip. She looked like she wanted to walk away, and his stomach clenched.

"And that means I'll show up?" she asked. "You think about me, and *poof*, there I'll be?"

He reached over and poked his finger into her thigh. "What I mean is that you were so full in my mind that I wondered if I was calling out to you, sending out vibes, my desperate plea for a friend, all that mumbo jumbo garbage." He released a slow, sleepy laugh. "And yet, I still hoped it might work. That you might appear. And here you are. Like magic. *Poof.*"

She pointed to the beer bottle. "Any particular reason you're drinking before the sun goes down? Rough day at the office?"

Judgment colored her voice, and his jaw clenched. "You're a smart girl, May. Woman. You're a smart *woman*." He finished off the bottle, dropped it onto the grass beside him like a bomb falling from the sky, and reached for another one. He pulled a bottle opener from his pocket and flipped off the metal cap. Then he drank before speaking again.

May watched him for a few seconds but then stared at the pond. Energy, frantic and angry, sizzled off him. The slats in between them released steam into the air.

Oliver shifted on the bench. "You're waiting for me to tell you, aren't you? But you *know* what it is. How do you do it? How *did* you do it?"

"Do what?"

Thunder rumbled in the distance. A solid concrete-gray sky stretched over them; even darker storm clouds, like clusters of thick, choking smoke, moved in. Warm winds pushed across the water. The weeping willow branches tangled together.

"How are you happy after going through a divorce? You said he was abusive, which sucks, but was the divorce easy? Were you both ready to give up so it was a relief to separate? I guess not having kids makes it really easy too—"

"Excuse me?" May asked, turning on the bench to face him.

The notebook slipped from her lap onto the wet bench as thunder growled in the distance. Nearby trees trembled in the approaching fury. Oliver felt his temper flaring, but he watched her pupils narrow, and he wondered if he'd lit a fire in her too.

"Did you just say that it must have been *easy*? Has *any* divorce ever been easy?"

Oliver's forehead wrinkled. He lifted the beer bottle to his lips, drank, and then wiped the back of his hand across his mouth. "It's a question, May."

"It's a moronic assumption packaged into the form of a question."

A laugh bubbled up Oliver's throat. "That's not an answer."

May turned away from him. She released her clenched jaw and placed her notebook back in her lap. She folded her hands together as the wind blew her auburn hair behind her shoulders. "I've never met anyone who thought divorce was easy. Even if both people understand it's necessary, it carries a heavy feeling of disappointment and regret. No couple ever agrees one hundred percent on *what* happened, so feelings are hurt and hearts break. But in regard to *my* divorce, no it wasn't easy, pleasant, happy, or any other ridiculous synonym that might be applied."

Oliver drank from the bottle and watched her. She glanced his way. He pointed the bottle neck at her. "So tell me. How are you happy?"

"How am I happy *now*? It's been years, Oliver. Time is the great healer, in case you haven't heard."

"You're sensitive about this," he said. "I can tell that I've struck a nerve. Maybe you aren't as happy as you're portraying."

"You implying that years later I can find happiness again because I didn't have a rough time with divorce, and your completely insensitive comment that not having children makes divorce easier for me struck a nerve, yes."

The rumbling thunder sent vibrations across the pond. Nearby birds quieted. The ducks on Jordan Pond huddled together among the reeds on the western bank. Even though a voice in his head told him to *back off*, the alcohol coursing through him made him bold and stupid.

"Is your happiness exaggerated then?" He twisted the bottle in his lap; the glass ground against a wooden plank. "I don't see how anyone could be happy during or after a divorce. It ruins your life. It destroys entire families. It makes men go broke, even when they're working their assess off to provide for their busted-up families. And women can just keep doing what they're doing, like they're *owed* everything. They've birthed the children, they've changed dirty diapers, and they've bathed and fed and nurtured everyone. So, why *shouldn't* they get everything? Then they are free to date again. They can share their sob stories about what a lonely marriage they had and how all they ever wanted was to have a happy home. And it's all bullshit, and the men are barely scraping by and still get guilt tripped about not being present enough for the kids."

Oliver finished his beer and hurled the bottle against the broad willow tree's trunk in an overhead pitch like a professional, yet

123

tipsy, baseball player. The glass broke into three large chunks. May flinched. Guilt erupted inside of him, and he wondered if her ex-husband had been just as much of an ass as he was being, smashing bottles like a child throwing a tantrum.

May placed her notebook on the bench and walked toward the litter. She picked up the glass shards and returned to the bench, stacking the pieces of glass between them.

"Your argument must feel valid to you. Maybe that's how you feel right now or how you're envisioning your future. You saying all men are the victims and the women are evil is a narrow view and leaves out many other stories. What about the women who are picked apart emotionally and psychologically? What about the women who are terrified to cook the wrong meal for dinner because of the rage it might ignite? Or the women who must apologize for everything, no matter the circumstances? What about when the verbal assaults turn into shoves and slaps, and the women who run down the stairs just so they aren't pushed? What about the women who move out, run away even, and sleep on the floor anywhere they can find just to get away? The ones who don't care about money because they just want to escape with their lives?"

The alcohol enlarged his anger. "It seems my version is more prevalent. I'm not denying that women suffer abuse and there are terrible husbands. But I think situations like mine are the norm. Women manipulate the whole situation until it's in their favor, and they unite other women with them so there's no way for a man to win."

May faced Oliver. "I don't think anyone *wins* during a divorce. Both people lose in a way. I'm not sure why you were 'calling' out to me because it seems you're unfit for anyone's company. So I'm going to leave, but you want to know how I'm happy now? Because I *choose* to be happy. I refuse to let one man or one relationship or one situation dictate the rest of my life. Nothing deserves that much control over my life. I also refuse to picture my future as one giant suckfest, the path you've chosen at present."

Rain approached in the distance, moving toward them, bringing raucous thunder and bolts of vicious lightning. The trees vibrated and branches swayed in the increasing winds, sounding like rolling ocean waves crashing onto the shore.

"What you make of your life and how you let your hardships mold you is *your* choice," she continued. "It sounds like you're leaning toward cynical and bitter, and that's a lousy, emotionally immature choice." May stood and grabbed her notebook. "There's a trash can beside the parking lot. Throw out your garbage when you leave. All of it."

Oliver listened to her stomp away and thought, *Damn.*

A quarter of a mile away from the Jordan Pond, the rainstorm caught up with May and pelted the car with drops that sounded like hail on the roof. She imagined Oliver sitting on the bench, letting the rain drench him while he fumed and cursed his life. May didn't know how to process this incensed version of Oliver. His reactions and words weren't as vile as Chris' had been, but his mood created a sour taste on her tongue. She finished off her water bottle, but still the taste lingered.

May drove to the farm, windshield wipers slapping on high, a nauseous ache in her stomach. Gone was the giddiness and promise she'd felt the day before when Oliver wrapped his fingers around hers. She parked her car and leaned her forehead against the steering wheel. Part of her wanted to go back to him, to tell him she was sorry for storming off, to tell him it was okay that he was angry and insensitive. Even though it was *far* from okay. *Old habits of trying to make someone else happy at my own expense.*

"What did you think, May? That you'd find love and romance in Mystic Water? That a man going through a *divorce* was a healthy choice?" She lifted her head and reached for the bags in the passenger seat. "I thought he was different, though." *Isn't that what everyone says?*

Later that night, when the storm finally quieted and Grandma Charity padded off to bed in her white cotton nightgown designed with tiny roses, May lay on the living room couch, mesmerized by the spinning fan blades. She'd been drifting in and out of consciousness, trying to relax her mind and read *Matilda*. She'd reread three times about Miss Trunchbull forcing Bruce Bogtrotter to eat a whole chocolate cake. May closed the book, placed it on an end table, turned off the lamp, and shuffled to her room.

May pulled the cool sheets up to her chin and rolled onto her side, letting her gaze drift toward the window. She'd forgotten to the close the blinds, and silver moonlight slanted into the room, creating stripes on the dark floor. May's cell phone lit up and vibrated on the desk. *It's nearly midnight. Who would be texting me this late?* Her heart jumped to Oliver, but her mind worked hard to shut down the thought. *What could he possibly say to change my mind? We need to stop seeing each other.* May rolled onto her back and stared at the ceiling. The phone vibrated again. *Maybe he wants to apologize.* "Who cares?" she asked out loud and rolled away from the light of the illuminated phone. May sighed. *You care, May.* But she didn't get out of bed, and the phone quieted. May drifted off to sleep thinking about Oliver and rain and bottles that broke apart like hearts.

ay stood at the small desk in the guest bedroom. A child's desk had been wedged into a nook in an otherwise awkward, unusable space, and it was the only place where the desk fit. The desk was also there to "block an eyesore," as her grandma put it. Behind the desk on the lower portion of the wall was a two-foot-tall wooden door with a knob perfect for children's hands. The door led to an opening that ran between the walls in the house, meant to serve as a way workers could access wiring and plumbing. When May and her cousins were kids, they pretended the tiny door led to another world, a bridge between this world and a more fantastical land. It had also been used as a place of punishment, a makeshift jail, for days when they played pirates or cops and robbers.

May slumped in the desk chair and reached out her toes toward the doorknob on the small door. Holding her cell phone in her hand, she read the text messages that had come through as she'd been falling asleep the night before. Both messages were from Oliver.

He wrote, *I owe you an apology. I wasn't my best self today.* Followed by, *Would you allow me to apologize in person? Sweet dreams, May. You're in my thoughts tonight.*

May reread the lines enough to sear them into her brain. When she closed her eyes, the words floated before her in the darkness. She longed for a day when she crouched in front of the tiny door, glanced over her shoulder at her cousins, and prepared to enter a world where the scariest challenges were scaly, fire-breathing dragons or wicked queens who cast spells on the innocent. In the world behind the door, broken hearts always healed, the good guys always won, and right versus wrong never blurred together. The doorknob felt cool beneath her toes.

May dropped her feet flat on the floor and pushed herself into a straighter position. The unforgiving wood of the chair felt cool against the backs of her thighs. She inhaled slowly, puffed out air, and texted Oliver, *What you're going through isn't easy. It's understandable that you will have a variety of "selves" appear, some less than ideal. Apology accepted. Meeting in person isn't necessary.* May hesitated before she hit send. She *wanted* to see him again; her heart thrilled at the idea of being near him. But was that what the old May would have done? Gone right back to someone who hurt her? *He wasn't himself. Maybe it's a one-time breakdown.* "Do you *hear* yourself? You're making excuses for his awful behavior." May hit send and pushed away from the desk, dropping the phone on her bed as she walked out of the bedroom.

Before she could walk ten steps down the hallway, her phone dinged. May paused, debated going back or going forward. Coffee percolated in the kitchen. The phone dinged again. She returned to the bedroom and read the new messages from Oliver.

Thank you for accepting my apology. I'd still like to see you. The next message, *Please.*

May squeezed the phone in her hands. Sunlight poured into the room, stretched across the wooden planks until it touched her toes. But May shook her head and glared at the sunlight. "No. Spending more time with each other will only connect us even more." May imagined wild vines strangling her. Part of her said, *So what? You know what your heart is saying, so listen to it. You see something in him you haven't seen before. You're feeling something stirring way down deep in your heart. He awakened that.* The other voice in her mind sounded panicked and desperate, *No, no, no, don't even think about it. Why would you want to be a part of something so broken? You know what they say about trying to save someone who's drowning...you'll drown instead.* Even as May responded to Oliver, *I don't think that's a good idea,* her stomach clenched, and the back of her neck tingled. Sunlight crept up her calves, warming her. Her breaths became shallow, but she hit send. Then she closed out of the text messages and rushed out of the room, frightened of a response that might change her mind.

Grandma Charity stepped out of the laundry room, and May nearly ran her over. May dodged her grandma but slammed her shoulder against the wall, rattling the hanging pictures. She was

128

almost into the kitchen before she could slow her momentum.

Grandma Charity stood still in the hallway. When May looked at her and asked if she was okay, her grandma tossed a thumb over her shoulder and said, "You can't outrun that, you know."

"Ma'am?" May asked, pressing one hand against her chest as she tried to slow her breathing.

"You can't outrun that problem. You'll never be fast enough or run far enough. It'll catch up with you if you don't deal with it," Grandma Charity said.

May squared her shoulders. "I'm not running from it."

Her grandma lowered her chin and gazed up at May through her thinning lashes. Then she looked toward the back bedroom where May's phone remained silent. "You're dealing with it?"

"Yes, ma'am, I am."

"Why are you running?"

May rubbed the back of her neck and stared at her feet. "Even though I'm dealing with it, I'm afraid it's going to catch me anyway. Because maybe...maybe I'm going to let it."

May ran around the farm and ventured into the neighbor's farm to complete a seven-mile run after she'd had peanut butter on toast with a cup of coffee. Running helped clear her head and released the nervous energy that pulsed through her like electroshock therapy. She hoped running would push Oliver right out of her mind, and it had for brief moments, but as soon as she realized, *I'm not thinking about him,* she was thinking about him. Why wasn't his apology enough for her to let go? Why couldn't she close the book on their story, mark it as complete? Was she being weak? Or was her connection with Oliver something she *shouldn't* let go of?

After showering, she drove to the Mystic Water library for research and for a change of scenery. In a back corner of the library, May sat at a table and flipped through a book written about the history of Asheville, North Carolina. To keep the book open, she weighed down the pages with two other books. Then she reached over and pulled photographs of the Biltmore Estate closer to her. A floor plan detailed the extravagant rooms and areas throughout the mansion. Pen-and-ink sketches of the majestic gardens were paired alongside color photographs of their current state.

May's fingers moved over her laptop's keyboard as she typed an article that described the must-see sights of Asheville, with a highlight on the estate. May had been to the Biltmore, but only once when she and her siblings were young. May thought she must have been nearly eleven, and the memory that stood out the most was of her standing in the grand foyer in awe of the magnitude and beauty of the space. She had imagined women in shimmering ball gowns floating down the stairs, while men in tailored suits stood around talking and pretending not to stare at the women joining the party.

A young woman approached the table, and May recognized her as Emma Chase, the librarian who assisted her nearly every time she'd visited the library. "Hey, May, Morty found these for you. He's always been fascinated with the Biltmores and their connection to our country's history. He says these books are rarer and most people overlook them, but they have a lot more detailed and personal history about Asheville." She placed three books on the table.

"Thank you," May said. "Tell Morty he's as 'with it' as Grandma Charity said he is. She said if you don't know something, you go to the library and ask Morty."

Emma smiled and shook her head. "I can already see the size of his noggin growing," she said and held out her hands around her head and puffed out her cheeks like a blowfish.

The soft sound of footfalls on the tile sounded behind Emma as someone else approached. Emma turned to follow May's gaze, and Oliver walked straight for them, holding a handful of oversize, yellow sunflowers.

"Those are beautiful," Emma said. She looked at May with raised eyebrows. "Let us know if you need anything else." Then she walked away, leaving Oliver standing at the end of the library table, looking down at May.

"What are you doing here?" May finally asked, unsticking her tongue from the roof of her mouth. She straightened in the chair and placed her hands in her lap.

He held the flowers out toward her. "Apologizing."

"I already accepted."

When she didn't make a move to reach for the flowers, he drew them back toward his chest. "But you won't accept my flowers." He pulled out the chair across from her and sat. He placed the flowers on the table, careful to not squish the fat petals. "You're still angry with me. I completely understand—"

"I'm not angry with you." She glanced away from his steady gaze.

Oliver folded his arms together on the table and leaned forward. "But you don't want to see me."

"No."

Oliver sat up and his mouth fell open. "I wasn't expecting that response."

May closed her eyes and pinched the bridge of her nose. "That came out wrong." She looked at him. "Oliver, it's not that I don't want to see you. It's that you didn't need to come all the way down here to apologize. Again. And how *did* you know I was here?"

"I drove out to the farm. Your grandma told me. I wandered around the library until I found you, hiding way back here in the corner."

"She *told* you I was here?" May asked, her eyes widening. *Grandma knew I was handling this. How is sending Oliver to me helping?*

"Why wouldn't she?" Oliver asked. "Be honest. On a scale of one to ten, how badly did I screw up?"

May stared at him. "Why does it only go up to ten?"

Oliver's lips twitched like he wanted to smile. "If you're not mad at me, then what is it?"

May saved her document and closed her laptop. She traced the symbol on the top of the case with her finger. "It's complicated."

"All the best stories are." Oliver's dark eyes watched her, and he sat still, waiting for her to respond.

May busied her hands by closing the books in front of her and stacking them. Then she shuffled together the photographs and loose papers. "I don't know what we're doing, but whatever it is, it needs to be put on hold or stop altogether. You're understandably in a bad place, and I don't want to imply that your feelings aren't valid or that this situation doesn't call for lousy behavior, but I'm saying that I don't need to toss myself voluntarily into the mix. It doesn't have to be more complicated than it already is. You need to...get through on your own."

Oliver leaned back in the chair and folded his arms behind his head. He stared up at the ceiling. "You're right about most of that. But you're wrong about one thing."

"Which thing?"

He leaned forward and reached across the table. When he grabbed her hand, she didn't pull away. "I know what we're doing. We're falling in love."

May flinched, but Oliver rubbed his thumb across the top of her hand.

"It hasn't been long enough for you to *fall in love* with me. You barely know me," May argued.

Oliver half-smiled at her, and the expression in his eyes caused May's skin to tingle. He *looked* like a man in love, like the whole world had turned into a blur while May sat before him in clear focus. "May, it took me less than ten seconds to fall in love with you."

"Eight point two?"

"What?" he asked.

May shook her head in response.

Oliver continued, "You want to deny that or shove it out the door because you *are* right that this is a crappy situation. To bring you into it, well, maybe that's wrong. But the truth is, I don't want you to leave. I'm aware that it's selfish. But I think you enjoy being my friend too. Tell me if I'm wrong, if you haven't liked spending time together. And I'm using the word *friend* loosely because otherwise I'd be straight-up lying. I'm not *only* interested in you as a friend, and you know that. I don't know what to *do* with these feelings, but taking you out of the equation makes me feel..." He rubbed his hand

132

across his collarbone. "Empty. You're the only highlight in my life right now, the only warmth I've felt for a long time."

Sunlight pushed through the wall of windows behind May and covered them in creamy light. Oliver gazed over her head, and the brightness caused his face to glow. His dark brown eyes lightened to a caramel hue, and she noticed strands of lighter brown in his hair.

Oliver smiled and leaned back in the chair, releasing her hand. "Like that. You pull sunlight toward you. Or maybe it's you stretching it over others. Whatever it is, I don't want to be without it." He reached into his pocket and pulled out a folded sheet of paper. He unfolded it and pushed it toward her.

"What's this?" She glanced down at what looked like an outline created by a high school literature student.

"An outline of my novel."

May's head lifted, and she gaped at him.

"You inspired me to write. I couldn't sleep last night so I spent hours thinking about my story, and I created an outline. I wrote a few paragraphs in the first chapter, but I was too drowsy to do more."

May's lips lifted. "You're writing? You're finally going to write your novel?"

"Looks that way." He pointed at her. "All because of you and your sunshine."

May sighed and slid the outline back toward Oliver. "I appreciate you thinking that I'm helpful for you to have around—"

"May, you're not my landscaper. You're not just *helpful* to have around. You're vital."

"That's dramatic," she said, but she was already smiling. A fluttering started in her stomach, and she stared at Oliver's folded hands on the table, tamping down the desire to reach out and take them in her own.

"Doesn't make it any less true. If you really don't want to hang out with me, tell me. I won't try and justify what I'm doing or feeling, but at the same time, Angelina and I have been unhappy for years, and we're heading straight toward not being together, so being in love with you doesn't sound or feel like this god-awful mistake. And it's not like I would feel this way about *any* woman. I'm not some lonely creep looking for a space filler. It's different with you. I've been looking for you my whole life, and now I've found you."

May's quiet laugh slipped out before she could cover her mouth with her hand. "Oliver, you have *not* been looking—"

"My whole life," he interrupted. "Yes, I have. Finding you feels like stumbling straight into a dream that I've always had but gave up on. I don't consider myself romantic or much of a dreamer, but you make me feel like both. I'll respect your need to stop seeing me, but I won't act like it doesn't make me unhappy."

May dropped her face into her hands. "Oliver, you're making it hard to say no."

"So don't say it." Oliver propped his elbows on the table. "I've been drinking too much. Not today, but in general."

May leaned back in her chair. She clasped her hands together in her lap. A memory of a liquor cabinet surfaced. Glass bottles—short and fat; tall, sleek cylinders; amber rectangles; classic and circular with long necks—sat shrouded in the dark, away from the light, which would spoil their sensitive blends. A sticky highball glass, left absently behind the night before, still held a few drops of brown liquid. May blinked, and the memory swept away like fog on the wind.

"It took you showing up yesterday for me to become aware of it, aware that it's a problem," Oliver continued.

"And it *is* a problem?" May asked. She remembered the stench of scotch on Chris' breath when he'd lean in close with his unfocused eyes and venomous words.

"Avoidance," he answered. "I can appreciate a well-balanced drink. Angelina and the kids left, and one glass at night turned into two, turned into two and a half. Then that eventually turned into two or three beers at lunch on the weekends. Then a couple more in the afternoon. And by dinner, I'd had more than a six pack of beer or finished off more than half of a bottle of wine. By myself. I knew I could stop if I wanted to, but I haven't *wanted* to. And I've been pissed off with Angelina for drinking too much.

"Yesterday it became clear that not only am I a hypocrite but I haven't wanted to deal with the deeper issues. Angelina's affair wasn't the only reason we aren't working. Our problems go back much further, and we're both guilty. We could have been better people and better to each other. But we got tired and lazy." Oliver waved a hand through the air as if to send away the negativity. "So I've been drinking because it puts a haze over everything. Makes it dull. Dull is easier to ignore. But you...you shined the light on it. And it's ugly. I don't want to be an alcoholic who hides from his problems. I threw away all the alcohol." He brushed his hands together. "Today is a new day to start again. Thanks for putting me in my place yesterday. I threw out the garbage, just like you said. Can you forgive me for being a complete ass?"

Chris had never apologized for his drinking. A vein had bulged in his neck as he'd denied he *had* a drinking problem. May had never brought it up again. But Oliver had not only admitted his problem, but he dumped any temptations that might keep him on the wrong road. "Yes."

Oliver smiled. "Thanks. While we're on the subject of new stuff, I have an idea. Our running group wants to create a team to run a 10K for a charity race raising money for the Leukemia and Lymphoma Society, not this weekend, but the next weekend. Al's wife had leukemia and beat it, so it's a cause close to their hearts. Al's company will match the total proceeds earned if he can form a team and complete the race. We're short one person to sign up as a group. Why don't you join us? Are you free next Saturday?"

"You've set me up," May said. "Only a jerk would say she didn't want to help raise money for that charity."

"So you'll join us? You're not going to cut me off just yet? We're still friends?"

"Only until after the race." She made a scissor motion with her fingers. "Then we're cutting loose until you're in a better headspace." It felt easier to joke about their approaching separation because accepting it as their future made her feel lightheaded and dizzy.

Oliver slapped his hand on the table and grinned. Then he apologized for being loud while glancing around to see if he'd disturbed anyone. He lifted the flowers and held them out for May. She grabbed them and said thank you. Oliver stood and pushed his chair up to the table.

"Fair enough," he said. "Unless I can convince you after the race to stay friends or I can come up with another way to set you up."

May chuckled. "Get out of here," she teased. "I have work to do, and don't you have a job?"

Oliver waved and turned to leave.

"Hey, Ollie," May called. He looked at her. "I'm proud of you for starting your novel and for tossing out the garbage."

"Thank you, lovely May," he said, "and thank you for turning your sunshine my way."

May tapped her pen against the tabletop. *I'm really* handling *this. I've agreed* again *to spend time with him.* A shiver shuddered up her spine. *What if I* can't *let him go?* Another voice asked, *But what if I don't* have to?

16

*O*ut in the library parking lot, Oliver walked to his car, dropped onto the driver's seat, and exhaled. That had gone better than he imagined. He'd half expected May to ignore him or explain in detail how much of an ass he'd been yesterday, but she'd done neither. Then he realized that's how Angelina would have reacted.

May had watched him with her pale, green eyes, unnerving him with her calm while drawing him nearer with the light and warmth that surrounded her. To Oliver, May was the reverse of a mythological Siren. She wasn't beckoning him to his death but calling him forth into a life that made him feel like his skin couldn't contain the energy and happiness. Spending time with May reminded him of when he was a child and he and his best friends would race to the ocean, full speed and hair blown back by the wind, smiling wider than the horizon. *That's* how May made him feel.

Even as his chest expanded, and he thought the feeling was too much, he still craved more. More time, more talking, more *everything* with May. They *had* to make this work. He couldn't have spent his whole life longing for a girl like May only to have it *not* work out. Fate wouldn't do that, would it? He wouldn't let it. What could possibly stop him from fighting for it?

Oliver texted May to say thank you again and to let her know that he would be traveling to see the kids for the weekend. For his sake, and for the kids, he hoped the visit would be less *screeching owl* and more civil. Oliver cranked the engine and drove to his office with a smile on his face. Lovely May had forgiven him, and he still had a chance with her.

May drove to the farm with the windows rolled down and singing a Trisha Yearwood song as though she were putting on a concert for the whole town. Country music wasn't a genre May listened to often, but listening to it while staying in Mystic Water created a sweet, nostalgic feeling, making her believe everything would be all right. Her cell phone rang just as she parked at the farm. May turned off the radio and then found her phone beneath the books in the passenger seat. "Hey, Mama," she said.

"Hey, honey, how are you?"

May shoved the loose books and papers into her canvas bag. She slid the sunflowers into the bag too, careful not to crush their blooms. A few bright yellow petals littered the floorboard. "I'm okay. Just finishing up some work and about to head inside Grandma's." May rested her hand on the keys dangling from the ignition, debating whether she should turn off the car. "How are you and Daddy?"

"Your dad should be finishing up his lecture about now, and I just got off the phone with your sister. She has some news I think will make your day."

"Really?" May asked. She dropped her hand from the keys and turned an air vent directly at her face. May closed her eyes and breathed in the artificial scent of plastic mixed with the air circulating through the car. "That must be *some* news. Let's hear it."

"She's coming to Mystic Water to relieve you of your duty." Her mama's voice was airy and gentle, like someone who knew her words were bringing peace and comfort with them.

May's eyes popped open. "She's what?" May stared straight out the window while the last few weeks sped through her mind in fragmented images, ending with Oliver handing her flowers in the library.

Her mama continued, "She wasn't sure she could work it out because of the kids, but she knows you've been there much longer than anyone else. She figures—well, we all do—that you could use a break. It's not easy to spend a week with Grandma Charity, and you've been there, what? A whole month? I know it's easier for you to work from anywhere, but that's no excuse for the rest of the family to put such a burden on you for so long."

May's mouth felt like it filled with desert sand. She tried to swallow and create spit before she spoke. "Mama, it's not been that bad. I don't mind. Grandma and I have found a routine that works for both of us. And coming here, that must be rough for Fiona. What's she doing with the kids?"

"The twins are off at camp for the next three weeks, and your dad and I are keeping Elizabeth. She's no trouble, you know. A little angel darling. And truth is, Fiona *needs* a break. She hasn't been kid-free in years, and Marcus is working long hours on a special project at the firm this summer, so she's actually excited to take a trip."

"Tell her to go somewhere else," May blurted. "The beach? Wildehaven Beach is close."

Her mama paused, and the only sound May could hear was the whoosh of the air conditioning in her ears.

"May?" Her mama said in a slow, drawn-out voice. "Are you okay, honey?"

May pressed her hand against her chest, feeling her pulse pounding beneath her palm. If she needed a way out, a way to leave Mystic Water and Oliver behind, this was the perfect chance. No lengthy explanations, no questions. Her stay in town had always been labeled *temporary*. Now that the opportunity for her to exit had arrived, a rising tide of panic rose up within her. She clutched the steering wheel with both hands and twisted her fingers around the leather.

"May?" her mama said again.

"Ma'am?"

"Are you okay? Is something going on?"

"No...no, of course not," she said. "I'm just a little out of it, I think. Working all day. You know how I get, laser-focused on a project. What I meant to say is that if Fiona has a break from the kids and Marcus, and I'm doing just fine here, maybe she would like to go somewhere more relaxing, like the beach. She doesn't have to come to Mystic Water and melt." *But this is my chance to leave, to "handle" this situation with Oliver. No one would blame me for ending it. He wouldn't even blame me.*

Her mama laughed. "She's actually excited about it. Said it made

139

her feel sentimental. Besides, she left here a few hours ago. She was going to take it slow, stop and go antiquing along the way, have lunch, but she'll probably get to Mystic Water in less than an hour. You can pack up and leave before it gets dark, head on back home."

"Yeah, home," May said. The words sounded flatter than notebook paper.

"Tell Fiona to call or text when she gets there, okay, honey? And let me know when you're heading back into town. Your dad and I have missed seeing you for dinners. We love you."

"Love you too, Mama."

Her mama disconnected, and May turned off the car. Days after her arrival in Mystic Water, she had imagined what it would be like to leave town. Now, a month later, even pretending she was going inside the farmhouse to pack made her queasy. Could she *leave* Mystic Water? Why did saying good-bye to the few friends she'd made there make her feel that instead of *returning* home, she was *leaving* home?

Fiona unhooked her seatbelt and pushed herself up inside the black Mustang convertible until she could prop against the driver's side headrest. She lifted both palms toward the sky, leaned back her head, and stretched. A tiny sliver of pale skin showed between her emerald green tank top and her khaki shorts. She waved with both hands and smiled at May and Grandma Charity, who stood on the front porch.

"I wasn't expecting a welcoming party," Fiona said, not bothering with the car door and swinging her legs over the door and sliding down the metal until her sandals hit the dirt.

May met her older sister halfway across the yard and hugged her. She peered around Fiona's shoulder at the sports car. "You've got your convertible and your sunglasses. Where's your riding scarf? Then you'd be a picture-perfect movie starlet. When did Marcus buy you a convertible? He seems *way* too sensible to do that. Have I misjudged him?"

"Don't be silly. I don't *need* Marcus to buy me anything. I could buy one if I wanted to, but," she hooked her arm through May's and pulled her toward the porch where Grandma Charity stood smiling at them, "he'd have a fit if I did. I can already hear him listing out all of the dangers of driving a convertible. I rented this one before I left town. What he doesn't know won't kill him."

Fiona greeted and hugged Grandma Charity while she fussed over Fiona's gorgeous, wavy red hair that fell past her shoulders. Grandma Charity had hair the color of Fiona's when she was younger, but no one in their Irish family tree had hair as gorgeous as Fiona's. Add in her pale green eyes, soft luminescent skin, and freckled cheeks, and Fiona could stop a man's heart one hundred yards away. If Fiona's soul wasn't more beautiful than her physical attributes, May knew she might have been eaten up with jealousy over her sister's bountiful blessings. But instead, Fiona had been, and often still was, May's hero and exactly the kind of woman May wanted to be: brave, kind, intelligent, and compassionate. The fact that she was also beautiful was more of a side bonus.

"Let me grab your bags," May said.

Fiona waved her off. "I'll get them. You're not the bellman."

"Lemonade or sweet tea?" Grandma Charity asked. "I made shortbread cookies. Come on in. Let your sister get your bag."

Fiona pressed her hands against her stomach. "Good heavens, I'm going to have to watch myself while I'm here. You'll have me chubbier than I was in elementary school if I'm not careful. But nobody makes shortbread cookies like you do, so I'll take the risk."

"Of course they don't," Grandma said. "And I don't remember you ever being chubby. Scrawny women aren't good for helping much. They're too fragile. MacAdams women are strong and resilient."

Fiona laughed. "We are most definitely *not* fragile. I'll help May, and we'll be right in. I'd love a glass of your lemonade. It's homemade, right?"

Grandma Charity huffed. "I'm going to ignore that because otherwise it's insulting."

Fiona laughed again and skipped off the porch with May. She

hooked her arm through May's again and lowered her voice to a whisper. "So tell me, are you going completely batty here? I can't believe you've been here so long. You're a trooper, you know that? Star student times a thousand. Has she laid off trying to get you to do your hair and makeup at level ten every day?"

May rolled her eyes. "She's relentless," she said with a smile. "She flat out told me that I would never catch a man unless I fixed up more."

Fiona choked on her laugh. "She did not. What do you *need* a man for? You have a dream job, you can travel and *do* travel anywhere and anytime you want. You're free and lovely and...and honestly I wish I had your life right now."

May scrunched her face. "You don't mean that. You have the kind of life that *everyone* envies. Handsome husband, adorable kids, a house with a pool. Do you remember when we used to sweat to death in the summers, wishing one day we'd have a pool? You grew up and fulfilled all our dreams."

Fiona sighed. "I don't remember dreaming about working my tail off and having no one appreciate it. It's like they think the house just runs by itself. Some days I think, 'What if I don't *do* anything today?' No laundry, no cooking, no cleaning, no nagging to do homework, nothing. What would happen? Would anyone notice?"

"I can already hear their complaints! Besides, whether they admit it or not, they really do know that you're the reason that ship is still floating." May stood by the car, and her smile slipped when she saw Fiona's expression. "Are you being serious? What's going on?"

Fiona shoved her hair over her shoulder. "Oh, nothing. We can talk about me later. Now tell me the honest truth. Are you completely losing it from being stuck here so long?"

May shook her head. "The first couple of days were an adjustment. But now, like I told Mama, Grandma and I are used to each other, and it's not bad."

Fiona's green eyes widened. Flecks of brown and gold were scattered around her irises. "Cousin Rickie said Grandma was a nightmare."

"Cousin Rickie has always been melodramatic."

"That's true." Fiona unlocked the trunk and lifted it. One medium-size suitcase and one fabric bag sat in the trunk. "I'd love to chat with you for a little bit before you head back. Do you have a few hours to spare? I don't feel like we've had a one-on-one conversation in—"

"Eight years," May said with a crooked smile. She grabbed the suitcase as Fiona reached for the bag and hooked it over her shoulder.

"Heavens to Betsey, you're right. That's pathetic, isn't it? We haven't really talked, just me and you, since Dustin and Allen were born. Eight years." Fiona grabbed the trunk lid and closed it. "Give me a second to close the roof so the blackbirds don't make this their personal Porta Potti."

May kicked around in the front yard trying to decide how to explain to Fiona that she wasn't sure she was leaving just yet.

Fiona turned off the engine and locked the door. "Can you hang around for a bit?"

May nodded. "I was telling Mama that if you wanted to stay here for a day or so and then drive down to Wildehaven Beach for a minivacation, you should."

"And leave Grandma alone?" Fiona shook her head. "I wouldn't do that. The point is to stay *with* her."

"I'd still be here," May said, walking toward the front porch.

Fiona frowned and grabbed May's arm. "What do you mean? Why would I make you stay longer? You deserve a break. I'm here to relieve you of your duty." Fiona paused, and they both stopped walking. "Something's going on. What is it? What's happened?"

"Nothing," May said, pulling out of her sister's grip and forcing a smile. "I wanted to offer you a real vacation, that's all."

Fiona hopped up the stairs to catch up with May. "Don't make me ask you what I always ask the kids."

One of the tractors' engines turned on, and the deep, vibrating rumbling startled a few squirrels. They chittered in the direction of the noise before disappearing up a pecan tree.

May held open the screen door for Fiona. "What's that?"

"Do you think I was born yesterday?" Fiona said. "I know you, Little May, and I know when you're not telling me something. Why don't you want to leave? You know what? Tell me later. Let's have lemonade and shortbread cookies and pretend we're kids again and stay up late and giggle and watch for shooting stars and—"

May snorted. "You'll be asleep by eight." She stepped aside so Fiona could enter the house.

Fiona narrowed her eyes, but then her smile returned. "Oh, let a girl dream." She stepped into the farmhouse and exhaled. "It's like stepping backward in time, if only for a little bit. It stills smells exactly the same in here. Like wood polish, Grandpa's Old Spice aftershave, pie dough, and that lemony clean scent." She leaned her head on May's shoulder. "Whatever the reason, I'm glad you're sticking around for a while. I've missed you. Having you around is like being all warm and cozy, slowly filled up with sunshine."

"Girls!" Grandma Charity called. "Don't let this lemonade get watered down with the ice."

They both snickered, dropped the luggage in the living room, and hurried down the hallway.

After a dinner of succotash and a fresh salad using lettuce, peppers, tomatoes, and herbs from the gardens, Fiona and May stood at the kitchen sink washing the dishes while Grandma Charity stood on the front porch talking to one of the field hands about her watermelon crop. The young man scuffed the rubber toe of his work boots against the porch boards as Grandma showed him dimensions with her hands. His responses were mostly head nods and yes ma'ams.

Fiona yawned and glanced around the kitchen, turning all the way around and frowning. "Where's the little clock with the birds on it? The one that used to hang in here and chirp every hour."

"Grandma changed the wallpaper in here last year. She took it

144

down and decided it looked better in the laundry room," May said, stacking the clean, dry plates in the cabinet. "I think she got tired of the cuckoo at noon. Whatever time it is, it's too early for you to be yawning." May pointed toward the window. "The sun is still up."

The lowering sunlight washed over the fields in deep golden bands, and the crickets tuned up for their nighttime chorus.

Fiona huffed and pushed her curls over her shoulder. "It won't be dark until after nine here."

"And?" May chuckled at Fiona's downturned expression.

Fiona fisted her hand on her hip, forgetting she had the soapy sponge in her hand, and sent a cascade of Dawn bubbles and water down her leg. "Good heavens." She tossed the sponge into the sink, and May passed her the hand towel. "Perfect example of why I need sleep." When Fiona stood straight again, she dropped the towel on the counter top, and for the first time, May noticed how worn down Fiona looked.

"No shame in going to bed early, if you need the rest," May said. "Close the blinds and those heavy curtains in your room. Should be mostly dark. Dark enough to fall asleep at least." May finished drying off the last plate while Fiona stared out the kitchen window in silence. "Hey," May said, lowering her voice, "you okay?"

Fiona sighed. "Oh, sure. I just haven't been to bed early since... well, I can't remember when. I normally stay up after the kids have gone to bed and try to get my own design work done. I have a lot more clients than I used to, which is great, but it's still a lot of work to juggle. After I finally get to bed, we're up, doing it all over again in the morning. My days are on repeat. They're a bit of a blur, if I'm honest, and real sleep feels like a luxury I haven't experienced in a while." She glanced over at May. "I'm glad to be here, though, and to see you. If I can squeeze another day with you, let's catch up with everything tomorrow morning. Would that be okay?"

May nodded, not pressing further. The topic felt itchy and uncomfortable, akin to the feeling of a poison ivy rash spreading over May's skin. Fiona guarded whatever it was, but it weighed her down and dulled her eyes.

"Tomorrow morning? You got it." May folded the damp hand towel and placed it beside the sink. "You can have me all day. I've nowhere special to be, so I can take a few days and spend with my favorite sister."

Fiona's smile lifted her cheeks. "I'm your only sister."

"Minor detail," May said.

Later that evening, after the fireflies twinkled to life, darting in and out of the crops and the trees and the blooming flowers, May passed by the second guest bedroom. Fiona sat on the edge of the double bed. The patchwork quilt had been folded over to reveal the pressed, white cotton sheets. Fiona wore a T-shirt with the words *Life happens. Coffee helps.* across the front. Her boxer shorts had miniature coffee mugs on them. Her curls sat atop her head in a messy bun, with a few long strands spiraling out like Easter basket accordion paper. Fiona stared at her cell phone before placing it on the nightstand.

"Good night," May said. "Get some rest, and try to sleep in as long as possible."

Fiona nodded. "Don't let me sleep all day. I don't want to waste it in bed."

May leaned on the doorjamb. "If you're not up by lunch, I'll come get you."

"Don't let me sleep past breakfast. Is Grandma still making her scrambled eggs with bacon and grits and biscuits?"

"She'll make anything for her darling Fiona," May teased.

Fiona rolled her eyes. "Wake up me. I mean it. I can't remember the last time I ate a decent biscuit or a biscuit at all. And we have some *stuff* to talk about."

May's eyebrows lifted. "That sounds cryptic."

Fiona slid back on the bed and folded the quilt over her legs. "Maybe, but I think it will do us both some good to air out the laundry. I have a feeling you have some baggage you need to put down."

May's back stiffened. In as casual a voice as she could muster, she asked, "What makes you say that?" Her smile wavered on her face.

146

Fiona lay back on the pillow and reached for the lamp. "Just a hunch. You're my baby sister. I've watched you for thirty years, and I've learned a few things about you. Until tomorrow, sweet dreams."

May told Fiona good night, and her sister switched off the lamp. May pulled the bedroom door closed before walking to her own room. Tomorrow she *could* tell Fiona all about Oliver and hear her sister's honest opinion about the situation. Or she could keep the conversation focused on Fiona, keep her sister distracted, so that May didn't have to explain *why* she had feelings for a married man who was in the middle of a messy, stressful divorce. May saw she'd received a couple of texts, both from Oliver. He wished her a good night and told her he had written more on his manuscript. He finished by saying she was on his mind, and he liked her there.

May plopped onto her bed and stared at the ceiling fan as it went round and round and round. The yellow sunflowers faced her, watching over her from a cloudy, antique vase. May sighed and pictured Oliver's smile as he offered the flowers to her. Five minutes later, she changed into her pajamas, turned off the light, and fell asleep before she could hatch a proper plan for how to avoid telling Fiona the truth.

147

17

After breakfast May leaned over the desk chair to boot up her computer. She looked away from the screen when she heard a knock on her open bedroom door. Fiona stood in the doorway, cupping a coffee mug in her hands. Her fiery red curls piled on her head in a messy bun, and she'd changed into a loose tank top and a pair of thin, linen lounging pants.

"Mind if I come in?" Fiona asked.

May shook her head, and Fiona sat on her bed, scooting toward the middle to sit cross-legged, cradling her coffee in her lap. "You wanna talk for real now?"

May walked over to the window and glanced outside. Her laptop's fan made a whirling noise as it opened her applications. Outside in the brightening morning sunlight, a farmhand carried a shovel and a five-gallon bucket out of the shed. She tried to imagine which vegetable he might be harvesting. *Or maybe he's on weed-pulling duty.* When May and Fiona were younger, weed pulling had been the chore reserved for grandchildren who needed punishment.

May looked over at her sister. "Sure. What's going on? I can tell something's up, the way you were skirting around some of Grandma's questions."

"Me?" Fiona asked, her voice pitching higher. She pointed a finger at her chest. "I meant *you.*" She pointed at May.

"Me?" May mimicked Fiona's voice. She sat on the end of the bed, bending one leg beneath her.

Fiona nodded and quirked an eyebrow. "I want to know why you're really staying in Mystic Water."

May's cell phone dinged, and she glanced toward the desk. Then she looked at her sister. "I told you. I'm working, and the Mystic Water Library is a treasure trove of books, not to mention the librarian and his assistant are walking, breathing knowledge banks. You know it doesn't matter where I work from, so why not where there's a nice place to stay and work with the bonus of a library."

Fiona narrowed her pale green eyes. "The university has a library three times the size of this one." She sipped her coffee and then pointed toward May's cell phone. "And who's that? Is it the same texter who's been sending you messages for the past two days?"

May grinned at her sister and chuckled, but her throat tightened. "Who are you? The cell phone police? I have friends who text me. Don't you?"

Fiona tucked a stray curl behind her ear. "Hmmm, but do I get all sparkly eyed when I read texts from my friends like you do?"

May laughed again, even as her breaths quickened. "I have no idea what you're talking about. Maybe my eyes have natural sparkle."

"Yeah?" Fiona asked as she focused on May so intensely that May felt as though her sister might be reading her mind. "Go check that one. Let's see if you can control yourself."

May huffed, but she slid off the bed and walked to her phone. She hesitated before reaching for it. *What if it's Oliver? What am I going to tell her?* When she lit up the phone's face, she exhaled. "It's Emily, the children's book author I told you about." May opened the text and read it. "She wants to go to lunch today." May started typing. "I'll tell her you're in town, and I can go another time." She looked at Fiona and batted her eyelashes. "Are my eyes sparkly?"

Fiona put her mug on the end table. "I've seen them sparklier. Let's both go to lunch with Emily. Grandma won't care. She already told me that one of her friends from church is coming by to pick her up so they can go to somebody's baby shower. It'll be fun to go out and have some girl time. Do you mind?"

"If you come with me? Of course not." May typed a new message to Emily. When the phone dinged again, May read the text and put the phone on the desk. "Lunch date at the Corner Pub. Emily loves their mini corndogs."

Fiona hummed. "Once all those biscuits from breakfast settle, I could go for a full-size corndog."

May's laugh punctuated the air. The curtains around the windows rippled. "And when is the last time you had one of those? The state fair when you were twelve?"

"Probably. Now let's get back to—" Fiona's phone rang in the other room. She jumped off the bed. "Pause this conversation! I'll be back!"

When Fiona's five-minute conversation turned into ten with no end in sight, May put on her running clothes, laced up her tennis shoes, and went for a run in the rising morning heat. Her playlist for the day included her favorite motivational, up-tempo running songs. She waved to the workers who were harvesting asparagus and pole beans. When she ran by Steve, who was putting away the last of the Vidalia onion harvest, he tossed an onion to her like a softball pitcher. May bungled it for a few seconds but grinned when she didn't drop it. She tossed it back to him.

"Nice arm," he said. "You been practicing?"

"Only with the watermelons."

Steve laughed and waved her on. She knew he'd carry the onions into a dry building where he'd lay them out in a single layer to further dry them, taking care not to bump or bruise them. Grandma Charity used to make a Vidalia onion dip for potato chips that tasted even better than the onion dip sold in grocery stores. May thought with Fiona's help, she might be able to convince Grandma to make them a batch. Then they could stay up late scooping up the dip with Fritos or Classic Lay's while they talked about anything. *Anything but Oliver.* That elephant was becoming more challenging to ignore. *Just a few more days. Convince her that I love the library and the quiet of the farm. Lower the sparkle when Oliver texts.* For someone who was intent on cutting him off after the race, why *were* her eyes so sparkly when she heard from him?

May ran by the muscadine vines and slowed her pace, jogging slowly up the rows, looking at the young fruit still ripening on the vine. In a few more weeks, she could sneak out here and shove handfuls of green and purple scuppernongs into her pockets. She remembered how she, Fiona, and their older brother, Conner, had held contests when they were kids for who could spit the grape seeds the farthest. The contests always ended with laughter, a lot of spit, and a mound of grape seeds not much farther away than the

151

tips of their tennis shoes.

May finished her run by circling the neighbor's cornfields and turning back for the farm. Fiona sat in the living room, tapping away on her laptop, while Grandma pulled cling wrap over a plate of finger sandwiches. When May breezed up the hallway, Fiona called out to her.

"Hey," May said, leaning in the doorway, fanning the bottom of her tank top back and forth to send cool air up her stomach and chest.

"Sorry about earlier," Fiona said. "We had a major leak in our upstairs master bath, and because Marcus is working crazy hours, I've been dealing with the plumbers and the contractors, and it's been a holy mess. For my clients, I hire all of this work out to people who know how to fix and build and reno. I've never had to live in the house that's being taken apart, and I've never had to know the difference between an S trap versus a P trap."

"Well, the reason why an S trap isn't—"

"Just an example," Fiona said with a wave of her hand. "I know the difference *now*. I've got to send off a few emails and look for a different floor tile because the one I chose is out of stock. The contractor is going to check with his suppliers too, but I've found it's best if I do my own research and calling around. Your job is always more important to you than it is to anyone else. I also need to find a good care package to send to the boys at camp. Evidently, it's shameful if you don't receive mail the whole time you're away. Mail time is a big deal."

May crossed her arms over her chest. "When we went to Girl Scout camp, we didn't get mail."

Fiona made an *L* with her forefinger and thumb and pressed it against her forehead. "'Cause we're a bunch of losers with loser parents." Then she and May both burst out laughing.

"I'm telling Mama you said that," May teased.

Fiona's eyes turned to slits. "You do that, and I'll tell her that you snuck out of the house with David Alexeev when you were in tenth grade to go to that senior party she forbade you to go to."

152

May gasped dramatically and pressed her hands against her chest. "You wouldn't dare!"

"Don't try me. I still can't believe you did that. I *never* would have dared sneak out. You were always a little bit too reckless." Fiona grinned at her. "And I was crazy jealous of that. But anyway, I know all your dirty secrets. You better keep mine."

"You don't know *all* of them."

Fiona pressed her lips together and nodded. "I *do* believe that. Make sure you give me at least half an hour to get ready for lunch. You know, in case I fall down the rabbit hole of care packages and bathroom tile."

May nodded. "I will pull you out of the hole in time. Although you could go just like that and everyone would *still* think you're a beauty queen."

Fiona looked away from her computer and her shoulders relaxed. Sunshine poured through the living room windows and highlighted her like it was shining down just to warm her with its light. She exhaled. "I wish we could hang out every day. I forget how great you are."

May rolled her eyes and shook her head. "How could you *ever* forget that?" She walked away listening to her sister's laughter and thinking, *If only she knew what I'm really up to, would she still think I'm that great?*

Fiona and May slid into the booth next to the window. Emily smiled at them from the other side and pressed back against the tall cushion behind her. Her poppy pink lipstick matched the pink roses on her sleeveless white blouse. She'd curled her blonde hair, and it cascaded around and down her shoulders. May and Fiona greeted her as they bounced their way across the dark leather bench seat.

"Well aren't you two twins?" Emily said. She grabbed two menus from the holder and placed them in front of May and Fiona.

"What? We aren't twins," May said the same time Fiona added, "Thank you. You just gave me two extra years of youth."

May looked at her sister and then at Emily. "Are you seeing what I'm seeing? Fiona is a beauty queen. Her hair is curly, and mine is straight-ish. She has China doll skin, and I don't. She—"

"Oh, give it a rest," Fiona groaned and elbowed her sister. She picked up her menu and flipped it to the lunch side.

Emily leaned over her menu and stared at May. "First, we need to work on your ability to take a compliment. Just smile and say thank you. It's good manners," she said as her smile widened. "Next, are *you* seeing what *I'm* seeing? You're too critical of yourself. I'll admit that Fiona is a knockout—"

"Thank you, Emily," Fiona said. "And it's very nice to meet you. May gave me a briefer on the way over, and I just *knew* I'd like you."

"Nice to meet you, too," Emily continued. "May, you look just like Fiona, minus those few, albeit minor, differences. As much as I'll admit that Oliver is attracted to that brain of yours, that's not what sucked him in immediately." Emily's expression conveyed the message, *Don't act like you don't know what I'm about to say.* "That, my sweet friend, is your beauty. You are stunning."

May's mouth fell agape. Sunlight pressed through the tinted pub windows and painted the dark-wood tabletop with sunbeams. Oliver's name floated in the air between them. May wanted to squash it back into Emily's mouth. Fiona reached over and pressed her fingers below May's jaw and pushed her sister's mouth closed. "Has anyone ever told you that you look just like a Barbie doll?"

Emily's husky laugh filled the pub. A few men at the bar turned and looked at their booth, pulled in by the sultry sound of it. "A couple of times. Thank you, though. You're sweet."

Fiona slid her sunglasses off her head and dropped them into her purse. "May said you love the mini corndogs. Would you rate them a must-have, or is there something else you think is their specialty? And who's Oliver?" Fiona continued to scan her menu.

Emily and May locked eyes across the table. Emily's pink lips parted, and her eyebrows rose in question. May shook her head slightly. Emily pretended to need something from her purse. The silence dragged on.

Fiona lowered her menu when no one answered. She looked at her sister when Emily didn't meet her gaze. "Who's Oliver?"

May forced a smile and shrugged. "Oh, he's just a guy here. He's Grandma's doctor, actually. Well, he's not her *real* doctor. But he saw her when Dr. Beatty was delivering a baby. And Emily likes to tease me about it. But it's nothing. I heard the club sandwich is pretty good. You could try that." May lifted her menu and stared at the words, registering none of them. She felt her pulse throbbing in her neck.

Emily swirled a red straw around in her ice water, clicking the ice together, creating a slow whirlpool. Fiona turned her body to face May and pressed her hand against the laminated menu, forcing May to lower her hands and the lunch selections.

"Ivylin May," Fiona said, "a doctor, huh? Is this who has you all sparkly eyed and babbling? I just added babbling because that's clearly what's happening right now. So, who is Oliver *really*?"

18

$\mathcal{A}$ young waiter wearing a black apron stepped up to the end of their booth at the Corner Pub and smiled. He held a black bill receipt folder and pen at the ready. The conversation halted.

"Can I get your drink orders?" he asked. Emily ordered a strawberry lemonade, Fiona ordered sweet tea with extra lemon, and May said the water already on the table was enough. She lifted her cup and gulped down half the glass to unstick her tongue from the roof of her mouth.

Once the waiter walked off, Fiona focused on May. "I'm ready whenever you are."

"He's a guy in town," May answered.

Fiona nodded. "You mentioned that already. Are you dating him? Give me the details. Why are you being so stingy with them?" She glanced between Emily and May.

"There aren't a lot of details, and it's complicated," May answered. She clasped her hands together in her lap.

"Isn't every relationship?" Fiona said. "He's a guy. He's a doctor. He texts you. And..." Fiona waved her hand in a rolling motion, encouraging May to keep talking.

May rubbed the back of her neck. She watched two young men stroll up the sidewalk and turn the corner. "And he's going through a messy divorce."

Fiona straightened in the booth. "Oh, well, that does make for complications. When you say *going through*, you're saying he's still married?"

May nodded. She caught Emily's eye but looked away.

"So there isn't much to talk about," Fiona continued, folding her arms on top of the menu. "He's a guy you know, but you aren't dating because you can't. But he's texting you. Why?"

That's a great question, May thought. She watched thin, see-through clouds drift in front of the sun. When May didn't answer, Emily said, "He likes her."

157

May glared at Emily before she could stop herself. "Whose story is this? Mine or yours to tell?"

Emily pressed her lips together and flipped her hair over her shoulder. She leaned forward and propped her elbows on the table. Her husky voice rolled out in a whisper. "You aren't telling it."

"Did it occur to anyone that I don't want to talk about it? There's nothing to tell. We're not together. We're not doing anything. It's over." May's voice sounded pinched and disappointed. The ice in their glasses melted. "Not that it can *be* over since it can't even begin."

Fiona's lips formed a small *o*. She sagged against the back cushion. "Oh, Little May, you like him too, don't you? And you're embarrassed to talk to *me* about it because it'll look as though you're pursuing a married man like a common tramp. You think I'll think less of you or be really disappointed?"

The waiter cleared his throat, and all three women looked over at him. A flush crept up his neck and created splotches of pink on his ruddy cheeks. He placed drinks on the table and took their food orders before scurrying away.

Fiona tucked her curls behind her ears. "You think I'm going to go all judge-y on you?"

May's exhale ruffled the paper napkin stuck to the bottom of her water glass. "Fiona, the worst thing you ever did was come home with a B in Chemistry in eleventh grade. And you *cried* because you were dead certain it was going to lower Daddy's affection for you. But you're the angel daughter."

A sarcastic "Ha" burst out of Fiona's mouth. Then she added, "You think I haven't done some dumb things? Made some mistakes?"

"Is that rhetorical? Because otherwise I'm going to say no," May said.

"I'm your *sister*," Fiona said. "I'm your built-in, judgment-free friend. I would hope you know you can tell me anything. Obviously, you've told Emily."

May fiddled with her wrapped silverware, pulling off the paper ring and folding it in half and then in half again. "She's been

158

present for it. It's hard to hide anything in a town this size. And she's Oliver's neighbor." She glanced at Emily. "No offense. I don't mean to imply that I wouldn't talk to someone like you. You've been a much-needed friend."

Emily waved away the idea. "I understand. Believe me, no one wants to be labeled a harlot."

May lowered her gaze and looked sideways at Fiona. "I don't really know how to explain the situation without it sounding awful, which is a major indicator that I shouldn't be involved in it. But it's not like I planned it. We haven't done *anything*, I swear."

"Other than emotionally attach," Fiona said. "If you'll allow me to play the devil's advocate, can I ask you *why* he's getting divorced?"

"Let me answer since I have seen and been around both people in the flesh," Emily said, "Oliver's wife, soon to be ex, is a troubled, difficult person to even be around. And they haven't been happy in years, which is why they aren't staying married. She had an affair with a doctor in his practice, and they moved to Mystic Water with their two kids a few months ago in an attempt to start again in a new place. But you can't fix a marriage if both people aren't willing to make big changes. Angelina wants what she wants, and right now, that is an expensive divorce. She hated Mystic Water. Oliver loves it. Something's eating Angelina up from the inside, and Oliver is wasting away. Then May shows up in Mystic Water, and Oliver is instantly charmed. If you're thinking it's a rebound thing, it's not. Women have been throwing themselves at him since he arrived—"

"What?" May's voice rocketed up an octave.

Emily offered an apologetic expression. "It's the truth, May. A handsome doctor whose wife is MIA? Women notice, and he never gave anyone a second glance. Until you." Emily looked at Fiona. "Now, you're caught up. And May has been picking herself apart over being a homewrecker—"

"I've never used those words exactly," May said in defense. She slumped forward in the booth. "Am I a homewrecker?"

Emily and Fiona spoke at the same time, "No!"

"You don't even really know the story," May said to her sister.

159

"I just heard a summary. And I don't have to know everything because I know *you*." Fiona looked at Emily. "Sometimes our timing is all wrong. We meet people we are attracted to, but it's not the right time or we're not in the right place." Fiona lifted her sweet tea and pulled out the straw. She squeezed in two lemons and then took a slow sip and put down the glass. "Marriage is hard. You know it just as well as I do," she looked at May, "and have they...have they been to counseling or tried to work it out? Have they given it all they can to see if it can work?"

May told Fiona and Emily all the rest she knew about Oliver's relationship with Angelina, right up until she'd found him half-drunk on the bench by Jordan Pond. Then she told them about him finding her in the library and how she'd agree to run the race with him next weekend.

"So it's not exactly over yet? You've made plans for next weekend. And I agree with Emily," Fiona said.

"How so?" May asked.

"I know *why* Oliver wants to be with you," Fiona explained. "Who wouldn't? But it's selfish of him to drag you into a situation that is so tangled up. What if Angelina found out? What would happen to him and the kids? To his time with them if there was a custody battle? Even if she doesn't want to be with him, she would be livid if she found out about you." Fiona pressed her hand to her forehead. "I would lose my mind if Marcus had a beautiful woman on the side."

Fiona's words startled May. She looked wide-eyed at her sister. "Marcus would *never* do that."

"Are you so sure?" Fiona asked with watery eyes. "Listening to you talk about Oliver's marriage, I can see how easy it is to drift apart until you don't even like each other anymore. Marcus works all the time now. He leaves before seven in the morning and doesn't come home most nights until after seven. I can't remember the last time we had dinner as a family, and it's been even longer since we've been on a date. He doesn't even *look* at me like he's interested in anything. It's not like I've *let myself go*. I work hard to stay healthy,

160

and I swear I don't spend all day in sweat pants. I don't nag him to do anything around the house."

The waiter approached their booth and cleared his throat. He dropped off their lunch plates. The air filled with the scents of fried food and crispy bacon. Once the waiter was out of earshot, Fiona slid her basket of mini corndogs and thick-cut fries out of the way. She grabbed onto May's arm.

Tears filled Fiona's eyes. "I'm sorry, May. We were talking about you, and I've just gone and made it about me. I hate that you didn't want to talk to me about Oliver. I hope you don't think I wouldn't understand or I'm some saint who would think you're a bad person. I know Mama and Daddy haven't always understood you as easily as they have me. They don't have that call to adventure like you do. *I* get it, though, and I love that about you. I love that you're different, and you're not as boring as Conner and I are. We're predictable. But not you. You've always been able to see the promise on the horizon where we've been comfortable staying put where it's safe and comfortable. I'm sorry if I've made you feel like I'm better than you."

May shook her head. "Don't apologize. I've never thought *you* thought you were better than me. I've just known it's true." May smiled sweetly at Fiona. "But it sounds like you need to talk about what's going on with you and Marcus. I had no idea you were going through a rough patch."

Emily unfolded a paper napkin and placed it in her lap. "Better out than in. You don't think he has someone else, do you? From the way May has talked about you and Marcus, it sounds like a storybook romance."

Fiona dabbed at her eyes with a napkin. She cleared her throat. "In my heart, no, I don't think he'd do that. He looks too exhausted to have someone else. From what I've heard about affairs is that they energize people and make them feel alive and reckless again. Marcus looks like a zombie most nights. He eats without talking. Some nights he doesn't even heat up the food. He eats it right out of the container standing in the kitchen. I want to talk to him about how I feel, but I also feel guilty because he looks like he couldn't handle *one more thing*." She grabbed the ketchup bottle from the table and squeezed a blob on her plate next to her french fries. "But hearing you talk about Oliver and Angelina, I can see how easily it happens. How two people can start living separate lives and then after so long, they are too far apart to even want to connect. I don't want that for Marcus and me."

"So don't let it happen," May said. "You've recognized there's a problem. Chances are that he notices too. You're going to need to talk to him, even if he is exhausted."

Emily lifted a mini corndog and pointed it at Fiona. "Is your marriage worth saving?"

"Yes. Definitely. I can't imagine my life without him," Fiona said.

"Then May's right. Talk to him. You and Marcus aren't like Oliver and Angelina. You don't want to imagine a life without him, but they are *only* imagining their lives apart. And you're right about Oliver being selfish to keep wanting May around during this time, but if you could see the way he lights up when she's around...you might forgive him just a little."

Fiona sighed and reached over to squeeze her sister's hand. "Oh, I can imagine that perfectly. Who doesn't light up when Little May is around?"

Fiona dipped her last small corndog into the ketchup and popped it into her mouth. She hummed and reached for a french fry. "My nutritionist says that food doesn't *really* offer comfort. We just *think* it does. But I don't think she's ever had one of these beauties. I already feel better."

"You think you'll stay for the full two weeks?" Emily asked Fiona. She dropped her wadded-up paper napkin into the red plastic basket that had held her corndogs and fries.

Fiona nodded. "I miss my kids, but I need this break. Mama doesn't mind watching Elizabeth, who is an angel baby and way more so than I ever was."

May lifted her water glass. "That is true. She's your gift for having the twins." She drank down the last of the water.

Fiona groaned. "Those two boys. They're more curious than May ever was, and they get into trouble faster than a knife fight is over in a phone booth. I can't even imagine what it's going to be like when they're teenagers."

May snorted. "You'll need to get those house-arrest ankle bracelets so you can monitor them 24/7."

May and Emily laughed as Fiona pretended to make a note in her phone to research ankle bracelets. "Do they sell those to regular people?"

After they paid the bill and May told Emily she'd call her later, Fiona drove them back to the farm with the Mustang's top down. The radio blasted the local station's mix of new and old country. As the sunshine filled up the interior of the car, May leaned her head against the headrest, closed her eyes, and let the summer wind tangle her hair as she worked to untangle her heart.

Fiona shouted over the wind and the music. "Do you love him, May?"

May rolled her head to the side and looked at her sister. "I know I shouldn't."

"Does he love you?" Fiona slowed down as they approached the newly paved road leading to the farm.

May nodded. "He said he was falling in love with me. And if I'm honest, it terrifies me. All that mushy stuff I've heard about how love gives people wings and love makes them feel like leaping off a cliff, cloud nine, walking on air, *all* that nonsense... This *thing* with Oliver, the way my heart races," she looked at Fiona, "the way my eyes sparkle, it feels like I'm on the verge of something huge. Like it could shoot me to the moon or swallow me whole, and it's not sure which it's going to do, maybe both. It's absolutely terrifying. Am I making sense?"

Fiona smiled and turned on the blinker, even though there was no one behind her. "Yes. That's exactly how I felt about Marcus when we first met. Those days when I couldn't get close enough to him. When all I wanted to do was breathe the air he was breathing."

May nodded and unhooked her seatbelt when they parked in front of the farmhouse. "I know the right thing would be to back off until the divorce is final, so that's what I'm going to do. I'll run the race next weekend because they need me to complete the team. But afterward, I'll pack up and leave." Her stomach squeezed as soon as she said the words.

Fiona's surprised expression had her turning to look at May.

"What? You don't think I can walk away?" May asked. *Can I?*

A blackbird swooped down and landed on the car hood. It bounced around on its feet, not able to stand in one spot for long on the hot metal. It cawed at May and Fiona before hopping onto the windshield.

"Can I be honest?"

"Sure," May mumbled. She had a good idea what arrow her sister was going to shoot into her heart.

"Walking away isn't your thing," Fiona said. "Which isn't always a bad characteristic. You don't abandon people. You don't leave them hanging out on the limb in desperation. You're dependable, and you stick around long after everyone else has gone. But—"

"I don't leave when I should."

"Exactly." Fiona's apologetic expression made it difficult for May to feel frustrated.

"You're referring to how long I stayed with Chris. I should have left at the first sign. I *know* that, and looking back on it, it's clear to everyone, even me. But I'm not the same person anymore."

Fiona faced her sister. "I know you're not. You're stronger and healthier and wiser. But your heart is so dang sweet, May. You're so forgiving. I just don't want you sticking around because you see the potential in this relationship because we don't always reach that potential. What if Oliver can't be the man you see when you look at him? What if he's stuck in this malfunctioning relationship?"

"I hear you," May said with a sigh. "And you're right. I don't *want* to leave, and even though I'm acting all tough, I worry that I won't be. Maybe Chris was right. Maybe I'll always be weak."

164

"No, ma'am. *Nothing* that man said about you was right. You are a lot of things, but you are *not* weak. Having a soft heart doesn't make you weak. I *know* you're strong enough to walk away, but the bigger question is, is Oliver going to let you?"

May opened the car door and swung out her legs. "You say that like I'm going to give him a choice." May wouldn't be able to allow there to be any alternatives. She would have to find her courage because staying in a town where she knew Oliver was nearby would only increase her suffering, intensify the desire she felt to be near him. She could already imagine herself giving into his invitations until she would never be able to leave him or tell him no.

Fiona grabbed her purse and followed May through the yard toward the front porch. "I've found that when I make plans and I truly believe everything will fall into place, well, that's when it all goes to pot. Just be hopeful for the best but know that your plans could go right down the crapper. All it takes it a handsome man to throw you *way* off track."

"Be prepared for the crapper. Got it." May glanced over at her sister, and they both laughed.

19

*T*he next week May and Fiona helped Grandma Charity give the farmhouse a deep clean. They smiled over children's toys found in the backs of closets, under beds, tucked into the corner of a bookshelf, all left behind from their younger days. They cried over old photo albums full of their family's black and white photographs and over their grandpa's folded winter shirts stored in a bankers box. They put unused items into boxes ready for Goodwill and cleaned out the attic that was like a museum full of oddities and worn-out treasures, most of which no one could imagine had ever been undeniably special. Except the boxes of baby clothes with smocked dresses, Easter-colored overalls with matching toddler button-up shirts, and miniature Sunday school shoes that were scuffed with thin black soles—those they kept for a future no one could predict.

The sisters picked bushels of blackberries and packed quarts of the sweet dark berries into the chest freezer. They spent time on the front porch eating berries fresh out of the basket, and they made half a dozen blackberry hand pies. They shucked sweet corn and peas, and while sweating in the kitchen for hours, they canned a few dozen jars of fat, juicy heirloom tomatoes from the garden.

The farmhands stayed busy, moving around the fields and gardens in small clusters like bees. Grandma Charity kept them full on lemonade and watermelon and the occasional BLT on her homemade sourdough sliced thick.

By the end of the week, May had managed to avoid spending time with Oliver by using Fiona as an excuse, even though an uncomfortable longing built in her body like a pot coming to boil. May and Oliver texted all during the days, which helped release some of the pressure. He also called her every morning on his way to grab coffee before work. He swore that starting his day with her positivity kept the whole day brighter. He'd asked her to lunch every day, but May had turned him down with one reason or another. So on Friday night when May and Fiona were sitting on the front porch stairs watching the fireflies emerge in the darkening skies, Oliver drove down the driveway and parked next to May's car.

Without thinking, she stood and stared as her heart galloped away in her chest, causing her to feel quivery inside.

"Who is it?" Fiona asked, looking up at her from the step.

"Oliver."

Fiona heaved herself up and twisted her hair into a loose bun. "Do you need me to distract him while you run off? I've taken self-defense classes. I know how to fight off a predator."

May snorted. "Are you serious?"

"Kinda."

"A predator? Really?"

Fiona shrugged and whispered. "I'm not sure which category he goes in yet. Predator is still on the list."

Oliver's car door opened. He lifted his hand and waved before reaching into the car and grabbing a blue plastic bag. Then he closed the door. May could see his wide smile from yards away, and her feet stepped off the stairs before she realized what was happening. How had she forgotten how handsome he was? How had she forgotten how seeing his face caused all of her other thoughts to quiet so she could focus only on him? She crossed the yard to meet him. Oliver strode toward her and pulled her into a tight hug. Without thinking she sagged into him like a rag doll, breathing in the clean scent of his soap. Her whole being responded to him like he filled a space she hadn't known was aching and empty. Her desperate need to be near him had her wrapping her arms around him like an octopus hug.

"I missed you," he said, pulling away, but only far enough to look in her eyes. He tucked a few hairs behind her ear and touched her cheek.

"Yeah?" she asked. Then she realized they'd never been this close before, not like two lovers reuniting after too much time apart. She moved back an inch. "What are you doing here?" Heat rose in her, squeezed her muscles, and made her sound breathless.

Oliver's eyes glazed as more heat radiated from him and curled around her, circling them, drawing them closer together. Oliver staggered backward and unwrapped his arms from her waist. He cleared his throat and handed her the plastic shopping bag. "Our team shirt for tomorrow's race."

Wisps of fog rose up at their feet as the ground heated beneath their passion. May sidestepped the swirly mist and pulled a purple T-shirt out of the bag. Their team name was on the front, and MacAdams was printed on the back. "You could have given me this tomorrow."

"I couldn't wait another day to see you," he said, touching her arm before lowering his hand. His fingertips left behind warmth and her pulse responded.

"I know you've been spending time with your sister, but I was losing my mind a little." Oliver glanced over her shoulder toward the house. "Is that her?" He lifted his hand and waved.

May turned. Fiona stood on the bottom stair with her hands crossed over her chest, staring at the two of them. Her expression looked like they were about to be scolded for staying up past their bedtimes. Oliver placed his hand on May's lower back.

"Introduce me," he said, moving her across the yard. As they neared Fiona, he said, "You two could be twins." He removed his arm from May's and held out a hand toward Fiona. "I've heard so much about you. I'm Oliver Bisset."

Fiona stepped down onto the grass and shook Oliver's hand. "Nice to meet you. I didn't realize you were coming over tonight. May, why don't you get us all something to drink, and we can sit out here and talk awhile?"

May offered her sister a blank expression. "What?"

Fiona turned her pale eyes toward May, giving her a look that May hadn't seen since they were kids. The expression yelled, *Scram!*

May blubbered, "I don't think that's—"

Fiona smiled, but her eyes didn't reflect the expression. "Please? I bet Oliver would like some of Grandma's lemonade."

"I'd love some," Oliver said, oblivious to Fiona's frozen smile and false sugary voice.

"See? He'd love some. Thank you," Fiona said, tilting her head slightly toward the front door.

May pressed her lips together. Then she hustled up the stairs two at a time, like she was performing football drills at the high school stadium. The screen door slammed three times against its frame after May rushed inside.

Oliver shoved his hands into his pockets and rocked back on his heels. Fiona's easy smile didn't fool Oliver into believing she wasn't about to grill him. The narrow slant to her eyes, which nearly matched May's in color, stared at him.

Oliver tilted his head toward the house. "Good use of lemonade as a way to get May out of earshot. Are you playing Good Cop or Bad Cop?"

Fiona laughed, surprising both of them. "Which one will make you the most honest?"

This time Oliver laughed. "I have no reason to be dishonest with you. There's nothing to gain there."

Fiona pushed her fiery red hair off her shoulder and crossed her arms. "What exactly do you think you're doing with my sister?"

Wow. Cut right to the chase. There's not a lot of shooting the breeze with the MacAdams women, is there? Oliver cleared his throat. A blackbird cawed. "What do you mean?"

Her lips parted and released a huff. "You're married, right?"

The crickets quieted. Lightning bugs gathered on the porch and flashed in front of the door, pulling Oliver's attention for a second.

"That's right," Oliver answered.

"So why is a married man driving across town at night to spend time with my sister?"

Oliver shifted on his feet and shoved a hand through his hair. "Fair question. May and I are friends. Would you be asking these same questions if Emily had shown up?"

"Of course not," Fiona said, "but Emily isn't in love with my sister. Well, I mean I don't *know* that you are either—"

"No, you're right," Oliver interrupted, sliding his hands into his pockets. "I *am* in love with May. The situation is complicated. I didn't set out to fall in love with your sister, but you've met her. You *know* her. Did I stand a chance *not* falling for her?"

"No," Fiona said. "May would never admit it, but I don't think anyone has a chance of not loving her once they've met her. Even Chris, who was evil incarnate, loved her in his own bats-in-the-belfry way. He was like a moth drawn straight to her light, but he also didn't want anyone else drawn to her so he tried to snuff it out. He almost succeeded. So you can see why I'm protective of her. May is special and has this way about her that makes you feel lighter and safer."

Oliver glanced toward the house. "You don't have to sell me on her. I'm aware she's different."

Fiona exhaled. Leaves on a nearby tree shivered. Two squirrels chittered and ran down the tree trunk. "You know she deserves better than this for a relationship."

Damn. His chest ached. "I know that," Oliver said. "Angelina and I aren't going to stay married if that's what you think. I'm not stringing May along for a summertime fling. I *want* to be with her. I think about her all the time. Hell, I've been waiting my *whole life* to find May. I don't want to give her up now."

"So what are you going to do about it?" Fiona asked.

"I'm going to be the best father I can and work damn hard to make this divorce as fair and neat as possible, and then I'm going to love May for the rest of my life," Oliver said.

A crash sounded from inside the house followed by the sound of splashing water. Someone gasped.

"May, what are you doing in there? You okay?" Fiona called.

"I'll be right out," May said.

Oliver watched lightning bugs fill the spaces on the front porch, flying and diving around the front door, waiting for May to come back out, just like he was.

Oliver leaned his hip against his car door, crossed his arms over his chest, and smiled up at the nearly full moon. Lightning bugs danced all around May and him. May held out her hand, and a lightning bug paused on her palm. It fluttered for a moment and then flew off again.

"It looks like even the stars come down to be with you," Oliver said.

May laughed. "You sound like a poet."

Oliver smiled at the sound of it, feeling like if he could make May laugh for the rest of his life, he'd die a happy man. "Add 'inspires poets' to your resume." He glanced over her shoulder to see a dark silhouette framed in the living room window. He pulled his car keys out of his pocket. "I don't want to, but I should be going. We have an early morning tomorrow. And your sister is going to hover until you come back inside. It's like having a chaperone when we were sixteen."

May gave Oliver a questioning expression, and he pointed toward the farmhouse. May looked over her shoulder. Fiona must have realized they saw her because she slid out of view.

"She's just trying to keep me honest," May said with a shrug.

"I don't think you're the one she's worried about keeping honest," Oliver said. Without overthinking it, he wrapped his arms around May and pulled her against him. Her body pulsed heat straight into his, and to stop himself from doing more, he pressed his cheek against the top of her head and pulled away. "Sweet dreams, Little May Sunshine."

The innocent expression on her face made him want to kiss her.

"Rest well, Overbold Ollie." May turned to the farmhouse, stopping him from reaching for her again.

She waved over her shoulder once to him before he climbed into his car and blasted the air conditioner. He needed to cool down. The leather seats smoked beneath him.

Fiona sat on the edge of the couch, trying to look busy with her phone and failing.

"What's up, stalker?" May asked her sister.

Fiona placed her cell phone on the coffee table. "I wasn't stalking. I was making sure you were okay."

"Keeping me safe from the predator?" May teased.

Fiona sighed. "You're joking, I know, but this is kinda serious."

May leaned against the wide living room doorframe and shoved her hands into her pockets. "How so?"

"I'll be honest. I was hoping that Oliver was going to be a sleazeball or exhibit some terrible flaw so I wouldn't like him. But he's actually great. He's handsome and smart and funny and charming, and you two have a lot in common. And he *adores* you."

"So the kinda serious part means what?" May pushed off the doorframe and pressed her teeth into her bottom lip.

Fiona gazed up at her with her eyebrows drawn together. "I don't know how you're going to stay away from him. And even more than that, how is *he* going to let *you* go?"

"He's going to have to," May said. Her stomach slipped toward the floor. When she closed her eyes, she saw his smiling face, so she opened them again. "Until after his life is settled."

Fiona shook her head. "See that's the thing. I think *you're* helping him feel settled. I think *you're* the reason he's not completely unraveling right now. You're anchoring him *and* buoying him."

"But you said so yourself that I deserve better than this type of relationship. I can't be his girl on the side. That's not fair to me."

"You heard that, huh? Did you also hear him say he is going to love you for the rest of his life?"

May nodded and dropped onto the couch beside Fiona. She slumped against the back cushions. "What am I going to do?"

"Love him for the rest of yours?" Fiona asked.

May looked over at Fiona. "Is that an option?"

"Do you *want* it to be?"

May grabbed a crocheted throw pillow and squeezed it against her chest. "I thought we'd decided that I couldn't be weak and stay. I *have* to leave him, but now you've seen why it's not that easy. Not only do I stink at letting *anything* go, you've seen us. He lights me up like a firework. It's like I'm mesmerized, and I can't think of anything else but the two of us. That's a slight exaggeration, but you know what I'm saying."

Fiona puffed out her cheeks and exhaled. "What do you need me to do? Help you leave? Drag you back home with me? Tell me, and I'll do it."

"Can I live without my heart?" May asked.

"Literally? No," Fiona answered. "Figuratively? Yes. But it'll suck for a while. You think Oliver has resurrected yours and when you leave—"

"I'll be leaving it here with him, yeah."

"Heavens to Betsey, May, can't you do *anything* the easy way?" Fiona groaned and collapsed against the squishy couch cushions.

"Now where's the fun in that?" They both chuckled, but May rubbed her hand across her chest, wondering how excruciating it would feel to live without her heart filling her life with joy and lightness and Oliver's heart touching hers.

20

May crested the top of the trail a few paces in front of Oliver. She peered down at the finish line crowded with smiling faces, waving hands, and streamers of rainbow confetti being tossed in the breeze. A man holding a bouquet of a few dozen purple balloons meandered through the crowd. Food and drink vendors were set up on the edges of the gathering area. May's eyes lit up at the sight of the finish line archway with a banner that rippled in the wind. It waited less than a tenth of a mile away at the bottom of the hill.

Classic rock music blared from a bandstand and mixed with the cheering voices. A small booth set up next to the finish line held two volunteers who called out the names of the runners as they crossed the line. More volunteers waited off to the side with bananas, power bars, energy gummies, bottled water, and colorful sports drinks.

Sweat soaked through May's purple T-shirt, and only her matching sweatband stretched around her head kept the sweat out of her eyes. Even with the steady wind, the air felt hotter than a cast iron skillet over a campfire. *Sweltering* was the word that looped on repeat in May's brain.

Oliver jogged up next to her as they descended the last hill toward the finish. "You switched to beast mode a mile ago," he huffed.

She glanced at him. Sweat soaked his face and dripped down his splotchy red cheeks and neck. He'd taken off his shirt and tucked it into his running shorts. May tried not to stare or glance down at his bare torso too often, but to say a shirtless Oliver was distracting was an understatement.

"What do you mean?" she said between sucking in air and trying not to pitch too far forward on the decline.

The crowd noise increased as they neared the end. The band covered Steve Earle's "Copperhead Road," and May jogged to the beat.

175

"I can barely keep up," Oliver puffed. "I feel like I've lost 50 percent of the moisture in my body."

May's laugh was brief and breathless. "You look like you've fallen into the pool. Hang in there, Doc. We're almost there."

"Do you know CPR? I might need it," he said with a wink, and May released a choking laugh.

They stumbled across the finish line to shouts and cheers. A blur of faces surrounded May, none recognizable. Oliver grabbed a water bottle, thanked the volunteer, and poured the whole bottle over his head. He bent double and stared at the patchy ground. He looked mesmerized by the dry, brittle grass mixed with bright green dandelion weeds and pebbles.

"You're not going to barf, are you?" May asked before drinking half a bottle of water.

Oliver shook his head and stood. May's eyes strayed to his glistening chest. *Ollie, for Pete's sake, put on some clothes. You're killing me over here.* Oliver looked too dazed to notice her staring. He grabbed a bright red sports drink and finished the whole bottle in less than a minute. May loaded up on two of every snack. The rest of their running team had crossed the finish line earlier, and they huddled together, sweating, drinking, and stuffing snacks into their mouths.

"Could you have picked a hotter Saturday morning? Can you imagine if we'd been running *later* than 7:00 a.m.?" Jill asked Al, the head of their team. She piled her sweaty auburn hair on top of her head in a tight bun and situated her florescent headband. Then she opened a granola bar and ate half of it at once.

Al slapped Jill on the arm and laughed. "I do what I can. This will make you tough. Put some hair on your chest."

"No thank you," Jill mumbled through a mouthful, and the rest of the team laughed.

Al looked around at the sweaty group and smiled. "Thanks, y'all. This means a lot to me and Sara."

Everyone nodded and offered various versions of "No problem" and "You bet."

Oliver used his shirt to wipe his sweaty face. "Why doesn't everyone go home, clean up, and come over to my place for lunch? My treat. Bring the family and the kids too. Let's say 11:30."

A chorus of yeses and thank-yous and see-you-soons arose from the sweaty team. May shifted on her feet. She'd intended to talk to Oliver in the parking lot. That would have offered her an escape right after she told him that she couldn't see him anymore. But now the group would wonder where she was if she didn't show up at his house. *Does that matter?*

Oliver pressed his arm against hers and pulled her attention. "You're coming, right?"

"Huh? Oh, sure, yeah I'll be there." May fluttered her lips with an exhale. Was this giving in or was this a new opportunity to plot a strategy for a better way to talk to him? Maybe this way she could wait until everyone was gone after lunch, and then she could talk to him in private at his house. *Yeah, that's much better. Because there won't be anyone to overhear, and we'll both be more comfortable alone.* May's mind then drifted to their hug the day before. Remembering his closeness caused goose bumps to rise on her arms. "What can I bring?"

Oliver grinned at her and draped his sweaty shirt around his shoulders like a fighter's towel. "Just you."

Lord, he doesn't make it easy to walk away, does he?

May slipped the still-warm peach cobbler into an insulated bag and left it on the kitchen table with a Tupperware bowl of fresh salad made from Grandma Charity's garden. In her bedroom she grabbed her keys and cell phone, dropped them into her purse, and walked past Fiona's bedroom where her sister typed on the keyboard, filling the room with a constant *click, clack clack, click, click, clack, clack, clack.*

"Hey, hey, hey!" Fiona called.

May doubled back and leaned into the doorway. "It's Fat Albert!"

Fiona chuckled. "No one but me would even get the reference."

May stepped farther into the doorway. She grabbed the doorjamb with both hands and stretched her body forward, lengthening the muscles in her arms. "That's sad, isn't it? Do you ever wonder why that is one of the only cartoons Daddy loves? Anyway, I'll work to keep it alive."

"When did you get home? You look cleaned up. Are you going out? Where are you going?"

"Whoa, there, cowgirl," May teased. "You look like you're waking up from a trance. I spoke to you when I got home, but you were too focused to hear me."

"It happens when I work," Fiona said, closing her laptop and swinging her legs off the bed. She placed the laptop on the quilt beside her. "Did you tell Oliver that it's over? What did he say?"

May sighed, let go of the doorjamb, and her shoulders sagged. "He invited everyone to his house for lunch."

"So?"

"The *whole* team. To celebrate," May added.

"So?" Fiona's green eyes narrowed, and she slipped off the bed, crossing her arms over her chest. "You didn't tell him."

May shook her head.

"Why? May, you can't keep putting this off," Fiona said. She paced across the room to look out the window.

Sunlight warmed the windowpanes and created heat ripples in the air that hung above the wood floor. May stared transfixed, unable to meet Fiona's eyes. "He invited *everyone*. How was I going to tell him no?"

Fiona twirled around and gaped at her. "You just say no. That's it. Nothing fancy. *No.* That was the word you were looking for. Even *no thank you* would get the job done. I was afraid you wouldn't be able to—"

"I'm going to tell him," May argued. "This afternoon after everyone goes home. I figure it'll be easier at his house anyway. No one to interrupt, and it'll be private. And...he was standing there shirtless."

"What?" Fiona asked, wrinkling her forehead.

178

May raised her hands in an exaggerated motion. "After the race. It was hotter than Hades out there, and he had his shirt off and I couldn't stop staring and he asked me to come over and—oh never mind, as I was saying, it's going to be better to talk to him at his house in private."

Fiona's eyebrows raised. "And you think you're going to have *more* willpower if you're alone with him in his house with no one else around? Just the two of you, all alone?"

"Yes," May said, tossing up her arms in frustration. Nerves crept in around the edges of her stomach and squeezed.

"I'm just being your big sister here. Your voice of reason. You asked me to help you do this. Putting it off *again* is not helping you."

"I know, okay? I get it. I'm procrastinating, but I froze when he asked me to come over. Then the idea came to me that telling him when we could really have a private conversation made more sense. It's a more mature option, rather than standing around sweating like pigs in a parking lot while I break it off with him."

Fiona nodded. "You're right. But you *have* to tell him today. No excuses."

"Have you talked to Marcus?" May countered. She fisted her hands on her hips.

Fiona looked at the floor before glancing at her phone. "Not yet."

"What's *your* excuse? Are you being a hypocrite?"

"You're being a jerk, May," Fiona said, her green eyes flashing. "It's different."

Sunshine shifted outside and pushed through the windows. It stretched across the floor until it highlighted the sisters in a beam of blinding yellow.

May sighed. "Of course it's different, but the feeling that the conversation is huge and uncomfortable and necessary are all very similar, aren't they?"

Fiona nodded. "I'm sorry for calling you a jerk, and you're right. Different characters, different storylines, but the same shared feelings, the same conversation that nobody wants to have because it's easier not to stir the pot."

May offered Fiona an apologetic smile. "I was being a jerk."

"And I was being a hypocrite," Fiona said and shuffled her feet. "Seriously, though, the longer you put off the conversation with him, the harder it's going to be and the more attached that man is going to be to you."

"You say that like he's the only one with something to lose here," May mumbled.

Fiona crossed the room and stood in front of May. "He has the most to lose, yes," she said quietly. "Because he risks losing his kids. Not to imply he could lose them altogether, but as a parent, even not being able to see your kids every day is a loss. And I *know* you, and I know you've already gotten attached to him, and it's going to sting real bad when you rip this off. But it's for the best. We both know that. Right?"

May nodded.

"You're going over there now?" Fiona asked.

May nodded again.

Fiona pulled her into a hug and caught May by surprise, squeezing the air out of her lungs. "I love you, Little May. I'm only trying to save you from more heartache. But it's not a forever good-bye." She pulled away and looked into May's eyes. May saw herself reflected in the pale green of Fiona's gaze. "That man is crazy about you, and when his life is sorted, he'll find you."

People, laughter, running kids, the aroma of grilling meat combined with the sticky sweet scents of summer honeysuckle and lemonade filled Oliver's house by the time May arrived. She knocked on the front door and then pushed it open. Two kids skipped barefoot through the living room and straight out the open terrace door.

Someone outside yelled, "Close the door, Murphy! Were you born in a barn?"

One of the younger boys made eye contact with May as she

stood in the foyer with her hands full of food bags. Then he closed the glass, terrace door before dashing off into the backyard.

Jill and another woman stood laughing in the kitchen and drinking flavored sparkling water out of silver cans. The kitchen island was cluttered with open potato chip bags, a couple cans of premade dips, a plate of fruit, store-bought cookies still in their plastic containers, and an assortment of sodas and sparkling water.

May walked into the kitchen, unzipped the insulated bag, and found a space for the cobbler on the counter. She put the salad container on another end of the island. May said hello to Jill and her friend. May had never seen Jill without her running gear on, and she was surprised at how different Jill looked. Gone were the tiny athletic shorts and fluorescent sports bra. Jill's auburn hair, almost the exact color of May's, tumbled down her shoulders in beachy waves. Her vibrant, colorful sundress accentuated her sky-blue eyes. With a light dusting of natural-looking makeup, she resembled a surfing beauty from California.

"May, this is George's wife, Kelly," Jill said.

Kelly, built like a ballet dancer, shook May's hand with a light touch. Her long, slender fingers displayed her pearlescent fingernail polish and an oversize turquoise ring.

May admired Kelly's white, lacy dress, which made her appear as though she would be leaping onstage at any moment. "Are you a runner too?"

"I'm most definitely *not* a runner," Kelly said with a sarcastic laugh. "I'd rather go to the dentist than go for a run." Using a large Frito scoop, she spooned up a dollop of salsa. "But I support it for George. It helps him release all his nervous energy, and you *don't* want to be around him when he's a ball of nervousness. The running keeps him operating at a more pleasant level."

"It's a stress reliever for most." May glanced around. "Is the rest of the group outside?"

Jill nodded. "The men are manning the grill. Because, you know, it takes all of them to make sure it's done right. They're making hamburgers, hotdogs, and some sort of beet-red veggie burger that Jo talked them into making. They're grilling an assortment of veggies at my request."

Kelly laughed. "I think *request* is a bit nicer than what you really said about those veggies."

Jill rolled her eyes. "Okay, so I didn't ask. I just told them that we weren't all cavemen who craved meat and they were grilling veggies or else." She walked to the end of the counter, leaned over, and breathed in the scent of the peach cobbler. "This smells delicious. Homemade?"

"Grandma's recipe," May said. "It's the best I've ever had, so save room after all those veggies." May grabbed a sparkling water flavored with lime and made her way to the backyard.

May stepped onto the springy, freshly cut grass. Two young girls were sharing a hula hoop and giggling. The clear circle, filled with glitter, sparkled in the sunlight as it looped around and around. A few more women, whom May guessed to be the runners' wives or girlfriends, stood in bunches, talking in low voices to one another, and then yelling at the kids when sword fighting went a step too far.

"Brian, do *not* hit your brother with that!" one woman scolded.

"David, take that out of your ear! I don't care what kind of alien you are," another woman said, waving her hand and motioning to her ear.

Oliver stood in a group of men near the gas grill. He looked away from the conversation, seeming to sense May was nearby, and he crossed the yard to her.

"I'm glad you could make it," he said. "It's not a party without you."

"I think the expression is that it's not a party without cake." The wind kicked up and blew her hair into her face. She shoved her hair back and spit strands from her mouth.

"Did you bring a cake?"

A male cardinal chirped from the nearest tree. A female cardinal flew over their heads and landed on a branch, chirping to the bright red male.

"Peach cobbler."

"Even better." Al called from the grill, and Oliver turned to look at him. "Be right there!" He focused on May again. "Relax, eat up, and save a dance for me."

As he walked away, May's inner voice piped up. *No dancing. Remember why you're here.* May rubbed her stomach, trying to push away the nauseous feeling that arose whenever she thought about telling Oliver good-bye.

After the party May grabbed a black trash bag from under the kitchen sink and shook it out until it ballooned open. She carried it outside where Oliver gathered up cups from the card table he'd set up, and he collected stray napkins that the wind had blown against the fence. May counted the pieces of garbage like a countdown to a ticking bomb. When the last bit of trash was thrown out, May wouldn't be able to procrastinate any longer. She'd have to tell Oliver. *Three pieces left.*

Oliver plucked a napkin snared by the thorns of the rose bush and dropped the wadded paper into the bag May held open. "The beet burgers weren't half bad, if you like crumbly fake burgers that stain your fingers pink."

"Not as good as your hamburgers," May said.

"You're just trying to make me feel better about how rare they were," Oliver teased. He grabbed the last two napkins and tossed them in the bag. Then he took the trash bag from May and motioned for her to follow him inside the house. "Finally, we can relax a few minutes, assuming you can hang around for longer. Can you?"

May's stomach rolled. "Sure," she said. A voice in her head told her to enjoy the moment and break it off with him later. *Don't spoil it. Have a little fun.* Another voice, angrier and more frustrated said, *No! Don't be weak. Don't give in. You have to do this!* "As long as he doesn't take off his shirt," she mumbled to herself, then choked on her laugh.

Oliver grabbed two other garbage bags from the kitchen and called. "What's funny?"

"Nothing!"

He returned to the foyer, where May stood staring, having an argument with herself. "You okay?" he asked. "You look...worried."

"I'm fine," May said, trying to smile but knowing it looked fake.

Oliver opened the front door and then looked over his shoulder at her. The mail truck rumbled to a stop beside Oliver's mailbox. The mailman shoved in a handful of mail and drove off with a wave.

"I'm going to toss this in the bin and be right back," Oliver said, slipping on a pair of flip-flops that were waiting beside the front door. "Then we can sit down and talk about whatever is on your mind."

"Nothing's on my mind," she lied.

"Uh huh."

May plopped down on the front stoop and watched Oliver walk around the house to toss the garbage bags in the large plastic container. She wrung her hands together and rehearsed lines in her head. She phrased and rephrased the breakup, working on different scenarios with Oliver's potential reactions.

May heard the plastic trash can lid slam closed. Then he walked around the house and down the stone path toward the mailbox. He glanced over his shoulder and smiled before turning around and leaping as he clicked his heels together like a chimney sweep from Mary Poppins. May's heart tugged with that terrible combination of aching love and distress.

Oliver popped open the mailbox and reached inside. He pulled out letters and an oversize manila envelope. As he shuffled the mail, he paused, and a blank expression locked on his face. His eyes scanned the words on the manila envelope, and he glanced up at May.

Sunlight shifted in the yard, rippling across the front lawn, pulling away from Oliver and pooling around the front steps where May sat. He walked toward her, looking like a sleepwalker, with glazed eyes and shuffling feet. He stopped in front of her and May stood.

"Everything okay?" May asked, feeling the gaping pit in her

stomach open even wider. She teetered on the slippery edge of it.

One corner of the manila envelope wrinkled in his grasp. "It's from the lawyer's office." He stepped around her and opened the front door.

May followed him inside like a shadow. She closed the door behind them. Oliver dropped the other letters on the table in the foyer, scattering them across the polished top. He ripped open the oversize envelope as he walked into the living room. He pulled out a thick pack of printed, legal-size white paper. The manila envelope dropped to the hardwood, then caught on the fan's breeze and disappeared under the couch. Oliver flipped to the back of the papers and stared. After a full minute of silence, while May shifted on her feet waiting, he finally looked at her.

"She signed them," he said. "Angelina signed for the divorce."

May stepped toward him, cautiously, feeling like she'd swallowed a mouthful of salt water, remembering that feeling of loss and relief and sadness and uncertainty when she'd looked at her own signed divorce papers. "I'm so sorry, Ollie." She touched his arm. "Is there anything I can do for you? How about I go? Give you some time to process?" *To let it sink in that your life has now changed in a way that can never be undone or repaired,* she thought. *You will never go back to who you were before this moment. That's what it was like for me.*

Oliver's hands lowered, the papers brushing against his thigh. "I didn't think she'd do it. I thought she'd say no just for spite. Just to keep me miserable because she is. But I worked hard to keep it civil last weekend. I tried to meet her in the middle for as many of her wants as I reasonably could. And she's...agreed. The kids...I can't even imagine what it's going to be like without my kids full time. This summer has been weird and hard to get used to without them."

May stepped backward. "Call me if you need anything?"

The wind blew open the terrace door, flinging it wide, hitting the stopper on the back of the door. May jumped in surprise. The strong breeze gusted through the living room, pulling sunlight in with it, filling the whole space with heat. May blinked in the bright light.

Oliver didn't move to close the door. Instead, he looked at May with a gaze so focused it pulled the breath right out of her lungs. "Don't go," he said.

"But..."

"Please. Stay."

A tremble started in her stomach and shot out, faster than lightning, so that her whole body shivered beneath his stare. "I don't have to go. What can I do? Maybe we should sit down? Do you want to talk it out? Breathe? Cry? Anything? I think I did all of those things, probably all at once." May patted the back of the couch cushion.

Oliver tossed the papers onto the couch. "You can let me do what I've wanted to do since I met you."

"What's that?" May whispered.

Oliver strode toward her, and May stiffened, dropping her hands to her sides like a soldier. He entwined his fingers with hers on one hand; he touched her cheek with the other. May watched him, mesmerized by his movements and the feel of his warm skin against hers. She held her breath through a few heartbeats. His dark eyes moved across her face as her stomach lifted like a helium balloon.

"Lovely May, I didn't know what it felt like to really be happy, not in a long time, until you. Now all I want to do is be surrounded by you and all that you are. If you'll let me. And right or wrong, I've wanted to kiss you ever since I saw you. Can I?"

May nodded.

When Oliver leaned toward her, she closed her eyes. And then his lips were against hers, and his body felt warm through the thin, cotton fabric of her shirt. Her chest expanded with air and anticipation. Oliver's kiss lifted her onto her tiptoes, and his arms wrapped around her waist as his hands slipped up her back and pulled her closer still.

*O*liver's body vibrated with excitement and desire and eagerness, and his heart pounded so hard against his ribcage that he couldn't inhale a full breath. His hands slid up the back of May's shirt and into her hair. Oliver had imagined this moment, but May's real-life kiss shot straight past what he'd expected, straight into the stratosphere.

Breath escaped May again and again, and the sound of it fueled his desire. The slow, almost hesitant first kiss shifted in intensity faster than Oliver's heartbeat. Energy pulsed through her, hot and burning like a hungry inferno, and everywhere she touched set his skin on fire. Oliver didn't know where to put his hands, didn't know how to move, so he and May were a tangle of hands, mouths, and limbs, everywhere, shuffling across the hardwood with no clear direction.

When Oliver pulled away from her, she stared up at him, and his bottom lip tingled. Her pale eyes looked dazed, lovesick with desire, and he saw the same expression on his face reflected in her eyes. "Damn, May," he whispered, leaning down to rub his cheek against hers.

May closed her eyes and leaned into him. She chuckled, sounding embarrassed, pressing into his T-shirt. Hot wind gusted through the room, and when Oliver looked toward the open terrace door, the manila envelope hiding beneath the couch slid out at their feet. May inhaled sharply as the reminder of Oliver's divorce papers tugged her a few steps away from him.

"Don't," he said, tightening his arms around her, pulling her gaze back to his. "Don't leave me just yet."

May furrowed her brow.

"I don't mean physically." He touched his fingers to her temple. His muscles tightened as desperation flooded through him. "Can we just be *here* right now? No thinking about those papers or tomorrow or next week? Just right here with you. Please? I've been waiting my whole life just to be caught in a moment like this."

Her slight nod was all it took for Oliver to lean down and kiss her again. May's kiss sparked the flame in him again, and they both gave in to the fire burning its way through them.

May and Oliver lay tucked into the oversize couch in the living room. May listened to Oliver's steady heartbeat from her spot on his bare chest. May's body pressed against Oliver's side, and his arm draped over her, holding her close to him. The sun had set hours ago, and a single lamp in the living room cast soft light, leaving most of the room in shadow.

May's body felt liquid, all the energy having moved out of her body and leaving behind a peaceful exhaustion. Oliver's arm loosened as his breathing deepened. *He's dozing off.* May lay still for another minute, not wanting to let go of the bliss that had surrounded them like a bubble of happiness. But on her next exhale, she shifted her leg off him, and Oliver stirred.

"No," he mumbled, tightening both his arms around her. "Stay."

"Ollie, I have to go home. It's too late to call now. I'll wake them up if I do. And they'll freak out if they get up and I'm not there." But she smiled at his request. May pushed herself up and looked down at his wild hair and sleepy eyes. She touched his cheek, like she'd been doing it for years, like this hadn't been the first time they'd ever lay like this in the darkness. Her heart swelled, and she pulled in a slow inhale, trying to breathe around the expanding emotion in her chest. She wondered if Oliver could see straight into her heart, if her expression reflected what she saw in his eyes.

"Best day ever," Oliver said.

May crawled off him and gathered her things, forcing herself to keep moving or else she'd never leave. When her arms were full of bags and shoes, Oliver pulled her into a hug and pressed his face against her neck. He left behind a line of kisses, working his way up to her jawline.

"Mmmmm, okay, Ollie, I have to go," she mumbled as her arms loosened at her sides.

He chuckled against her neck and let her go. "Text me when you get home." He walked her to the door and held it open. "If I die tonight, I'll die a happy man."

May's eyes widened. "Don't you go dying tonight. That would be awful."

Warm summer wind blew down the shadowy street. No house lights lit front yards, and the neighborhood was silent except for crickets chirping from the bushes. Lightning bugs emerged from the shadows and flashed along the stone path to the car.

Oliver shook his head. "Nah, I plan on spending the rest of my life repeating this day over and over again."

May looked down at her feet and laughed. Her whole body felt filled with light, as though she could lift off the ground at any moment and be pulled into the stars. "We'd eventually have to do something else. You have a job. I need to be fed and given water periodically."

"Different versions of this day then," he said, leaning against the door while May walked down the stone path guided by the flashing bugs. "As long as you're a part of my day, every day will be better than all the days before you."

"Good night, Ollie." May tossed her bags into the car and looked one more time at him. He stood on the front stoop, watching her with an expression May could get used to. He lifted his hand to wave and then blew her a kiss. May grinned; she couldn't remember anyone ever blowing her a kiss, and she found it endearing. As if she needed another reason to adore Oliver Bisset.

When May arrived at the farm, all the lights were off, even the flood lights on the corners of the farmhouse. May did a quick check of her hair and face in the sun visor's mirror before getting out of the car. She pulled her fingers through her tousled hair. Then she crept into the house, careful not to slam the screen door or step on too many creaking floor boards. Just as May eased past Fiona's room, her sister whispered her name.

May froze. Maybe Fiona was talking in her sleep, something she had done when they were children sharing a bedroom.

The bedsheets rustled, and the bedframe shifted. "May, I know you're out there."

May stepped into the dark doorway. "I didn't mean to wake you. Go back to sleep. I'm heading there myself."

The bedside lamp turned on, and Fiona squinted in the light. She looked at May, blinking, and waited for her eyes to focus. "You've been gone all day. And you look…"

May's back stiffened. She smoothed a hand down her shirt. Her cheeks warmed, and her neck prickled. Fiona continued to stare. "I look what?"

"Rested," Fiona finally said. "Not at all like someone who went to break it off with Oliver."

May felt her elation dimming. "Can we talk about this in the morning? I'm exhausted." *And I don't want to spoil the best evening I've had in forever.*

"What happened, May? I'd swear you look like someone in love, but that doesn't make sense for what should have happened according to the plan. What changed?" Fiona swung her feet out from the covers and dangled them over the side of the bed. Her fiery red hair fell in tangled curls around her shoulders.

"Short version. The signed divorce papers arrived today. She's agreed to all the terms."

Fiona gasped and covered her mouth with her hands. When she lowered them, her lips twitched like she wanted to smile. "That's a shock, right? What kind of magic did he work on her last weekend? So now it's really going to happen, and sooner rather than later. And what did he say? He wants to be with you. He wants to get through this mess and then spend the rest of his life with you?"

May rocked back on her heels, smiled at the hardwood, and nodded.

"Did you kiss him?"

May looked at Fiona and her lips pulled up in one corner.

Fiona bounced on the bed. "I *knew* it! You don't look rested. You look like you've been up to something." Fiona giggled, sounding like she did when they were little girls talking about school crushes. "I

190

know it's awful to feel excited when such a heartbreaking thing is happening simultaneously, but if they both want it, then maybe it's not so bad. So...how was the kiss?"

May closed her eyes and sighed. She pressed her hands against her heart. "Breathtaking." May dropped her hands. "And I sound like a lovesick teenager."

Fiona spread her arms and fell back onto the bed. "Oh, those are the moments to hang on to forever. I *love* that feeling of falling in love." Fiona started singing "Danced All Night" from *My Fair Lady*. May tried to shush her so they wouldn't wake Grandma Charity. Fiona giggled again and said, "Go get in bed so you can replay it over and over until you fall asleep."

"Good night," May said as her sister sung the chorus again.

Fiona rolled her head to the side to look at May. "Love looks good on you. Your eyes are extra sparkly. Sweetest dreams."

Sunday morning sunlight crept over the horizon, splashing the fields with sweetheart pink. May stood on the front porch, cradling a coffee mug in her hands, staring at the sunrise, while it darkened to a passionate fuchsia. She thought about Oliver. The screen door squeaked open behind her, and Fiona shuffled out in her pajama pants and tank top.

A crease ran down her cheek from her left eye to the corner of her mouth, looking like she'd slept with her face mashed against the cotton pillowcase all night. She plopped into one of the rocking chairs. "Couldn't sleep?" she asked May, her morning voice hoarse and deeper than usual.

May sipped her coffee. "I'm normally up early. I love this time of day before the world wakes up. It's quiet and peaceful. Just me and the chickens."

"Here I am busting up your quiet meditation with the farm fowl," Fiona said with a chuckle. "I talked to Marcus yesterday."

May sat in the rocking chair beside Fiona. "What did he say?"

Fiona reached for May's coffee mug, and May handed it over.

Fiona sipped, swallowed, and exhaled. "He said he'd noticed too."

"Noticed what?"

Fiona rocked her chair. "That we've been drifting past each other for weeks, not really connecting. He apologized and said he felt guilty, but he also felt stuck. He *has* to get his job done. But at what cost?" She took another sip of coffee before handing the mug back to May. "We're going to work on it, on us, with purpose. He loves me. He said so. And his lack of engagement has nothing to do with me or with him cavorting with another woman, and he actually laughed for a whole minute about that. He asked me where I thought he'd get the energy for another 'job.' And he said if he couldn't be with me, he didn't want to be with anyone because he already had the best girl."

May cherished the sight of the sweet smile spreading across her sister's face. "Marcus is a smart man."

"Thank you," Fiona said, pressing back against the chair. She gazed out at the sunrise. Birds chirped and sang from the trees. A monarch butterfly hovered in front of them before landing on a coneflower.

"For what?" May asked.

"You gave me the courage to talk to him," Fiona admitted. "I've been putting it off for weeks. But knowing you were going to talk to Oliver and that it was going to suck gave me the courage to be brave. Of course *you* didn't go through with it, but I didn't know that."

May rubbed her neck. "Do you think I'm being stupid?"

"Because you didn't talk to him? No. I worry about you, of course, but what would I have done in your position? The same thing. Technically he's not single yet. I get that, and I understand why that's not appropriate, but this is your life, May. You and he are adults, making your own grown-up choices. You're not out to tear apart his family like some harlot. And it's nobody's business what you're doing. The man is going through a divorce. In a few months, he *will* be single. So minor details to me. If you're happy, I'll support you."

"What do you worry about?" May asked. "Do you think he'll change his mind?"

"About being with you?" Fiona shook her head. "I think he's sincerely in love with you. I worry there are pieces that we don't have, that we can't see the whole picture so our—your—decisions aren't completely informed."

"You think he's hiding something?"

"No. I think the future is unpredictable. So my worries can be applied to any situation. Are *you* worried? Other than being nervous about being vulnerable again?"

"That's all I worry about. Opening myself up," May said. "But if I remain closed forever, then I'll miss out. Logically, I know that. It doesn't make it feel any less scary."

"Is he worth it?" Fiona asked. "Is he worth putting yourself out there? Is it worth being with him as he goes through a difficult season? Can you ride this out?"

"He's worth it. Giving us a chance is worth it," May said. "But maybe that's the lovesick teenager talking."

Fiona reached for May's coffee. "I like lovesick teenage May. She's one of my favorite versions of you."

22

$\mathcal{O}$nce the realization that May and Oliver had a future together sunk into May's heart and brain, the days burst wide open with glorious sunshine and enough laughter to uplift the whole town. Lightness filled her steps, like walking on a moving sidewalk, going hands free. May's constant smile buoyed not only her spirits, but everyone's. She became an unintentional sunshine dealer, spreading her light and drawing people into her warmth.

Crops on the farm doubled in size, and summer rains came and went, giving enough water for growth without waterlogging. Temperatures lowered, and Mystic Water's townsfolk whispered about the reason behind the sweet relief, nodding their heads in May's direction and smiling at her whenever they saw her in town.

Fireflies danced all night around the farmhouse and even at Oliver's house, as if drawing near to a boundless energy surge that brightened their nighttime flashes. And May fell more and more in love with Oliver Bisset.

Her joy didn't mask the difficulties they faced. She and Oliver weren't pretending that his divorce didn't drain him some days. They weren't ignoring how it created a new species of sadness inside of him. But handling each day together allowed them to approach the days with a sense of comfort and joy, even on the most difficult days. As soon as May was near him, his body pulled in the light she offered, and his tension eased, he breathed deeper, and the sharp edges softened.

Even though May wasn't leaving Mystic Water, Fiona stayed at the farm for the whole two weeks of her original plan. She and May spent hours walking the fields, baking with Grandma Charity, talking about their lives, and having lunches and dinners with Emily, as well as with Andy and Oliver.

At the end of her stay, Fiona packed up her bags and loaded the convertible, and she and May hugged as though they'd never see each other again.

"For goodness' sake, you two, you live in the same town. I imagine May will head home soon too," Grandma Charity said. Then she wrapped her arms around Fiona. "You be careful out there in that fast car. And you come back and see me anytime. Having you and May here for so long has been the best few weeks I've had in a long time."

Fiona gave Grandma Charity another tight hug. "I love you." She looked at May. "I'm going to miss you, so expect me to text or call you every day until I stop feeling so needy."

May and Grandma Charity waved as Fiona drove away. May waved until she couldn't see the car anymore and the dry dust settled.

"Do you think you'll go home soon?" Grandma Charity asked.

May lifted one eyebrow in question. "Ready to give me the boot?"

"The opposite. It's useful to have another pair of hands to divide the work," she said, opening the screen door.

"Good to know the main reason you're keeping me around is to give me chores," May said, following her grandma into the house.

Grandma Charity stopped in the foyer and slipped her arm around May's waist. "That's the least of the reasons I'm glad you're here, Little May. You bring much-needed life to the farm. Lord knows I'm no ball of sunshine. But you are. Now come help me get the linens out of Fiona's room and get them clean."

As with most of Grandma Charity's commands, this was not a question. May followed her up the hallway and into Fiona's vacant room as she hummed "Danced All Night."

The next few weeks with Oliver made May feel as though she'd tumbled into her favorite romantic movie. She saw Oliver nearly every day. They left notes—poems, writings, and letters—on each other's cars. They took early morning runs through the park. They met their running group on weekends. Some nights they lay in the backyard staring up at the stars, talking about all the adventures they would take with and without the kids. Other nights they sat squished together on the couch watching movies. The euphoria surrounding their relationship had them forgetting to eat, not needing much sleep, and waking up already happy before their feet touched the floor. Sunshine followed them everywhere, and Oliver basked in it. The idea of May letting herself fully love Oliver thrilled her. As a teenager, May had never experienced that first puppy love that other people talked about. But now, with Oliver, she felt as though she were reliving her teenage years when the world felt full of possibility and heartbreak would never be an option.

They didn't flaunt their relationship around town, but May didn't feel like she was a dirty secret either. Oliver assured her he was not ashamed of her or of their relationship. Still they decided to keep a low profile until the divorce was settled. Because the state required a mandatory waiting period before finalizing a divorce in court if children were involved, it would be another few months before the divorce became finalized. So far the only people who were aware of them being more than friends were Emily, Andy, Fiona, and Grandma Charity. May wasn't sure what the town thought, but so far, she hadn't heard any whispers about what might or might not be going on between her and Oliver.

Oliver kept their line of communication open at all times. May wasn't ignorant about the messy parts of the divorce, and he didn't hide his emotions that fluctuated. Keeping their relationship open and honest was crucial to him because he didn't want them building a relationship on sinking sand. Oliver encouraged May to talk with him about how she felt and about the state of her heart as well. Even though he was the one going through the changes, making sure May felt comfortable was a top priority for him. He'd already admitted to May that she had become not only the love of his life but also his best friend and the only person he wanted to talk to every day. Opening up to someone on a day-to-day basis was new for May, and it took her a few days to get used to the idea. But once she started sharing her life with him, he was the first person she wanted to talk to whether she had good or bad news.

One evening May and Oliver sat at the table on Oliver's back patio writing. May worked on an article for *Wanderlust*, a magazine based out of the United Kingdom, and Oliver wrote on his novel. She glanced up from her computer and noticed him looking at her.

"What?" May asked. She reached for her glass of water.

"I could get used to this," Oliver said, reaching his bare feet under the table and touching her feet with his.

May tapped the tops of Oliver's feet with her toes. "Writing?"

Oliver sat up straighter in his chair. "Yes, but mostly being with you while I'm writing. I don't have to entertain you or worry that you're feeling ignored. I love having you here with me. This house finally feels like home since you're in it."

May slid her hand across the table, and Oliver grabbed it, giving her hand a squeeze.

Other nights Oliver came home from work mentally exhausted because he'd spent the day on and off the phone with the lawyer, with Angelina, and with his kids. Those nights May would bring over food, sit with him for a little while, and then return to the farm, giving Oliver enough space to sort through the pieces.

There were evenings spent at Emily and Andy's house, where they dined on fried shrimp and hushpuppies, drank Coca-Cola and local beer, and churned homemade ice cream. On those days, May felt like they were just two couples who'd known one another for years. It was easier to forget the divorce stress when they pushed it off to the side for an evening with friends. Other evenings brought Emily and Andy over to Oliver's house, and the men grilled while Emily and May laughed over glasses of sweet tea and chips and salsa.

"You two look so happy," Emily said one evening as the tangerine sun was setting. Her azure blue eyeshadow highlighted the blue in her eyes. Her blonde hair was pulled into a high ponytail, and she'd wrapped a white ribbon around the rubber band in her hair. The pink and white checkered shirt she wore was rolled at the sleeves up to her elbows and tied in a knot at the front. She resembled a picture-perfect pinup image of a southern belle.

"We are." May spun the glass around in her hands and smiled in

Oliver's direction. Lightning bugs danced a waltz around the yard, blinking on and off, mesmerizing May.

"I knew he was going to be crazy about you," Emily said. "I could tell from the first time he brought you to the house. He was so excited to tell us about his *new friend*. He's fallen in love with you. Total faceplant into it."

"Have you ever been so happy about something, you're afraid to give all in to it? Afraid that it might vanish? So you hold back a little in case you have to let go?"

"You can never prepare your heart for that sort of break," Emily said as she scooped salsa onto a chip. "Holding back now won't make letting go any easier. It'll just keep you from loving him to your greatest potential. Lots of people don't allow themselves to be truly happy or open to possibilities. Worrying about the what-ifs is a waste of time, don't you think? Even if you could create a million scenarios in your head, you'd probably still be wrong about the future. I try to focus on where we are right now and not worry about tomorrow."

"Right now, I'm in love and I want to be happy. Ridiculously happy with a gorgeous man," May said.

Emily clinked her glass against May's. "I can toast to that. And besides, Oliver's already told me he's going to love you for the rest of his life. What could change that?"

23

*M*ay met Oliver downtown a few days a week to have lunch during his break from the clinic. One early afternoon as summer neared its end, May and Oliver ordered sandwiches from Cavelli's Deli and ate in the park, shaded by an oak tree.

May had spread out one of her grandma's worn, outdoor quilts on the soft grass. The patchwork quilt frayed at the edges, and there were a few picnic stains—red Kool-Aid, blueberry pie filling, green grass—that Grandma Charity had been unable to wash clean. But the material felt cozy and soft like a comfort blanket you want to hold against your cheek.

In public, May and Oliver kept a friendly, acceptable distance between each other. They didn't look like more than friends. But their quiet conversations revealed the depth of their relationship.

Unless they can see the attraction in our eyes, May thought from her side of the quilt. Sitting near Oliver and not touching him challenged May's resolve most days. She wanted to slide right up next to him and entwine her fingers with his. She wanted to run her fingers through his dark hair or touch the stubble on his cheek when he hadn't shaved the morning before.

As if reading her mind, Oliver said, "I want to be able to walk down the street with you in public."

"You do walk down the street with me in public."

"But I want everyone to know that I love you, so sitting here, pretending I don't want to be close to you kills me."

May offered Oliver the other half of her potato chip bag. "Builds the anticipation in the story."

"Can we skip to the good parts?" Oliver teased.

"These *are* the good parts."

He dumped her chip bag onto his sandwich paper. "You're right. These are my favorite parts."

A thin, blonde woman stood across the park from Oliver and May. May would have thought the woman was staring at them if she hadn't been standing around while her poodle sniffed the grass. *She was probably in a daze,* May thought. May looked away from her when Oliver spoke again.

"I've never read a romance novel, but I'd read about this story. You and me." He pointed to himself and to her, back and forth, a few times.

"We're like a love story?" May asked, thinking their story had a few hurdles and moments when May wasn't sure being with Oliver right now was the best idea. *But all good love stories have points of conflict, right?* When she and Oliver were together and happy and lost in kisses or doubled over with laughter, she felt like she might burst from the joy taking up so much space in her body.

Oliver nodded. "*I* love this story. Don't all romance novels end with the couple getting together?"

"Definitely. Otherwise it's a crappy love story." May laughed.

Oliver leaned toward her. "I know the ending of this story. You and I together. Happily ever after, right?"

May smiled at him. "You're a fortune-teller now, huh?"

Oliver leaned back on his hands, stretching his long legs across the quilt. "Only about this."

After lunch, May and Oliver crossed the park and stopped by Bea's Bakery for a cookie to go. While standing on the sidewalk, May broke an oversize chocolate chip cookie in half and gave the larger piece to Oliver.

They finished off the cookie as they talked about their afternoon and evening plans. The sunshine poured down from the sky, and May tilted her head back, closed her eyes, and smiled up at the sky. "It's not as hot as it has been." She opened her eyes and looked at him. "I always feel a little sad when summer starts to end."

Oliver dropped the cookie paper and napkins into a trash bin on the sidewalk. "But the fall will come right behind it, and that means football and sitting outside by the firepit under a blanket with you."

May lifted an eyebrow. "Under a blanket?" She made a humming noise in her throat, and Oliver grinned at her.

"I meant that in an innocent way. Kinda." Oliver reached into his pocket for his car keys. "Until next time." He looked like he wanted to wrap his arms around her.

May pressed her arms against her sides, nodded, and dug her car keys out of her purse. She watched him walk down the street toward his car. He waved at her from the end of block, and she waved back. When she walked in the direction of her car, she saw the blonde woman with the dirty-white poodle from the park. The woman walked up the sidewalk toward her. May moved out of the center of the path, but the woman mimicked May's movement, making a straight line for May. The dog wiggled on its pink leash, and May stood still and waited.

"Calm down, Bubbles," the woman said, tugging on the leash. She stopped a few feet away from May and pushed her oversize sunglasses up onto the top of her head. "You *do* know he's married, don't you?" the woman blurted.

May stared, not speaking. Up close, May saw that the woman's cheeks were splotchy from the heat, creating red patches all over her face and neck. May couldn't gauge her age, but she looked older up close, with dozens of lines stretching from the corners of her eyes and around her frown. She might be in her late thirties. Her dyed blonde hair was pulled back into a severe ponytail that tugged the skin at the corners of her eyes. Sunlight reflected off the diamond studs in her ears.

"What's that?" May asked. *Maybe I misheard her.*

"That man," she pointed up the street, "Dr. Bisset, he's married. He has a wife and two children."

May nodded. "Yes, I know all of that." Her heart slammed in her chest so hard that she feared the woman could see the thumping through her thin blouse. Blood pounded in her ears, making her feel like a thief caught in the act of stealing someone's precious jewels.

"Then what do you think you're doing?" She gave the leash a tug to pull her dog away from the bench's legs where it was scrubbing its face against the metal. Bubbles looked over at May, and she noticed a darker stain near its snout. Bubbles trotted in her direction, but the woman yanked the dog backward.

May inhaled and straightened her shoulders. She and Oliver hadn't been doing anything wrong. Standing on the sidewalk, eating a cookie, was hardly an illegal activity. "Right now, specifically? I'm standing on a sidewalk."

The woman's frown deepened. Lipstick collected in the corners of her mouth. "With him. If you know he's married with kids, then what are you doing with him? I know his wife. She's a nice woman. She loves her family." Bubbles whimpered at the woman's feet, but she continued to glare at May while tugging the leash tighter.

May wanted to back away slowly and then take off running, but to do that would be to admit that she was doing something terribly wrong. A hot summer wind blew down the street, kicking up dust and rattling the trees. Clouds rolled across the sky in fat, bulbous packs and blocked out the sunlight, throwing darkness onto May and the angry woman.

"Not that it's any of your business what I'm doing with my time, seeing as how I don't even know who you are, but Dr. Bisset and I are in the same running group. A running group his wife is aware of. If you want specifics, a few minutes ago we split a cookie from Bea's Bakery. You should try the chocolate chip ones. Maybe it'll add a bit of sweetness to your disposition. Now if you'll excuse me, I have work to do." May pushed past the woman but turned around to look at her once more.

The woman's lip curled into a scowl, and the dog's whimpering intensified.

May glanced down at Bubbles and pointed. "You might want to pay more attention to yourself and to Bubbles. She has poop on her face, which she's been trying to tell you the best way she can." May spun on her heel and strode away with her shoulders straight.

But once she got into her car and cranked the air conditioning, she noticed her hands were trembling on the steering wheel. *You've spent the entire summer avoiding this type of confrontation, someone accusing you of being what you were afraid of becoming—a homewrecker, a shameful adulteress. It was bound to happen. Maybe this is a one-time incident. Now that it's happened, I can stop dreading it.* Telling herself that she was *not* a horrible person for loving Oliver didn't help lessen the seed of unease that sprouted in her heart and grew long, prickly tendrils.

May didn't mention the woman to Oliver, because she didn't want to breathe any more life into something so toxic, but it left her feeling restless for days. The woman's words spread through her like a slow-acting poison, causing a low-grade ache in her stomach, stealing her appetite and bits of her joy. It followed her like a shadow of shame. Being with Oliver distracted her, but when they weren't together, her expression reminded her of when her grandma stood on the porch watching a storm approach. A wary look lingered in her green eyes, and by Saturday morning, literal storm clouds crept into Mystic Water, ready to pummel the town with a deluge.

May bounced on her toes and stretched her neck side to side. Oliver jogged up to meet May and the others in their running group. He cast a glance toward the sky.

"Think we'll make it?" he asked.

"A little rain won't hurt us," Jill said as she pulled her auburn hair into a high ponytail.

May's temple throbbed, and she rubbed her fingers in a slow circle on it. "Looks like a thunderstorm."

"Let's get going," Al said. He stepped closer to Oliver. "Are we having lunch at your house? Or you wanna cancel if the weather's bad?"

"We can eat indoors. I'll order pizzas," Oliver said. He moved closer to May and lowered his voice. "You okay?"

She shrugged. "I feel off today." She rubbed her fingers across her collarbone. The sky darkened, and the forest quieted.

Just before Oliver could question her further, the group took off at a jog, and May and Oliver fell into pace behind them. With the charcoal gray skies and the tree canopy, the poorly lit trail made it feel as though they were running at nightfall. May's steps were more cautious, and she and Oliver barely spoke. May questioned her anxiety. *Is it the weather?* Her thoughts kept drifting back to the woman on the sidewalk. *What do you think you're doing?* The woman's voice became shriller in her head. How could one angry woman taint a summer of love and fun?

A half mile before they finished a six-mile run, the air filled with the stink of sulfur, and the hairs on May's arms lifted. Seconds later torrential rain fell from the sky. The storm soaked them, pelting their bodies with drops that felt like a paintball war they were losing. They shouted words to one another as they jumped into their cars. By the time May sat in her car, the ominous feeling tripled, and thunder boomed, rattling the car like a miniquake. A nagging feeling in her gut told her to drive to the farm and stay put, but she'd already told Oliver she would go straight to his house to help him prepare for the group lunch.

Oliver texted, *See you at the house. Be careful!* May swiped a towel over her face, neck, and arms. Then she tossed the towel into the passenger seat. She was the last person to pull out of the parking lot. As she shifted the car into drive, lightning bolted out of the sky and struck a pine tree less than fifty yards away. The trunk split apart, throwing sparks; bark blasted off the tree, sounding like a bomb exploding; and the entire top of the tree separated from the trunk and crashed to the forest floor with a loud *boom*. The shockwaves threw pine needles and mud against May's car. She gasped and sat trembling. The tree trunk sparked a minute more before the rain beat out the fire, but the sound of the lightning strike echoed in her ears.

A voice whispered, *Go to the farm*. But May inhaled a few times to calm her shaking hands. Then she drove to Oliver's house, ignoring the nagging voice in her head.

24

May stepped out of Oliver's shower and wrapped a towel around her body. She tucked the towel flaps beneath her arm and combed through her wet hair. Using a hand towel, May swiped it across the steam-coated mirror. A wary face stared at her from the silver glass. She rolled her head on her neck and told herself everything was *fine*. Another round of wind howled around the house.

Oliver stood beside his bed and buttoned a pair of khaki shorts. "I never get tired of seeing you in my house, and definitely not when you're dressed like that."

May smiled at her feet. "I'm not sure this is considered dressed."

"Even better." Oliver crossed the room. He circled her waist with his arms.

May pressed her hands against his warm, bare chest. Thunder rumbled outside. "You're pretty tempting yourself."

He pulled her toward his bed, picked her up, and dropped her on the bed. May's breath came out in a rush of laughter.

Oliver reached for an empty Mason jar on the end table. "Don't move." He moved the jar through the air like an airplane and then screwed on the lid.

"What are you doing?" May asked, still giggling.

"Bottling up your happiness so I can keep it with me always." Then he jumped onto the bed beside her.

May scooted up toward the pillows, and Oliver crawled up after her, placing his hands on either side of her shoulders. Her wet hair fanned out across the pillow. Hovering above her, Oliver smiled. She saw desire in his eyes, and heat flamed out from low in her belly. Oliver tugged at her towel.

"The group will be here soon," May said, pressing one hand against the cotton fabric to hold it in place.

Oliver kissed along her jawline. "I love you, May. Have I told you that today?"

May hummed in her throat and closed her eyes. This time when he tugged at her towel, she didn't stop him. When she exhaled, she felt her body sink deeper into the mattress as her body reacted to his touch.

"Let's stay like this forever," he said, kissing her cheek and then her lips. "Promise me? I can't bear to think about a life without you."

May slid her hands up his bare back as rain pounded against the bedroom windows. "So don't."

Oliver caught May in a deep kiss, and moments later the towel and khaki shorts dropped off the side of the bed. "What about the group?" she murmured.

"They can wait on the front porch. A little rain never hurt anyone."

Oliver drowned out the sound of May's laughter with his kisses.

The doorbell rang and Oliver shouted, "It's open!" He sat on the couch eating pizza and talking with George and George's oldest son.

May refilled her water glass at the kitchen sink. She'd changed into a pair of khaki shorts and a T-shirt with her university's football team logo on the front. Her hair was twisted into a bun and still damp from the shower. It seemed silly to blow dry and style her hair when the rain continued to sweep through town. Jill walked into the kitchen carrying a giant-size plastic bowl full of salad. Her auburn hair was down and curled at the ends.

"Hey, Jill. Did it stop raining?" May asked and then drank from her glass.

Jill put the bowl on the counter, popped off the plastic lid, and straightened her striped, red sundress. "A small break, but there are more dark clouds coming this way."

"I'm amazed at how good your hair looks in this weather." May pointed to her own hair. "I didn't even try." She passed Jill a paper plate. "We have veggie pizza, cheese, meat lovers, margherita, and Al requested a Hawaiian one. No one is eating it but him."

Jill smiled. "I know why. It's gross." They both laughed. Jill filled half her plate with salad and then stacked three pizza slices on the other side. "I guess it's okay to eat in the living room?"

May nodded. "Everyone else is already in there. I'll be right behind you. I'm going to pull the ice cream cake out of the freezer so it'll have time to thaw before we cut it."

May opened the freezer and grabbed the cake box. She removed the frozen cake from the box and straightened a tilted Oreo on the top. As soon as Jill stepped out of the kitchen, thunder bellowed outside like an angry monster. Windows rattled, and the children released nervous shouts. Lightning blasted from the sky and threw flashing light into the house.

Jill stopped walking and turned to look at the front door. Her hair blew back away from her face and shoulders as though a powerful wind whooshed through the house.

The sound of squeaky rubber soles slapped against the hardwood. Oliver stood up from the couch, and his expression stopped May's heart.

Seconds later two kids bounded into the living room and wrapped their arms around Oliver. May gripped the edge of the countertop to keep her knees from buckling beneath her. *Is that Jackie and Michael? Does that mean that Angelina—*

A small blonde woman stomped into view, halting right beside Jill. She tossed her wet umbrella onto the kitchen floor. The formfitting tank top and matching skirt accentuated Angelina's petite frame. Light caramel accents highlighted her blonde hair. From her frozen spot behind the kitchen island, May watched Angelina's blood-red lipstick shine in the lights, drawing attention to her full lips.

"Having a party?" Angelina asked, glaring at Jill. Her words slurred, sounding like someone who'd already spent a couple of hours strangling a wine bottle. She scowled.

Jill looked at Angelina and then toward Oliver. The edges of the paper plate in Jill's hand shriveled as though she stood too close to flames. The room fell into an awkward silence, everyone watching Angelina and Jill.

More thunder boomed, and rain slapped against the terrace windows, sounding like rocks pelting glass.

Oliver let go of Michael and Jackie and stepped around the couch. "I wasn't expecting you," he said as he moved toward Angelina. His voice sounded calm, yet his tense posture betrayed his unease.

"I can see that," Angelina said. She faced Jill and looked her up and down with a snarled lip. "I bet *you* weren't expecting me either."

Jill laughed, a distressing sound, and May's heartrate burst into a sprint. *She knows about Oliver and me.*

Oliver reached for Angelina's arm. "Let's take this somewhere else." He looked at Jill. "I'm sorry about this."

"You damn well *should* be sorry!" Angelina yelled and pointed a manicured fingernail at Jill. "Who do you think you are?"

Angelina's poisonous, angry words spread through the house like an airborne plague, and May felt the pizza burning in her stomach, burning up her throat. The cake drooped on one side like a mudslide as the ice cream melted. The rest of the group in the living room stood and started inching away from the scene. Michael and Jackie watched, and May's heart lurched again when she saw their faces. Tears filled Jackie's eyes, and Michael rubbed the back of his neck and glanced at the faces around him as though searching for help.

"I asked you a question," Angelina continued, slapping the plate of pizza and salad out of Jill's hand.

The room gasped in unison. The salad seemed to fall in slow motion, like feathers tossed from a rooftop. Two slices of pizza landed on Jill's sandaled feet. She gaped at Angelina.

"That's enough," Oliver said, his voice taking on a darkness May had never heard before. Oliver squeezed Angelina's arm and tried to pull her out of the room.

"Don't you dare!" Angelina yelled, stumbling to the side. She wobbled and stretched out her arms as if to steady herself against a wall. "Don't protect her," she spat. "She's just as disgusting as you are. I can't *believe* you would have an affair with *her*."

Jill's eyes widened as waves of heat rose up from the floor

around Angelina's feet, blurring her image.

"I'm not having an affair with Oliver," Jill blurted.

"Party's over," Al called out over the noise of the driving rain. He clamped a hand on Oliver's shoulder. "We'll talk later, okay?" He squeezed Oliver's shoulder and then released him. "Let's head out. We'll get our stuff later." He put his hand on Jill's lower back and ushered her away from Angelina and Oliver.

May grabbed her cell phone and moved through the kitchen. Oreo and vanilla ice cream created a marbled, melted pool on the island and dripped onto the tile floor. Oliver glanced at her, and she saw panic combined with embarrassment in his eyes. She slipped past Angelina and breathed in the nauseating scents of ashes and liquor.

Oliver spoke to the kids, but May didn't understand his words. There didn't seem to be enough air in her lungs for all her senses to remain alert. May stumbled outside onto the stone porch right behind the rest of the group. Rain pounded the earth so hard that May couldn't see five feet in front of her. The others ran to their cars, looking like streaks of color that disappeared in seconds. Soaking-wet May collapsed into her car and sat shivering, gripping the wheel as if she would shatter into pieces if she let go.

May backed out of the driveway. *How does Angelina know? Why does she think he's with Jill? Who told her? What happens now? She knows. She knows. She knows.* The windshield wipers slapped furiously back and forth, back and forth, unable to clear enough water from the glass. May leaned forward, squinted into the storm, and drove below the speed limit. Angelina's face accompanied by her bitter words and shrill voice looped in May's brain. Her pulse pounded at her temples.

May turned onto the main road that led out of town and whipped the car onto the side of the road. She crawled over into the passenger seat, opened the door, and vomited up her lunch. Rain fully soaked the top of her body in seconds. She fumbled for a half-empty bottle of water and drank, swished it around her mouth, and spat it out. She closed the car door and pressed her forehead against the window. After a few minutes of deep breathing, May returned to the driver's seat.

Oliver's body shook with fury born from deep in his core. He clenched his jaw and formed fists at his sides. He turned toward the kids who stood slack jawed and trembling in the living room. Tears streaked down Jackie's cheeks. Oliver opened his hands, palms up, and walked to them.

"Hey, guys, why don't you two go upstairs?" he said. "Your mom and I will sort this out. It'll be okay."

"Like hell it will," Angelina snarled. "Don't want them to know the truth? I thought you were *all about* honesty and being open with them."

Oliver's voice was quiet but commanding when he said, "Please go to your rooms."

Without waiting to hear their mom's response, they scurried toward the stairs. Michael tripped over the rug in the foyer. Jackie reached back for him, keeping him from falling, and they disappeared up the stairs.

Oliver's jaw clenched and released. "You have no right to barge into this house and speak to my friends like that."

"This is *my* house too. Or did you forget that since you've been screwing around with someone else?" Angelina stomped into the kitchen and opened the fridge. Not finding what she was looking for her, she scanned the countertops. She grabbed an open bottle of wine near the sink and popped out the cork. Pointing the bottle neck toward Oliver, she said, "Think I wouldn't find out? Well, I have eyes everywhere. People here *like* me, and they tell me things."

"Your *people* are liars then," Oliver said, following her into the kitchen. He reached for the wine bottle. "I think you've had enough. I don't even *want* to talk about the fact that you drove *our* children here when you're wasted because I just might lose it."

She hugged the bottle to her chest and batted her fake eyelashes at him. "Oh, poor, wittle Ollie might lose it. Don't patronize me. I know what I'm doing." Angelina pressed the bottle to her lips and drank more. "A friend of mine saw you two in the park—"

Oliver's back stiffened. "I have *never* been to the park with Jill. She's in my running group. Everyone *here* today came over after a race. Your 'contact' is full of shit. Now give me the bottle."

"Why would she lie to me? Why would she say she'd seen you with another woman in the park? Laughing and looking like two idiots in love?" Tears welled in Angelina's eyes, and she swiped them away, scratching her long nails against her cheek. An angry red welt formed. Her breath hitched.

Why *would* some woman say that? Then Oliver's eyes widened. Someone had seen him with May in the park. "What did she say?"

"Other than that you were practically *all over* her? That she was an ugly red-headed girl she didn't know. Why? Wanting to admit the truth now? I can't *believe* you would do this to me!"

May and Jill both had auburn hair. What would have happened if Angelina had spotted May first today? Bile rose in Oliver's throat. "I am *not* having an affair with Jill." It wasn't a lie.

"You're a liar, Oliver Bisset, and I can't wait to be through with you."

Lightning flashed outside, and the electricity flickered. A bulb in a living room lamp exploded. Oliver flinched at the sound. Angelina shoved past him.

"Where are you going?" he asked.

She snatched up her car keys from the foyer table, and Oliver lunged for them. They wrestled for the keys. There was no way Oliver was going to let her drive away drunk.

"If you're going to stand there and lie to me, I'm going to make her admit it," Angelina screeched. "I'm going to make her say she's sorry. We have a family, and she's trying to destroy it."

Oliver laughed, releasing his grip on the keys. "Are you kidding me? I think you're doing an excellent job of that right now. And what about a few months ago when you were screwing Mike Vaughn like there was no tomorrow? What would you call that?"

Angelina stumbled backward, taking the keys with her, and

roared like a possessed banshee. She flung the wine bottle at Oliver's head, and he cussed, barely ducking in time. The bottle shattered against the wall, staining the wall paint with deep purple liquid. Angelina opened the door and ran out into the driving rain. The electricity flickered again.

"Son of a—"

"Dad, is everything okay?" Jackie called from the staircase.

Oliver looked up at Jackie, who gripped the railing. Michael stood a few steps above her, watching him with a strained expression. Oliver pointed. "Stay there." He raced after Angelina.

A car door slammed. The engine turned, and Oliver grabbed at the driver's door handle. It was locked.

Rain drenched him, and he wiped the water from his eyes. Slapping his palm against the window, he yelled. "Open up, Angi! Come on. Don't do this."

Thunder growled, and lightning ripped the black sky in half.

She glared up at him and shifted the car into reverse.

He pounded on the hood as she backed out of the driveway. "Please, Angi!"

She floored it, barely missing the curb as she reversed onto the street. Water flew off the tires as they spun on the wet pavement before catching, and she sped off.

Oliver tilted back his head and let the rain pound against his face. He pressed his hands against his chest and inhaled a broken breath. Even as his worry for Angelina grew, his concern for May and how she must be feeling caused his knees to tremble.

"Dad?"

Jackie and Michael stood in the open doorway, silhouetted by the interior lights. Oliver walked to them and opened his arms. He motioned for them to get inside. The door clicked closed behind him.

"Who's hungry?" he asked. "There's leftover pizza." He picked up the broken bottle pieces and dropped them into the kitchen trash can.

Ice cream oozed across the island and onto the floor. He yanked the paper towels and unwound a dozen before snatching them off the roll. "There *was* ice cream, but I'm pretty sure there are still cookies somewhere." Oliver knelt and wiped up the mess.

"Dad?" Michael asked.

"Yes, son?"

"Is Mom okay? Why did she leave?"

Oliver sighed and rocked back on his heels. "Your mom has a temper, and she's blowing off steam. She'll be okay, and she'll be back once she cools down. It's going to be okay."

"What about that lady?" Jackie asked, kneeling beside him and helping wipe up the melted cake.

"What lady? Jill?"

Jackie's blue eyes studied him. "Yes, sir. Are you in love with her?"

Oliver shook his head. "I am most certainly not in love with Jill. Someone told your mom a lie."

"I don't like when you and Mom fight," Jackie admitted.

Oliver reached out and tucked her hair behind her ears. "I don't either, baby. Your mom and I don't always get along, but we both love you and Michael very much, and we're going to get through this. This is stressful for everyone, and sometimes that means we have bad attitudes. Your mom will cool off, and then she'll be back. It's going to be okay, I promise."

Jackie nodded and tried to smile, but guilt stabbed in Oliver's stomach. Why did he feel like a liar when he promised Jackie it would be okay?

Thunder roared and bolts of lightning lit the sky. May looked around at where she'd pulled over and realized she'd made a wrong turn. Instead of driving toward the farm, she was on the road out of Mystic Water. She checked to make sure no one was coming, then she pulled a U-turn on the road and headed toward the farm. May slowed as she went around the next sharp curve, and a black car burst into view, having been obscured moments before by the wall of driving rain. May's lips parted, she tightened her grip on the wheel, and she saw the black car leave its side of the road and head straight for her.

As though watching from outside her body, May saw the black car crash into hers, saw the hood of her car fold together like an accordion as the vehicle lurched forward. The feel of burning skin on her face and arms followed a huge explosion of sound and force as the airbag deployed. The seatbelt tightened against her chest, crushing the air out of her lungs, and May bit through her tongue. *What is happening?* Powder, reeking like gun smoke, filled the car and blurred May's vision.

Rain pounded against the shattered windshield that crumpled forward into the car like melted plastic. May tilted forward, and blood pooled in her mouth. Splinters of pain shot up her left leg. Both her legs were pinned beneath the crushed car. The other car shot off the side of the road, flipping twice and landing upside down in a deep ditch. A wave of water surged out of the ditch, displaced by the overturned car.

May's vision tunneled.

$\mathcal{M}$ ay felt pressure on her hand. Muffled voices moved around her. She heard shuffling feet and the squeak of rubber against a tile floor. Her eyelids felt glued shut, and when she tried to swallow, a nauseating ache throbbed in her tongue. May groaned.

"May?" a soft female voice called to her from the blackness.

An image appeared in May's mind, rising out of the abyss. May wanted to ask, "Mama?" *Why is Mama at the farm? Why is it so cold in my bedroom?* But when she opened her mouth, her tongue felt ten sizes too big. She tried to lift her hand, but someone had replaced her arm with a lead pipe, and she lacked the strength to move it. May groaned again.

"Hey, baby," her mama cooed and squeezed her hand, "it's okay. Don't try to talk or move too much just yet. You've been sleeping for a while."

May blinked open her eyes, feeling a stickiness on her eyelashes and lids. She squinted in the florescent lights. Three white walls came into focus with one wall of windows to her side. The open blinds allowed in muted light that reflected off the shiny white floor. *I'm in a hospital.* May's mama stood beside the bed wearing a sleeveless dress spotted with sunflowers. May's daddy sat in a mustard-yellow chair near the windows, and Fiona gripped the railing at the end of the bed where May lay. A black headband held back her red curls.

A round table, no bigger than a large pizza, held a couple of colorful, propped-up cards. A helium balloon tied to the back of her daddy's chair read Get Well Soon. It's silver mylar backside rotated toward May and shot a beam of sunlight in her direction.

Why am I in a hospital? May shifted on the bed, trying to push herself into a sitting position, but when she moved, her ankle ached, and her left wrist wouldn't support her weight. May groaned again, which caused a shooting pain to stab in her mouth. She lifted her other hand to her lips as her eyes widened. The terrible idea that she'd had her tongue removed sent a wave of panic shuddering through her body.

"It's okay, baby," her mama said, touching May's shoulders and pressing her against the bed. "I think the numbing medication is wearing off. Riley, would you see if you could grab a nurse for us?"

Far off in a murky back corner of May's mind, more images and sounds emerged in her memories, drifting forward like fog. She heard a thunderstorm, saw flashes of car lights, and recalled the sound of metal crunching.

May's daddy stood, walked across the room with his tennis shoes squeaking against the tiles, and disappeared out of May's view.

Fiona hurried to May's other side. "Hey, Little May, don't panic. You're okay." As if reading May's mind, Fiona added, "You've still got all the things you were born with minus your baby teeth."

A car wreck. May pointed to her mouth.

Fiona and her mama exchanged glances. Her mama shook her head, and Fiona frowned. "Mama wants to sugarcoat this, but you'll find out soon enough. You almost bit off your tongue. Gross, but it's the truth. Good news, you *didn't* bite it off. Bad news, you did a number on it, and it's gonna hurt like the dickens. They don't normally stitch the tongue, so it's gonna feel awful while it heals. Talking will be awkward because it's swollen. But they have numbing medication to help you be more comfortable."

May closed her eyes and exhaled. A swollen tongue she could deal with, even if it felt like she had an engorged slug in her mouth. She garbled the word *water*, but her mama understood her well enough and held a straw to May's lips. May drank and struggled to swallow the water without spilling it out of her mouth. "What happened?" she mumbled, feeling like someone whose mouth was still asleep. *There was another car; it flipped through the air like a toy car shoved off the edge of a stair.*

"Do you remember anything?" her mama asked.

"A little," May responded, which didn't sound at all like those words did in her head. Still her mama and sister understood. She recalled an image of a black car crossing into her lane.

218

"You know you've been in a car crash?" Fiona asked.

May nodded.

Her mama said, "They'll want to know what you remember because it's not completely clear what happened to cause the wreck. The police, I mean. They've been by a few times to check on you, but it was hours before you regained consciousness. We were really scared that you..." Her mama paused as tears filled her eyes, and she covered her trembling lips with her hand.

Fiona picked right up where she stopped. "You were out longer than anyone was comfortable with, but you *did* come back to us. You were out of your gourd when you came to, trying to talk, but we couldn't understand you. It was like drunk May from college." May's mama gasped, and Fiona laughed. "Mama, I'm kidding. May never babbled when she was drunk." Fiona dodged her mama's flying hand. "Anyway, they gave you something to help you sleep, and here we are." Fiona lifted May's left arm gently. "You sprained your wrist pretty badly, so they've wrapped it up like a mummy. And your ankle was twisted at a weird angle. No one could believe it wasn't broken. Maybe you're half Gummi Bear." She smiled at May. "You now have an award-winning cankle until the swelling goes down." Fiona tapped her sister's forehead. "This was the main concern, you being out for so long. But your brain is firing on all neurons, even though you were concussed. They kept you overnight."

Overnight? Another stabbing pain, this time in her heart, caused her to moan. May remembered being at Oliver's—the storm, Angelina's arrival, Michael and Jackie, the burning anger. "Oliver?" she garbled.

"Who?" her mama asked.

Fiona pressed her hand against May's arm. "He knows." Fiona looked at her mama. "Her running group. She was with them right before the wreck. And Emily and Andy came by too."

"Oh, yes, of course," her mama said. "You've made some sweet friends here. They've all been by to check on you."

May nodded and looked at her mama and then at Fiona. "The people in the other car? Are they okay?"

Fiona looked away and fiddled with her wild hair. May's mama cleared her throat.

"It was just one woman, and she's in pretty bad shape, baby," her mama said in a quiet voice. "They had to take her into surgery. She was thrown out of the car. She wasn't wearing her seatbelt, so it's a miracle she's even alive."

"Let's give May a break for a few minutes," Fiona said. "She's just waking up. You want to see if Daddy found a nurse? Now that she's awake, maybe she can have something to eat? Soup? Are you hungry, Little May?"

May closed her eyes and sunk into the lumpy pillow. She shook her head. Her stomach squeezed. *The running group came by? Did that include Oliver? What happened with Angelina? How is he? How are the kids?* May felt someone press a finger between her eyes and rub at the tightness.

"Relax, May," Fiona said. "You don't have to do anything right now but let your body recover. We'll get all the other stuff sorted soon enough. Don't worry."

"I'll see if I can find your dad and a nurse. He might have gone to get Charity too since she's been anxious to see you awake," May's mama said.

When only Fiona and May were in the room, May said, "Oliver."

"That too. We'll figure it out," Fiona said. When May opened her mouth to speak again, Fiona shook her head. "Don't make me use my mom voice. Relax. Rest. Okay?"

May exhaled and nodded. The press of exhaustion settled into her bones, and her body felt heavy, as though she were sinking deeper into the mattress. *I'll just close my eyes for a few minutes, then we can talk about Oliver, and I'll tell Fiona what happened. She'll help me figure out what to do. She'll know...*

The next time May opened her eyes, Grandma Charity stood at the end of the bed explaining to a nurse the right way to bandage a head wound if someone fell off a tractor. She'd done it dozens of times on the farm, she said.

Grandma Charity caught May's movement and their eyes met. "Good afternoon, Little May. They're here to check your vitals, and then we hope they're sending you home."

Home, as in the farm? Or back with Mama and Daddy? I need to talk to Oliver.

The nurse raised May's bed until she was in a sitting position. He checked her blood pressure, temperature, and heart rate and asked if she felt hunger or thirst. He logged her information into a computer and then rolled his equipment out of the room, telling her the doctor would be in shortly.

Grandma Charity stepped up beside her and patted May's hand. "How're you feeling?"

May's eyes scanned over her body, noticing all the bruises and scratches for the first time. Her arms had strips of raw skin from the airbag's deployment. She flipped back the covers to see her legs. The short hospital gown stopped mid-thigh, and her legs revealed similar marks. "I look about how I feel. Beat up," she said, trying to get used to the feel of speaking with a numb tongue.

Her grandma touched May's forehead gently. "Got a few minor burns from the airbag. It's good to see you awake. You scared the pants off us. What happened out there? Did you lose control in the rainstorm?"

May shook her head. "The other car, it swerved into my lane, and I think she was driving too fast. She came out of nowhere."

"That makes sense since she was—"

"May!" Fiona said, breezing into the room and interrupting Grandma Charity. "You're awake again. I just heard the news that you're going to be set free after the doctor gives his okay."

May nodded and looked at her grandma again. "What were you saying about the other driver?"

"Oh, she was—"

"Hey, Grandma," Fiona said, "Daddy and Mama were talking about maybe staying over at the farm tonight. Daddy wants to talk to you about it."

"Of course that's fine," Grandma Charity said. "Why *wouldn't* it be?"

Fiona shrugged. "He wants to talk to you...now."

"Good heavens," Grandma Charity said, huffing. She patted May's hand. "You'd think he was still an impatient child."

Grandma Charity stomped out of the room, and then she looked at Fiona. The light shifted in the room, pushing back toward the windows. May's hollow stomach followed the light pulling away from her. "What's going on?"

"What? Nothing. Why would you ask that? You're going home soon!" Fiona said in a saccharine voice.

May pressed her lips together and inhaled. She rubbed the swollen bump on her forehead. "You're a terrible liar. What's happening? Am I dying and no one wants to tell me?"

Fiona's laugh burst out and surprised both of them, but it sounded nervous and tight, echoing off the white walls. "No, you're not dying."

"Then what is it?"

Fiona pinched the bridge of her nose. She stepped closer to the hospital bed. "I wanted to wait to tell you, wait until you weren't lying in a hospital. You've already been through a lot—"

"Fiona, spit it out!" May said, muddling the words together, but her sister understood. Her pulse quickened in her chest, and her blood pounded through her, causing her whole body to ache.

"The driver in the other car...it was Angelina, Oliver's wife."

$\mathcal{M}$ ay felt as though she and the hospital bed had been shoved off a cliff. She was free falling into blackness, leaving her stomach high above, her heart stopping in her chest.

Fiona's panicked expression hovered in front of her face, but May couldn't respond. Fiona's mouth opened and closed. May was aware that her sister was speaking, but she couldn't hear Fiona's words over the sound of her heart pounding. Fiona pressed her cold hands to May's face, and the chill pulled May back.

"May, can you hear me? May!"

May's eyes locked on Fiona's identical green ones. "How is she?"

Fiona stepped back and exhaled. "Dadgumit, May, don't *do* that. I thought you were having a heart attack. You're paler than Wednesday Addams. I'm so sorry. I didn't want to tell you. I *wanted* to wait, but you—"

May pressed one hand to her heart. "How is she?"

Fiona glanced over her shoulder to see if they were still alone. "She's not good right now. I *think* they believe she's going to be all right, but last I heard she's still in the ICU, and there are a few more surgeries she'll need. Fixing multiple broken bones, her breastbone, both legs, one hand. Part of her face shattered. It's really awful." Fiona started crying. "Good Lord, I'm so sorry, May. I feel terrible for Oliver and the kids, and I feel guilty because I feel even worse for you because I know the future you two have been planning, and it doesn't mean it's not going to happen now but..." Fiona's voice trailed off.

But...but now it's all changed. The future, shining and sparkling like a beautiful star on the horizon, went full-on supernova in May's mind. Then her body numbed, as though the medication for her tongue had leaked into the rest of her. She closed her eyes. "It's okay."

"Biggest lie ever—" Fiona started.

May's grandma and parents returned to the room with the

doctor. Autopilot engaged. May responded to the doctor's questions, and she moved her body as asked. Fiona stood at the end of the bed and fretted, biting her fingernails, but May couldn't access her emotions when she tried.

"Did you hear me, Oliver?"

Oliver sat with his hands clasped together behind his neck, leaning over in the chair and staring at the floor. The second time he heard his name, he looked up. His mother-in-law, Cassie, stared down at him with her downturned lips. Jackie and Michael lingered off to the side, both avoiding looking in the direction of Angelina who lay silent in the bed surrounded by a half dozen machines that were working overtime to keep her alive.

"What?" Oliver asked.

"I *said* I'm taking the kids home. Rosa is going to stay here with Angi," Cassie said. She tightened her grip on her purse straps.

Oliver stood and stretched. "Good idea. Thank you, Cassie."

Jackie hurried over to him. "Daddy, we don't want to go. What if something happens? What if you get lonely? Michael and I can stay with you."

Michael looked ready to bolt from the room at any excuse. The kids had been there for hours, and the stress showed on their faces. Angelina's condition, swinging like a pendulum of doom, changed every few hours.

"Baby, I'm okay," Oliver said. "Nothing is going to happen. Go on home with your grandma."

"I'll pull the car around. Michael, do you want to go with me?" Cassie asked and turned before Michael could answer, but he mumbled good-bye, glanced at the hospital bed once, and rushed out of the room.

Jackie stood in front of Oliver, unmoving with her mouth set into a tight line.

"Jackie, go on with your grandma," Oliver said.

But Jackie's bottom lip trembled, and she rocked back and forth, toe to heel, toe to heel. "Are you—are you going to leave us?" she blubbered. "If Mama has to stay here forever, are you still leaving us?"

Oliver wrapped his arms around Jackie, and she cried against him. "Baby, I'm not leaving you. I've never been leaving you. Just because your mom and I are separating doesn't mean I'm not going to be your dad anymore." He held her away from him so she could see his face. "Do you understand what I'm saying?"

She nodded. "But maybe we could still be a family. Me, you, Mama, and Michael. Maybe you two could work on it. Michael wants that too, for us to stay together. And Mama's story about the other woman you love isn't true, is it? You're not leaving us for her, are you? Because now that Mama's so hurt...she'll need us, all of us, and maybe she'll feel better inside too. She'll see how much you love all of us. You love us, don't you?"

Part of Oliver's heart crumpled as the sunshine fled from the room. He glanced at the windows, and his whole body shuddered. "I love you very much—"

Rosa, Angelina's sister, walked into the room and cleared her throat. "Jackie, come on with me. I'll take you down to Grandma so you can go home for a bit."

Oliver nodded his okay, and Jackie shuffled away from him. Rosa slipped her arm around Jackie's shoulders.

In the silence punctuated by the steady whir and beep and ticking of the machines, Oliver pressed his hand against his chest and leaned forward, desperate to hold his heart together.

Thirty minutes later May sat in a wheelchair wearing an emerald green sundress that belonged to Fiona. May's daddy pushed her out into the hallway, following her mama, grandma, and sister. Oliver rounded the nearest corner and nearly ran into them. He stared at May; she gripped the cold, metal armrests. Autopilot disengaged. She exhaled, sending an empty stretcher rolling down the hallway toward the elevators. A nurse rushed after it. A suffocating ache expanded in her chest.

Deep brown stubble darkened Oliver's face, and his hair was neat and combed. His blue T-shirt and khaki shorts looked clean, but his haunted eyes sunk in and betrayed his exhaustion. He pulled his hands out of his pockets and stepped toward May.

"Why don't we go get the car?" Fiona suggested. "Hey, Oliver, we're heading home. I bet you want to talk to May before we go, don't you? Would you bring her downstairs when you're done?" Fiona had to drag her mama along with her because she looked like she wanted to wait with May.

"I will," Oliver said. Without speaking, he wheeled May into a small cubby with two chairs and a window that overlooked the parking lot. Then he knelt in front of her and touched her face. "Oh, sweetheart, I'm so glad to see you awake, and you're going home. Even better news." He touched the bump on her forehead and brushed her hair back from her face. His words sounded sincere, but his expression revealed exhaustion and disquiet.

May reached for his hands and held them in her lap. The sunlight coming through the window retreated, leaving them sitting in the gloom. "I'm thorry my voith ith weird, but my tongue..."

Oliver shook his head and rubbed his thumbs across her hands. "I can understand you."

"How're you? How're the kids? And how...how is Angelina? Oliver, I'm so sorry. This must be terrible for y'all." May's throat tightened, and she squeezed her eyes shut.

Oliver leaned forward and pressed his forehead against her legs. May rubbed his head and waited. When he lifted his head, his eyes were watery and sad. "It's a miracle you weren't both killed. Maybe I'd deserve that—"

"No you don't," May said. "Don't say that. This isn't your fault."

Oliver pulled his hands out of hers and sank into a cold, plastic chair beside her. "She was *way* past the legal blood alcohol level. She's been charged with an aggravated DUI, and you could claim damages in a civil lawsuit, but your parents assured me you'd never want to press charges against her. So even when she's out of here,

226

she won't have to face legal consequences. I'll be paying all her fines."

"What happened? I left your house, made a wrong turn, and then turned back for the farm. She must have left right after I did."

Oliver's shoulders slumped, and he rubbed his hands down his face. He explained how Angelina's rage continued to build, about their shouting match, and how they'd wrestled for the car keys. Then he described how just as he'd calmed the kids and they sat in the living room playing a game, an officer knocked on their door.

May wanted to ask, "What's going to happen now? Are we over? *Shouldn't* we be?" But she felt terrified of the answer. Instead, she said, "It's going to be okay."

"Is it?" he asked. He reached out as though he were going to touch her, but he pulled his hand back, and it dropped into his lap. "The kids are worried I'll desert them and leave them without a father and possibly a mother too. *How* is it going to be okay?"

"One step at a time, that's all we have to do." A thread unraveled in May's heart; she felt the frayed ends being pulled in opposite directions. She inhaled a shuddering breath.

Oliver leaned forward and kissed her cheek. She inhaled the clean scent of him. "You're a good person, May. The best, really. I don't know what I did to deserve to find you. I wish I'd found you years ago, way before this catastrophic mess. But it does me a lot of good to see that you're okay. I better get you downstairs so your parents don't wonder what I've done with you."

Disappointment and distress knotted her stomach. She wanted Oliver to say more, to tell her they *were* going to be okay, that they would get through this *together*. But he didn't.

They rode the elevator in silence. May stared at their warped reflections on the silver elevator doors. Her face appeared long and smeared, like someone melting into nothing. Oliver's facial features blurred, fading away. *Is this our future?* May wondered.

Oliver stood under the concrete overhang where people picked up released patients in the U-shaped driveway. Fiona and her mama bundled May into the car, and Oliver waved, watching them as they drove off. Fiona reached over, grabbed May's hand, and squeezed. May's bottom lip trembled, so she pressed her teeth into it. She heard Oliver's voice ask again, *How is it going to be okay?*

May propped the crutches against the bedroom wall. She sat on the edge of the bed and sighed. Leaning over toward her nightstand, she checked her phone again. Still no messages from Oliver. The thorns in her stomach twisted deeper. His silence injected devastation through her veins.

Fiona stepped into the room, catching May staring at her phone. "You know he's probably overwhelmed, being at the hospital nearly twenty-four hours a day. Every time I saw him, he looked exhausted. He'll call or text soon."

"He has more important things to worry about," May said. "But everything has changed."

Fiona sat on the edge of the bed. "What do you mean? What do you think has changed? He still loves you, and he still wants to be with you."

May slumped forward and stared at her bandaged wrist and at the bruises and scratches on her arms. "How do you know that? It felt different being with him today, like all the joy had been sucked out, replaced with a broken version of us. I *know* this is a terrible situation, and it makes sense that he would be distant and distracted. But I wanted him to comfort me, to tell me that he *does* still love me." May's smile broke on her face. "I wanted this to work out. I was so happy with him. We had started talking about me meeting the kids. But now..."

Fiona pressed tissues into May's hand. "Why can't that still happen? I know it can't right now since Angelina's not in stable condition, but why not later? Did he tell you that?"

May shook her head. "I can feel the shift inside of me. I talked about letting him go for weeks, but then the signed papers arrived, and we acted like that gave us permission to be together. We acted like we *knew* we'd have a future together. But we never imagined how that one decision would affect everyone else. Now look where we are. If I'd broken it off, then Angelina wouldn't have found out that Oliver was having an affair, and she wouldn't be dying in a hospital bed right now—"

Fiona grabbed May's hand. "You can't carry all the blame."

May shifted on the bed and lay back on the pillow. She squeezed her eyes shut. "I have to let him go."

Fiona inhaled sharply. "Why? He told you that he loves you and wants to be with you. Angelina will get well. The doctors at the hospital are incredible, and they're going to fix her. Oliver isn't going to want you to let him go."

Tears pushed their way out. "That's the thing, though. If he doesn't already, he'll feel like he has to choose me or the kids, and there's no way I'm going to let him go through that. It would tear him apart."

"Why can't he have both?" Fiona argued.

"That's not how this is going to play out." May's voice hitched, and she swiped at her tears. Her mind was already creating dialogue for how the end would be.

"How do you know that?"

May tapped a finger against her chest. "Today in the hospital I could *feel* the separation happening. He's already starting to realize how this changes our future. Angelina needs him. Even when she pulls through all of the surgeries, it's going to be a long road to recovery."

"She has a mom and a sister here. They can take care of her just fine," Fiona said. Her anger warmed the sheets around her.

What May wanted to say was, "I feel like my heart is being ripped out of my chest." But instead, she said, "I'm tired."

Fiona stood and walked toward the door. "He'll fight for you and fight to be with you," she said. "And if he doesn't, then he's not worthy of being with you. I hate what happened to Angelina, but that doesn't change the fact that they had a miserable marriage. This shouldn't change any of the plans you and Oliver were making."

More tears traveled down May's cheeks. Thinking about Oliver

229

fighting to be with her pushed a sliver of hope into her heart. But perhaps that possibility had been left behind in the twisted wreckage.

The next morning May woke up to text messages from Oliver. He wrote, *You've been on my mind every minute. I need to see you. Angelina's mom and sister are with her at the hospital. Emily and Andy are going to watch the kids. Would you meet me at the willow at noon?*

May replied that she would see him soon. Grandma Charity, May's parents, and Fiona sat at the kitchen table by the time May had showered and dressed for the day. The kitchen filled with the earthy smell of freshly ground coffee and the sweet scent of pancakes with maple syrup.

May half listened to the conversation and responded when she needed to. Fiona had made a fresh-fruit smoothie for May, but after a few sips, the cup sat untouched. Her parents wanted May to leave when they headed back home that morning, but May explained she needed to meet with a friend.

"Honey, you need rest. You don't need to be gallivanting all over town after what you've just gone through. Can't your friend come here? Then you could still leave with us. I worry about leaving you here without a car. It'll take days before the insurance company totals the car and you get the money to buy a new one. We can do all of that from home."

"Mama, I'm okay," May said. "Grandma said I could borrow her car anytime I needed to. And I can drive. It'll do me good to get out of the house. I don't want to be cooped up all day."

Fiona understood May's vagueness and offered to stick around with her so she could take her home. "We can head home this afternoon. I don't mind hanging around a few more hours."

Her mama's lips released from their thin line. "I'm hovering, aren't I? I can't help it. I know y'all are grown, but you're still my baby girls."

After breakfast, Fiona followed May back to her bedroom.

"When are you meeting Oliver?"

"Noon," she answered, "but I'll probably go earlier. I need to get out of the house. I'm having an Alice in Wonderland moment—everything feels like it's shrinking around me. I'm going crazy not knowing what's going on in his head."

Fiona chewed on the side of her thumbnail. "What's your plan? What are you going to tell him? That it's over?"

May's exhale sent a shiver through the curtains. "I don't know. I have a hundred different scenarios in my head, but I need to know what he's thinking. I don't know what he needs or how I can help. I just want to get on the same page with him. Or I need to know that it's over. This in-between is turning my stomach into a rolling pit of acid."

"Do you think ending it right now is the best idea? He's been through a lot in the past few days."

And I haven't? May stared out the bedroom window. "Mama wants me to *leave* Mystic Water. But leaving here means leaving him. I don't know what to do or say or how to feel." May clenched her jaw as tears burned in her eyes. "And I'm scared that I gave my heart to someone who can't take care of it."

"Don't give up on him just yet. You have no idea what he's going to say, but I bet that he loves you and wants to be with you and he's been sorting out how to make that happen."

May thought back to the hospital when Oliver kissed her cheek. She pressed her fingertips against the spot, not wanting to admit to Fiona that it had felt a lot like the beginning of a good-bye. *What would Oliver want to talk about at noon?*

$\mathcal{M}$ ay drove Grandma Charity's silver Lincoln to Jordan Pond. The interior smelled like her grandpa's aftershave—a mix of nutmeg, cedar, and vanilla—and the dashboard on this older model car had a cassette player. Grandpa Ramsay's country music cassette tapes were stacked neatly in the console. May removed a Johnny Cash tape from the plastic case and pushed it into the player. The overcast sky matched May's mood, faint sunshine and more gray than light.

The closer May got to Jordan Pond, the more her body tensed. She felt thankful she hadn't eaten breakfast because her stomach churned like a volcano bubbling to life. She parked near Oliver's car. May inhaled and exhaled a few times before she grabbed her crutches and hobbled her way down to the bench.

Oliver heard her coming, and he stood watching her for the last few steps. He held out his hand and took the crutches. He propped them against the side of the bench and then pulled her into a tight hug, squeezing her like he hadn't seen her in days. She breathed him in, hoping her body would relax, but her muscles remained tight with tension. May sat and clasped her hands together, feeling the soft fabric of her worn cotton skirt against her skin. She turned to look at him.

"The color of your shirt matches your eyes exactly," he said.

May didn't look away from his gaze. Fiona had chosen the spring green shirt for May to wear, saying, *This color looks beautiful on you.* May responded, *It doesn't matter what I'm wearing.* Fiona scoffed, *How many men's decisions do you think have been swayed simply by a woman's beauty? How many battles won and lost?*

"You look beautiful," Oliver said, then his expression shifted. "Thanks for meeting me," he continued, sounding both relieved and exhausted with his voice more hoarse than usual. "It's good to see you. Really good." He scooted closer to May and reached for her hands.

Oliver's energy felt restrained, perhaps dimmed by the last few days, perhaps by something else. His controlled expression set off alarms in May's mind. He looked like a sailor who was watching his love standing on the dock while his ship sailed out of the harbor.

"How are you?" he asked. "It gave me a lot of peace yesterday to know you were home with your family."

May studied his face, his eyes, looking for the man she'd fallen in love with during the last few months. "I'm okay." She stared down at Oliver's hands in hers, memorizing the shape of his fingers and the feel of his warm skin. "How are you? How are the kids?"

"We're doing okay," he said. "Angelina had a rough night after surgery yesterday, but she's resting now, and the doctor says the outlook is better than he thought. The next few hours will tell us more. I took the kids out for pizza last night, just to give them a feeling of normalcy." Oliver met her gaze and tucked a strand of hair behind her ear. His fingers brushed across her cheek. "I miss you."

"I miss you." She grabbed his hand in hers. "It's been a weird time. It feels like a dream."

"Being with *you* felt like a dream." Oliver almost smiled. Then he said, "This feels more like real life. This total breakdown. This lack of light."

"Not everything is falling apart, right?" *Not us, right?*

"I don't share your optimism. I wish I could, but I don't," he admitted.

"What about us?" May blurted. Oliver's hands squeezed around hers before he lightened his grip.

"What about us?" he repeated, pausing on each word. "I want to be with you. I've never felt this way about anyone. I love you, May."

May's heart relaxed for a few seconds, and when she exhaled, the willow rustled above them.

"I love you too," she said, more breath than sound.

Oliver released her hands and looked at the pond. "But I don't know what to do."

May's back stiffened. "About what?"

"About any of this," he said without looking at her. "I have to

234

focus on my family. I have to make sure the kids are okay. And with Angelina in the hospital and the schedule of upcoming surgeries, I don't know how..." He stared at his feet and gripped the back of his neck with both hands. "I have to get my family settled first. I'm— I'm so sorry, May." He reached for her hand, but May didn't react. His fingers wrapped around hers, and she sat stiff like a wooden doll.

Oliver's watery eyes stared at her, pleading with her to speak, but everything May wanted to say blew away like shredded notebook paper in a gust of wind.

"I wasn't thinking clearly. I wasn't thinking about the consequences," he stammered, still staring into her eyes. "You were right to want to stay out of this mess. But I pursued you. I didn't want to *stop* being with you. You have every right to hate me. I dragged you straight into a trap, into a situation neither one of us could win. And now here we are." His voice sounded squeezed.

A ripple of hope still moved inside of her. "And where are we?"

"I don't know what's going to happen with my family now. I wasn't prepared for this. I want to be with you, but I want to do what's right too. I need some space to figure this out."

May pulled her hands away and leaned slightly forward as her lungs constricted. She nodded, not trusting herself to speak yet. On her next exhale the last bit of hope exited and sent shivery ripples across the pond. May reached for her crutches.

Oliver grabbed her hands. "Where are you going?" A panicked expression dashed across his face.

"Home." Numbness spread out from her heart, injecting a cold, dead feeling into her veins.

He nodded. "You need rest. It's been a hard few days. I'm so sorry, May. Sincerely. Get some rest at the farmhouse with your family. That's the best place for you right now."

"No, I'm going home. I'm leaving Mystic Water." She stood on one foot and positioned the crutches beneath her arms.

Oliver stood, staggering in his haste. He gripped the back of the bench. "What? You're leaving town?"

Tears pooled on his lower lids. May felt her insides collapsing like a sand castle at high tide.

"Your family needs you, Ollie. You said it; you need time to figure out how to make this right. Your family is much more important. This," she said, motioning between the two of them as her voice cracked, "this was a summertime fling, a bad decision."

Oliver's expression fell, and he stepped toward her, pulling her against him. He cupped the back of her head, and May stood straight and still, not moving her arms to hug him in return. The crutches dug into her ribcage beneath his grip. "You're *not* just a summertime fling." He released her and put his hands on her cheeks. "I *love* you, May. I'm going to love you for the rest of my life. I don't want you to go. I don't *want* to lose you."

His dark eyes stared into hers, and his warm touch burned her skin. May trembled so hard the ground shook, sending more ripples across the pond that caused waves to roll onto the banks, pushing back the cattails.

May moved away from him, away from his touch, and turned toward the parking lot. Oliver stood staring at her, arms dangling at his sides, eyes full of sorrow. The clouds split apart just enough to let a ray of sunshine reach down from the heavens and highlight only May.

"You're really leaving?" he said.

May looked at him and nodded, standing in the shaft of sunlight, wishing he'd hold her again and tell her he'd fight for her, that he'd take care of his family *and* her. May wanted him to refuse to let her go and promise to find a way for them all to be a family together. But Oliver didn't say any of those things.

Instead he said, "I understand. I'll walk you to your car."

"No," May said, holding up a hand, telling him to stop moving toward her. "I don't want you to."

"I can respect that," he said with a nod.

Still she hoped he would change his mind, that he would chase after her. But as May limped up the hill toward the parking lot, the gravity of the truth, of the end of their relationship, nearly suffocated her. Oliver didn't follow. Even as she unlocked the car door and cranked the engine, he remained standing beside the bench, watching her with his downturned eyes and the same haunted expression she'd seen when they first met. She felt certain his expression mirrored her own.

May drove away in silence. The tears did not come because her heart could not process the end of her summer with Oliver, of her *future* without Oliver. May parked her grandma's car in the garage. When she walked past the living room, Fiona called out to her. May stood in the doorway.

Fiona and Grandma Charity sat on the couch looking at her with expectant faces. Fiona closed her laptop, and Grandma Charity lowered the cookbook in her hands.

"What happened?" Fiona asked.

"It's over," May said.

"What do you mean?" Grandma Charity asked.

"He didn't fight for me," May said. "But keeping his family together is what matters." She nodded like a puppet.

"Why does it have to be you *or* his family?" Fiona asked, sounding angry as she stood. Grandma Charity reached for Fiona's hand and tugged her back onto the couch. "Why can't you have both?"

"He doesn't know what to do. Or what he wants. He needs time to figure out what's best for his family," May said. "And I'm an additional complication."

"That's bull. You're not a complication—"

May lifted her hand to stop Fiona. Grandma Charity's expression was unreadable. "He doesn't *want* to fight for me. He wants space to figure out what's best. I don't want to talk about it anymore. I'm ready to leave Mystic Water as soon as I pack my bag."

May hobbled to her bedroom, sat on the bed, and stared at the floor. Still her tears remained locked away inside. It felt as though her heart had removed itself from her body because her mind could not process the intensity of the heartbreak just yet.

Fiona spoke from the doorway. "I'm so sorry, May. I can't even imagine how you're feeling right now. I know how happy y'all were.

Maybe it's not really over. Maybe he'll come to his senses once life here settles down. Are you sure you want to leave?"

May gazed up at her sister. "I can't wait around for him to want to be with me, and I can't stick around and destroy his family. It's over. I'll never return to Mystic Water. I can promise you that."

"Don't make that kind of promise," Fiona said, swiping at her wet cheeks, shedding the tears May couldn't. "You don't know what the future holds."

"I know it won't find me in Mystic Water. I'm never coming back, I promise."

A month later an early autumn breeze gusted through May's open living room windows, ruffling papers on the couch and flipping open May's passport. May reached down and closed the booklet. Then she dropped it into her purse.

"Mama, it's only for a month," May said in the phone. "And I'll be working most of the time. I'll be fine. I'm a grown woman." Afternoon sunlight filled the room, and May warmed her bare feet on a patch of sun on the hardwood.

"Don't use that tone of voice with me, Little May," her mama said. "I've heard stories about Italian men. They're not like American men. They're—"

"Gorgeous, charismatic, and did I mention gorgeous? They understand fine wine and fresh foods and eat pasta anytime they want. They stay up late gazing at the stars and laughing. They believe dancing is perfectly acceptable after dinner. They think woman are delicate, beautiful creatures—"

"May!" her mama scolded. "You keep talking like that and you'll have me worried that you're never coming back."

May walked to a window, pushed aside the curtain, and gazed out at the blue sky. *Would that be so bad?* May wasn't imagining any sort of romantic affair with an Italian man, no matter how handsome he might be. When she closed her eyes, she still saw Oliver's face. She felt the memory of him sliding across her skin, felt the lingering fire from his touch. "Mama, I'll call you as soon as I get there, which won't be until late tomorrow for you. It'll take me a while to get from the Leonardo da Vinci airport to the house."

"Call me as *soon* as you get there. I won't sleep well until you do."

"I love you, Mama," May said, watching the mailman slip a stack of mail into her box. He gazed up at May and waved. She waved in return.

"You're going to have a wonderful time," her mama said in a wistful voice. "I love you too. But after a month, come home, May."

Home. The word hung in the air, drifting through the room with no sure place to land. May waved it away. "I'm going to grab the mail, finish packing, and head to the airport. I'll talk with you soon. Tell Daddy I love him."

May pulled her oversize sweater cardigan tighter around her body as the autumn chill rushed down the city streets, tossing fallen leaves onto the sidewalks. She opened her mailbox and removed the stack of mail. Walking back to the front door, she flipped through the letters, shuffling one envelope behind the next.

Then she stopped.

On an oversize white envelope, written in black ink in thin printed script, Oliver Bisset had written her name. In the top left corner, he'd scribbled his name and return address, using his clinic's location in Mystic Water.

May closed the front door, dropped the mail on the coffee table, and stood in the living room staring at the letter. She slipped her finger beneath the flap and tore through the thin paper. Inside the envelope was another smaller one. Oliver's handwriting had scrawled *Lovely May* on the outside, and he'd drawn a sun with beams stretching across the envelope.

May unfolded the letter inside, which had been written on notebook paper, and read the last words he ever wrote to her.

Dear Lovely May,

These last few weeks without you have been difficult. I didn't truly realize how much light you brought to my life until it was gone, and I have stumbled along as best as I can.

It hasn't been easy to put my family back together, and I'm not sure it will ever look the way any of us hoped. Maybe that's for the best. But we are doing what we can to hold ourselves together and take care of one another. We still have a long way to go here.

I've been writing on my novel, thanks to your inspiration and encouragement. If I ever finish, it will be because I hear your voice in my head telling me to keep going.

I cherish the time we had together. I feel so thankful to have had you in my life even for a short time. I didn't even know I was searching for someone like you until I found you, and now I can't imagine not having experienced such happiness and love. You are so very special, May, and I will love you for the rest of my life.

Love,
Oliver

May read the letter two more times. There was no indication or buried hint that Oliver was working toward being with her again. The final paragraph sounded like what someone would say during a eulogy, which felt accurate. The day she'd said good-bye to Oliver, May had imagined she'd left a part of her soul there, sitting on the bench by Jordan Pond.

The idea that he had not fought to keep her or find a way to be with her and *still* wasn't going to caused her jaw to clench. She folded Oliver's letter and stuffed it back into the envelope. May knelt on the floor in her closet and grabbed a gray Nike shoebox. She sat the shoebox on her desk and removed the lid. She placed Oliver's letter inside on the stack of other letters and cards he'd written to her in Mystic Water. With a trembling breath, she exhaled the rest of her love and hope into the box. Then she sealed the lid with packing tape. May stuffed the shoebox into a back corner of her closet and closed the door. A hollowness had filled her for weeks now, so she couldn't have cried, even if she wanted to. Besides she had a plane to catch.

She clenched her fists at her sides. *I can't imagine anything in the world ever dragging me back to Mystic Water.*

240

28

*Y*et here she was, with Fiona's words echoing in her head, *Don't make that kind of promise. You don't know what the future holds...* May blinked in the fading sunlight and glanced up at Honeysuckle Hollow's second-floor balcony. The wind flapped the French doors inward, causing the doors to hit the stoppers on the baseboards. *Thunk. Thunk. Thunk.* May's cell phone rang, and the muffled sound coasted down from the balcony and found her on the grass. *How much time has passed?*

May grunted as her stiff legs ached when she tried to stand. She pressed her hands against the oak tree's trunk and pushed herself up. She hobbled toward the house until her limbs loosened. Jacqueline's number showed as the missed call on her phone. May dialed her number and apologized for being sidetracked.

Fifteen minutes later, as May sat in the car in the driveway, she glanced over at the passenger seat, imagining John sitting beside her, buckled in and staring down at a folded, paper map.

"John, what am I doing? I wish you were here so I could tell you about Oliver. So I could explain *why* I never told you about him. About how loving him and then leaving him was one of the most challenging, most heartbreaking lessons I've ever learned. Then you could tell me that it's okay to visit an old friend, even if I had loved him desperately at one time. You'd tell me that life is short, and we have to love as many people as we can and as much as we can."

May sighed and leaned her forehead against the warm plastic of the steering wheel. When she pulled down the sun visor and looked at herself in the mirror, she didn't see sixty-year-old May. She saw the young woman who had slept under the stars with a man she hardly knew, a man whose soul felt connected to hers just the same.

May turned on the car engine, backed out of Honeysuckle Hollow's driveway, and blasted the air and the radio. An oldies station played songs from her childhood, which she supposed classified her as "old." But how could she be old when her heart and mind had morphed her back into a young woman?

She drove toward the hospital on autopilot, with half her mind on the road and the other half trapped in a thirty-year-old summer romance. No matter how hard she tried to imagine Oliver as an old man, she couldn't. She could only see his boyish face and hear his quick laughter. A splinter of panic arose when she imagined *not* recognizing him once she stood in his hospital room. What if he were bald or overweight or as skinny and sickly as a yellow string bean? What would *she* look like to him if he were awake? What in heaven's name would they even *talk* about if he were lucid? *Nice gown you have there. Bit breezy in the back?* She snorted as she rolled to a stop at a four-way stop sign. Or Oliver would say, *Goodness, May, you've gotten old. You have more wrinkles than a bedsheet left in the dryer.*

"Does anyone iron bedsheets anymore?" May asked aloud as she turned on her blinker. She smiled for a moment thinking about how Grandma Charity had given her a lesson on how to properly arrange a guest bedroom for company. Ironed sheets were a necessity.

May's nerves churned her stomach into a mess while she sat in the hospital parking lot. She realized she hadn't eaten lunch, which was perhaps the best option given the nausea rolling through her and shooting chills up and down her arms. She could drive away and maybe the fear would ease. But through the years one of May's life rules was never to let fear control her decisions or her *lack* of making a decision.

Inside a hospital elevator a young man stepped in behind May. He clutched a bouquet of wildflowers. He looked twitchy and shifted his gaze. "What floor?" he asked.

"Four please," May said.

He nodded, saying, "Sure, sure. I'm going to five. The maternity floor. My wife. She just had a baby. *Our* baby. A son. I can't believe it. I mean, I'm not ready. I don't think I'm ready. What if I mess up? What if I'm a terrible dad?"

May's gaze met his. "How are they? Mom and son?"

He grinned so widely at May that his eyes nearly closed. "Great. She's amazing. And he's...do you have kids?"

May shook her head.

"Well, it's...words kinda leave you, ya know? Ever had something happen that's so big, that words just..." he made an exploding motion with his free hand, "poof?"

"Many times." *A bit like right now.*

The elevator dinged. May congratulated the young man and stepped around him. She walked slower than necessary as she read the numbers posted beside each door.

May hesitated outside room 402. The low hum of voices slipped out through the partially open door. She lifted her hand to knock but lowered it.

I can't do this. She turned to leave. The room door swung all the way open, and a thirty-something young woman inhaled in surprise to see May standing there. The woman's dark hair framed her pale face. Her downturned, brown eyes looked just like her father's. She stood a few inches taller than May, and her long arms and lanky frame reminded May of the women in the running group she'd been a part of in Mystic Water that summer.

"Mrs. May?" the woman whispered, placing both hands over her heart.

May nodded.

Jacqueline reached out and grabbed May's hands. Tears filled her eyes. Then she threw her arms around May and hugged her; May stiffened in the embrace, but she patted Jacqueline's back.

"It's okay," May said, not able to think of anything else.

Jacqueline swiped at her cheeks. "Thank you so much for coming. You have *no* idea how much this means to me. To Dad," she said. "He's awake. Would you like to come in?"

Jacqueline pulled May into the room before May could argue or explain that all she really wanted to do was drive away.

Blood pounded in her ears; her heart leaped forward, and she stumbled after it. The overhead light was off, keeping the room cool and shadowy.

As soon as May stepped into the room, sunlight poured in through the open blinds, stretching across the bed, the machines, the tiles, until it reached May's feet.

The older man in the bed had his face turned toward the windows, but when the light entered, he turned his face toward May.

29

Oliver's mind cleared minute by minute as the pain medication wore off. His back ached from lying on the lumpy hospital bed for days, and he dreamed of going home to close his eyes in his own bed. But he wasn't a fool; he'd been a doctor long enough to know going home might not be in his future.

Sunlight rushed in through the windows, filling the room with sparkling light. Oliver's pulse quickened, causing his breath to catch. A machine near his head kicked on and whirred, and his fingertips tingled. He turned his head and saw her.

May MacAdams stood bathed in sunlight, and Oliver's weak heart expanded with so much love that his body trembled.

$\mathcal{M}$ay stopped walking. Jacqueline moved toward the bed, but she blurred in May's vision like a phantom in a dream.

Oliver's dark eyes met May's, and goose bumps traveled up and down her skin. He closed his eyes for a moment and smiled. Her stomach fluttered. When he opened his eyes again, he said, "Lovely May, I've missed you."

May covered her mouth with her hand because her bottom lip trembled. She stepped toward the bed, moving to him without thinking, drawn forward by Oliver's familiar voice. He held his hand out to her, and she covered it with both of hers.

Wires and tubes connected Oliver to the machines around his bed. An IV ran from the top of his left hand, and the purple bruising all around the medical tape told May they'd had trouble finding his vein. Oliver was propped up slightly in the narrow hospital bed, with his long legs stretching all the way to the end. His once dark hair was mostly white with a few faint streaks of brown remaining. Lines scored his face, fanning out from his eyes, across his forehead, and framing his mouth where he'd been smiling his whole life. He looked too thin for his tall, lithe frame.

"Hey, Ollie," May said.

"You haven't changed a bit," he said in a voice made hoarse from an oxygen tube. "You look beautiful."

May's laughter surprised her. She gazed down at their joined hands, noticing how pale and spotted her skin was against his darker complexion. She touched her hair. "I'm old, Ollie. I look like an old woman," she said in a quivery voice.

Oliver shook his head. "You look just like I remember." He reached up toward her cheek. "That smile...I've missed that. You could always light up a whole room just by smiling."

Oliver closed his eyes and lowered his hands back to the bed. His body shuddered, and Jacqueline rushed to his side.

With her hands on his arm, she said, "Dad? Dad, can you hear me?"

Tears leaked out the corners of his eyes and shined in the sunlight. "Thank you," he rasped. He pulled in a trembling breath and opened his eyes. His face turned toward May. "Thank you for coming. I...I didn't think you would. Not after what I did." His body shuddered again.

May leaned against the bed and hesitated for a few seconds. Then she touched his face. "Hey, Ollie," she said in a soft voice. "Don't think about that. It's all in the past, a million years ago." She tried to smile as words climbed up her throat and slipped back down. She swallowed and said, "Let's focus on getting you well and out of here, okay?"

"I've never been able to leave it in the past," he said. "I haven't been able to forgive myself."

May and Jacqueline made eye contact before May looked at Oliver. "Oh..." May grabbed Oliver's hand again. "Ollie, we were doing the best we could back then. Just two lost people trying to keep our heads above the water."

"All these years, did you hate me?"

The heartbreak in his eyes unwound the last of the knots in May's heart. She rubbed her fingers over the thin skin on his hand. "I never hated you," she admitted. "I was angry, but that faded. None of that matters now. You shouldn't be holding on to that. Everyone deserves forgiveness. And if you've not forgiven yourself, then that's long overdue."

"Every day," Oliver said.

He pressed her hand against his heart. She felt its weak but steady beat.

"Every day," he repeated. "I thought about you every day. You've been with me since the day we met. And as the voice in my head, you've been directing me for years and years." His eyes closed when he exhaled. His heartbeat drew a steady thump-thump rhythm on the monitor.

A nurse knocked on the door and pushed a cart into the room. May stepped away from the bed.

"Time for your next round of meds," the nurse said.

"I'm not ready to sleep yet," Oliver argued. "May just got here. I've been waiting for her—"

"Get some rest, Ollie," May interrupted. "We can talk about all of this later."

"Are you leaving? You just got here," he said as a panicked expression filled his eyes. "You're not leaving town, are you?"

"No, Dad," Jacqueline answered. "Right, Mrs. May? You're going to stick around for a few days." Jacqueline's eyes pleaded with May.

"That's right," May said with a gentle smile. She touched Oliver's arm. "I'm staying in Honeysuckle Hollow."

Oliver's dark eyes widened. "The mansion?" A whistle escaped his dry lips. "Every princess needs a castle."

May chuckled. "That's exactly what Emily said."

"I better get well, then," Oliver said. "So we can have a proper conversation when I'm not wearing a gown and looking like an octopus with all these tubes."

"I'd like that," May said. "A proper conversation. Now get some rest. We'll let the nurse do her thing."

A young man walked into the room, and Jacqueline greeted him.

"Mrs. May, this is my brother, Michael. Michael this is Mrs. May."

May shook Michael's hand. She wouldn't have recognized him because he'd lost all of his little-boy features, and his blonde hair had darkened through the years. With the addition of a well-trimmed beard, he looked too different from the chubby-cheeked boy she'd seen thirty years ago.

"It's nice to meet you, ma'am," Michael said. "So you're the one we've been trying to find?"

May tilted her head and wrinkled her brow. "I guess looking for Oliver's old friends has been challenging."

Michael mimicked May's expression. "What old friends? We've been trying to find *you* for months. *Find May* has literally been written at the top of our to-do list forever."

Jacqueline gave her brother a look that said, *Shut up*, as she ushered May out of the hospital room and told Michael they'd be back later. Jacqueline tapped at a down arrow in the elevator lobby. "Do you have dinner plans? I'd love to have you over to the house for dinner. Nothing too fancy, but it would be nice to have company and not eat hospital food again. Are you free?"

May stepped onto the elevator and pressed one hand against her pounding heart before touching her neck and then patting down her hair. *Stop fidgeting.* She lowered her hands. May wanted to speed back to Honeysuckle Hollow, grab her bags, and hightail it out of town. Seeing Oliver again cracked open her insides, resurrected a part of her heart and life that had taken her years to bury. A deep-set sorrow mingled with a trembling joy while forgiveness weaved through all those wounds, stitching her back together, healing her. Healing *them.*

Jacqueline watched her in the reflection on the elevator doors. "Are you free tonight?" she repeated.

As if responding to Jacqueline's question, May's stomach growled. "Yes, dinner sounds nice. Thank you. What time?"

Jacqueline's smile lifted her cheeks just like Oliver's did. "An hour? I'll swing by the grocery store and grab a few things. I'll make something easy. Grilled cheese okay?"

May almost laughed, thinking about the first time Oliver had cooked for her. They'd eaten grilled cheese while sitting on sleeping bags beside a family-size tent they'd pitched in his backyard. The elevator doors opened, and May gripped her purse straps. "It's perfect. I'll see you in an hour."

May's body vibrated the whole drive back to Honeysuckle Hollow. Just seeing Oliver again shoved her straight down a rabbit hole littered with colorful memories and complicated emotions, and her heart swelled, uncomfortable and bristly in her chest.

May sat on the edge of the master bed and hugged Timothy O'Conner's *Locust Winter* to her chest. The orange sun deepened to crimson as it set behind the trees. *Locust Winter* was her go-to book whenever she needed comfort or needed to turn off her brain. She'd memorized large passages of the book now, and through the years, she'd hosted one-sided conversations with the author about his work. But today she couldn't focus on anything but the image of Oliver lying in a hospital bed looking aged and frail yet still so much like the man she'd fallen in love with. *His eyes,* she thought, *those same dark, haunted, beautiful eyes.*

A half hour later May stood on the front stoop of the Tudor house Oliver had owned when she'd met him. Standing there made her feel just like she had the first time she'd come over for dinner, with a fluttering heart and antsy stomach. The doorbell chime echoed through the foyer.

Jacqueline opened the door with a smile. "Come in!"

The wrought iron chandelier lit the foyer, sparkling light onto the dark wood staircase. Two rooms branched off, one to the right and one to the left. Straight ahead was the living room where they'd sat laughing and talking many nights. French doors led to the outdoor terrace. May remembered the feel of the backyard grass beneath her bare feet. The house emitted a steady pulse of warmth and comfort with a low-grade trace of loneliness, like a hollow ache in the stomach.

May stepped past Jacqueline and into the living room, walking with her mouth open and the breath lodged in her chest. "Did he— did he decorate this place just like it was before?"

Jacqueline ran her hand along the back of the couch. "I haven't decided if it's sweet or disturbing."

May turned full circle in the room, darting her eyes into every corner, across every wall, pulling all the light from the room toward her. With one hand pressed against her heart, she whispered, "It's like I never left."

"For him, I don't think you did. Come with me, please. I want to show you something else." Jacqueline motioned for May to follow her into the room that had been Oliver's office.

The desk was smaller than the one before, but still made of a dark wood that matched the built-in bookcases that stretched all the way to the ceiling. Books filled the shelves, and Jacqueline dragged her fingers across the spines on a row of books.

"Recognize these?" Jacqueline asked.

May slid one of the books off the shelf. "These are mine." She returned the book and pulled out another and then another. "Even first editions. Even this one with the hideous cover." May laughed, but it hung in her throat like a strangled cry. "You knew? You knew we were more than friends, but on the phone you kept saying you were calling *his friends*."

Jacqueline stared at the rug anchored beneath the writing desk. "I knew the depth of it only after he told me." She looked up at May. "I knew when I was calling you, yes. I was afraid...afraid if I made it sound too important, afraid if I told you the whole truth that you wouldn't come. Michael said I should frame it like I thought you two were old friends from Mystic Water and nothing more. And it worked."

May nodded, sliding her novel back onto the shelf. "Clever kids." More chills washed over her as she reached for a mason jar acting as a bookend on one side of her books.

"I have *no* idea why he kept an empty Mason jar," Jacqueline said.

When May's fingers wrapped around the jar, it lit from within with a soft glow.

"Whoa, that's never happened before," Jacqueline said, moving in closer. "Do you know what that is?"

The glow radiated in the jar, faintly, almost as though the sunlight were glinting off it as May turned it in her hands.

"Ollie said he was bottling my happiness," May said and laughed. "Sounds crazy, doesn't it?" May's eyes fell on the shelf above the one that displayed her titles. Oliver also had every copy of Timothy O'Conner's books. He even had duplicates. She returned the Mason jar to the shelf and reached up, pulling out a book. She showed Jacqueline the cover. "He reads O'Conner too?"

Jacqueline exhaled. "Yeah, those are Dad's."

May blinked at her.

"I mean, those are Dad's as in, he wrote those. *He's* Timothy O'Conner. His penname, like yours is May James."

May squished the book against her chest. Her tears surprised her, springing forth too quick to stop. "He is not."

Jacqueline nodded. "His dad's name was Timothy, and his mama was an O'Conner before she married."

May covered her mouth and leaned forward as the air whooshed out of her lungs. She wobbled toward the desk, and Jacqueline reached out to steady her.

"What's wrong?" Jacqueline asked in a panicked voice. "Are you okay?"

May's tears dripped onto the cover of the book, and she swiped them away. "I've loved Timothy O'Conner's books. Every one. I felt like I *knew* him. I've been carrying his books around for years, rereading them, cherishing them, waiting for the next one to publish. And...it's been Ollie this whole time."

"So you and Dad are in the same boat, then? You've still been loving each other for years, even when you didn't realize it." Jacqueline propped her hip against the desk. "You're one of my favorite authors, so tell me, Mrs. May, how does this story end?"

31

Each new day brought another sunrise that painted Mystic Water in blushing pink and joyful orange. May drank coffee and sat spellbound by the early-morning displays. And each day May told herself she would make one more stop by the hospital, speak to Oliver, say good-bye, and then head back home. But five days later she hadn't dropped one item into her empty suitcase. She'd extended her rental car twice, and she had yet to book a return flight.

During his waking hours, May sat in a chair pulled up beside Oliver's hospital bed. They talked about what they'd done, what they'd seen, and all the adventures that stood out the most during the past thirty years. Every conversation created new thoughts, and it seemed they might never run out of topics to discuss. Laughing and talking with Oliver was a rhythm that felt easy to fall back in to, like they hadn't gone thirty years without speaking.

May had also spent nearly every evening having dinner with Jacqueline. Last night after Oliver had experienced a restless day full of discomfort, the nurse gave him something to help him sleep. Then May, Michael, and Jacqueline had gone to the Corner Pub for a late dinner. Years ago May had dreamed of what it would be like to finally meet Oliver's kids, to have them *know* she existed, and now after all these years, there was a quiet peace that accompanied that dream coming true.

The next morning May's cell phone vibrated, and she jerked awake. She sat up, disoriented and groggy, in a dark room. The light from her cell phone cast flashing, blue light toward the ceiling. "Hello?" May looked around and thought, *Where am I?* She turned on the bedside lamp. Honeysuckle Hollow's master bedroom illuminated in the light.

"I'm sorry I woke you," Jacqueline said.

The thought *Oliver has died* raced through May's mind. "Is everything okay?"

"The doctor just left, and he says—" Jacqueline's voice broke.

255

"He says Dad can go home."

"Home because he's getting well?" May asked, glancing at *Locust Winter* on the nightstand. *Or go home so he doesn't have to die in a hospital bed?*

"He still has a ways to go before he's recovered, but, yes, he can go home because he's improved so much overnight. He'll need cardiac rehabilitation. His lifestyle habits aren't the problem. He eats well, still exercises regularly, and he's never been a smoker. The doctor said half his heart just stopped working, but now, now he's firing on all cylinders."

May swung her legs off the bed and rotated her ankles, drawing circles with her toes. "That's great news. I bet he'll be glad to go home. What time do you think they'll release him?"

"Later this morning, before lunch, though. It takes a while to process the paperwork. I can call you," Jacqueline said. "He's been asking about you this morning. He seems afraid that you'll leave without saying good-bye."

May shuffled toward the French doors and pulled open the heavy blackout curtains. When she stepped onto the balcony, two cardinals chirped from the oak tree. "I'd never leave without saying good-bye. Let me know when you're home. I can walk over."

After a late breakfast and a large Americano at the local diner Scrambled, which had been built after Bea's Bakery burned, May felt the urge to drive to Jordan Pond. Would their bench still be there? Would it have washed away or crumbled to dust like their relationship had?

May parked in the lot and walked down the hill toward the massive willow tree. It had grown in immensity during her absence. It's long, narrow limbs brushed against the ground, swaying in the breeze. The green grass felt springy beneath her shoes as she walked to their bench. Its weathered wood was almost gray now, and one slat on the seat had been replaced with a darker plank, creating a line like a scar on skin.

As she walked, May pictured a much-younger Oliver standing beside the bench, staring at her while he let her walk away. She pictured the two of them sitting on the bench, heads close to each other, talking. Then she replayed the day she'd found him drunk, throwing bottles at the willow. May sat, slipped out of her shoes, and crossed her legs at the ankles. A mallard swam across the pond, quacking and ruffling his tan feathers.

A few minutes later the breeze strengthened into strong gusts. The puffy clouds separated above the pond, revealing the bright sun and an azure sky. The wind changed directions and pushed against May's back, blowing her hair into her face. As she shoved it back, she heard movement behind her. May looked over her shoulder.

Oliver, leaning heavily on a cane, had stopped a few feet behind the bench. "Jackie thought I was crazy to want to stop by here. She was determined to take me home to rest, but really I know she was just eager to call you and tell you to come over." He stepped closer. "I was thinking about you."

May smiled. "And that means what? You think about me, and *poof*, there I'll be?"

He sat and propped the cane beside him. May studied his profile.

"What I mean is," he continued, "that you were so full in my mind that I wondered if I was calling out to you, sending out vibes, my desperate plea to be near you again. Sounds like I'm losing my mind, doesn't it?" He laughed. "And yet, I still hoped it might work. And here you are. Like magic. *Poof.*" He placed his hand, palm facing up, on the space in between them. May put her hand in his. "I'm sorry, May."

"For what?"

His fingers tightened around hers. "I'm sorry that I didn't fight for you back then. I was a coward—"

"Ollie—"

"Let me finish. Please." He released her hand. "I was a coward. Too scared to make a decision because I thought it would be the wrong one. I was paralyzed, incapable of doing anything other than keeping the kids safe and happy. All these years, I kept them safe,

257

but I couldn't keep them happy. And I was so sure that if I gave into the weakness I had for you that I would be dragging you straight back into a mess. And you deserved better than that. I knew you were too good for me the moment I met you, but I was selfish. Once Angelina's body mostly recovered, when she could have lived on her own, I should have called you. I should have reached out to you again. We were miserable. That never changed."

Sunlight sprinkled down on them, dotting them with glittery light. "Why didn't you?"

"Emily kept me up to date on you." Before May could speak her surprise, Oliver held up his hand. "I swore her to secrecy. But I *had* to know May. I needed to know you were happy and okay."

"Well, I wasn't," May argued. "I wasn't happy *or* okay for years—" Anger resurfaced, sending ripples out across the lake, so May paused and pressed her hands against her thighs.

"Then you met John, and he did the thing *I* should have done. He was so much smarter than me. Married you as fast as he could. And you *were* happy with him. I was sorry to hear about his passing. Sincerely."

Oliver reached for her hand. Her hand fit into his just as she remembered, like they were two halves of one whole.

"We *were* happy." May closed her eyes and let the breeze toss her hair around her face. "He was a good man and so good to me."

"I know," Oliver said. "You deserved it. All the happiness life could give you. I *wanted* to be jealous of him, but I wasn't. Emily promised me that he was the best fit for you, that you two were traveling and you were writing and that kept me going too. It was like your happiness could still fill me with enough to keep me moving forward."

May turned her body toward him. "Speaking of writing, I saw your books, *Timothy*."

Oliver's cheek lifted when he grinned, and May saw the young man she had loved. "You saw those, did you? Remember five years ago when our books were wrestling for the top spot? One week you were number one, then I'd edge you out by a breath?"

May chuckled. "If I had only known. *Locust Winter* is one of my all-time favorite books. If I'd have known it was yours—"

"You never would have bought it," he finished, and they both laughed.

Oliver scooted closer to her on the bench and covered May's hand with both of his. "Thank you for coming back. Jackie has a way of getting what she wants."

"Like her dad."

"I didn't get *everything* I wanted," he said, brushing auburn hairs from her cheek. "Until now."

May's stomach fluttered, and her cheeks warmed. "Are you trying to charm me, Dr. Bisset?" Her eyes met his.

"Is it working?" he asked. "Will you stay a while? You don't have to keep renting Honeysuckle Hollow. There's plenty of room at the house."

May's mouth opened in surprise.

"I'm not asking you to move in, May," he said as his smile widened. "Not yet. But a few more days? A week maybe? Emily mentioned that she and Andy could drive down."

"Using my best friend as leverage. I see you still pull out the heavy artillery when needed," May said, but she was smiling too. The thought of spending a few days with her best friend *and* Oliver caused her heartbeat to quicken. Joy pulsed through her, warm and delightful. "I can stay a few more days."

"And when that time is up, I'll ask for more," Oliver said. He lifted her hand to his lips and kissed the top of it. "I think you should write a story about us. We can talk about it while you're here. It would fit right in with your other novels. Love lost and found, forgiveness, restoration, all the good stuff."

May's eyebrows rose. "You've given this some thought already."

Oliver nodded. "I even have a title."

Sunlight beamed down on them, and May soaked up the light, warmed by Oliver's presence. She stared at their interlaced fingers. The word *home* drifted into her mind, and when she looked at Oliver, the word settled into her heart.

"What's the title?" May asked.

Oliver smiled and leaned forward like he had a secret to tell. May mimicked his movement. With their foreheads nearly touching, he whispered, "Finding May."

Acknowledgments

Thank you to Karissa for being such a kind, efficient, and amazing editor. Your feedback and support helps Mystic Water sparkle and shine. Thank you for taking such good care of my characters.

Thank you to Hank for always, always being my early reader for everything. Mystic Water wouldn't have made it this far, nor would it be as mature, magical, or vibrant without your support, advice, encouragement, and honesty. Thank you for being such a fantastic friend who loves Mystic Water and its townsfolk. I am endlessly thankful to have you on my team.

Thank you to my bested buddy, Julianne, for creating another gorgeous, magical cover. You are a blessing in my life, and I hope everyone will find a friend like you.

Thank you to Jason for your support, for always having words of encouragement just when I need them most, for talking me back from the cliffs of despair, and for making me laugh. Thank you for brainstorming for hours during car rides and for being so kind that you never tell me to zip my lips.

Thank you to Daddy and Ma. I wouldn't be here without you. Literally and figuratively. When a world of people laughed at my dreams, y'all never did. In fact, you told me to rub some dirt in it, ignore the naysayers, and get to work chasing my dreams.

Thank you to May, who showed up a few years ago, sitting on a bench, waiting patiently for me to tell your story. Thank you for waiting, May, and thank you for sharing your story with me. As you healed, so did I.

About the Author

While growing up in southern Georgia, where honeysuckle grows wild and the whippoorwills sing, Jennifer became a writer in elementary school. She crafted epic tales of adventure and love and magic. She wrote stories in Mead notebooks, on printer paper, on napkins, on the soles of her shoes.

She considers herself a traveler, an amateur baker, and a dreamer. She can always be won over with chocolate, unicorns, or rainbows. She believes in love—everlasting and forever.

Jennifer has published six enchanting novels based in Mystic Water, *The Baker's Man*, *Little Blackbird*, *Honeysuckle Hollow*, *The Legend of James Grey*, *Wednesday's Child*, and *Finding May*, and all are available in print and as ebooks. *Full Moon June*, *Average April*, and *Starry Sky July* are short stories available as ebooks.

Jennifer also co-created and wrote an illustrated young adult fantasy, *The Wickenstaffs' Journey*, with co-creator and award-winning illustrator Julianne St. Clair. To learn more about Jennifer, visit her website at www.jennifermoorman.com.

Want More Magical Adventures?
Do you love free treats?

Looking to add more sparkle and magic to your life? Go to www.jennifermoorman.com, and subscribe to her newsletter. It's completely free. Never spam. Always fun!

All month long she posts delicious recipes based on books she's reading, including recipes inspired by the Mystic Water series. Her Cooking Through Fiction literature-inspired dishes will transport you into the pages of some of your favorite novels and wrap you in nostalgia for our most-loved stories.

By subscribing to her newsletter, you'll also be a part of Jennifer's insider group and the first to hear exciting news, like her upcoming novels, book sales, and freebies! Come on and join in the magic!

CONTACT JENNIFER

Connect with Jennifer on Instagram @jennifer7478.

If you're interested in hiring Jennifer for a speaking engagement, please send an email to info@jennifermoorman.com.

Thank You!

*Y*ay! I had so much fun introducing y'all to Mystic Water, and I hope you enjoyed reading this story as much as I enjoyed writing it!

If you did enjoy this story, please consider writing a review. I appreciate any feedback, no matter how long or short. It's a great way of letting other magical realism fans know what you thought about the book.

Being an independent author means this is my livelihood, and every review really does make a super-big difference. Reviews are the best way to support me so I can continue doing what I love, which is bringing you, the reader, more stories from Mystic Water!

Thank you for spending time in Mystic Water, and I hope to see you on our next adventure!

Made in the USA
Lexington, KY
26 September 2019